Captured by the BEASTS

KELLY LORD

Cover Design by Sky Designs:
skydesignsofficial@gmail.com

Formatted by Phoenix Book Designs:
lizzie@phoenixbookdesigns.com

I'm dedicating this book to my readers.

Thank you for all your encouragement, your kind word, and for taking my characters into your hearts. You are welcome to visit Whitehaven anytime you like. The quads will be happy to give you a guided tour.

Also, I would like to thank L. P. Dillon for giving me a nudge to publish. And lastly, a massive thanks goes out to my beta readers, Rikki, Henri, Jael, Rachel, and Ashlie.

TRIGGER WARNINGS

This book includes some mild kidnap thanks to one wolf's idiocy, and plenty of smoking-hot sex.

CHAPTER
One

"**M**iss Isobelle Harding," our principal, Mr. Saunders, called me to the stage.

Shaking with adrenaline and sweating like a bitch in heat, I ascended the steps with the sound of applause ringing in my ears. All my focus went into not tripping in my graduation gown and looking like a complete dickhead in front of all these people. The pressure of having a hundred pairs of eyes following me across the stage scorched my face with embarrassment. I wasn't exactly an outgoing person and despised being the center of attention. Perspiration formed across my upper lip like a sweaty mustache, making me feel sticky and gross.

Why did this gown have to be made from black polyester?

With temperatures seeming to be in their eighties, the heavy material was suffocating. By the time I had walked across the stage floor, I was a flustered mess. As subtle as I could muster, I wiped my damp palms against my gown before accepting the diploma. The principal grasped my clammy hand as we exchanged an awkward handshake. I couldn't get away quick enough, scampering off down the opposite steps to wait for my best friend, Joanne.

A beaming smile spread wide across her face as she walked off the stage. "We did it!" she squealed jubilantly, bouncing on her heels.

"I know," I gushed, relieved that the torture was finally over. "Thank fuck for that. No more essays. No more exams. We're fully-fledged adults. Productive members of society," I expressed, reminiscent of all the caffeine-infused nights we had endured over the last few years.

"Soon-to-be taxpayers you mean," Joanne replied, bursting my bubble.

My heart dropped. "Oh, yeah. And repaying the student loans." The thought was daunting.

"Fuck the loans. I can't believe you're going away

tomorrow. I'm gutted I can't come with you," Joanne grumbled, pouting her lips to display her envy. "You're such a lucky bitch."

It was true. I was lucky to have been chosen out of all the other candidates. The university had secured a grant for one person to travel abroad to study a rare species of *Canis lupus*, more commonly known as wolves. An unknown species was found in the faraway state of Whitehaven, and I had been chosen to research them. All the necessary equipment, also food and lodging, would be provided. I didn't have to worry about anything. When the information pack came through the mail, I obsessively scoured through it to find out anything I could about the place, the culture, and whether I'd be staying in the wilderness or a town with lots of people. I decided to run a Google search to see if it would bring up a street view, but each time I tried, the search engine didn't recognize the location. Whitehaven was so remote there weren't even any news articles available. It's like it didn't exist.

"I know . . . I've only ever been to Spain," I replied. "I've always wanted to go to America. Now my dream is becoming a reality." I clapped my hands with excitement, feeling proud of myself.

My mum was concerned about me traveling

alone, which didn't ease my anxiety. As much as I craved my independence, I was nervous about taking this giant leap, and it surprised me when my professor mentioned I would be going alone. It would have been nice to have a companion. Joanne was visibly disappointed. Not that she wasn't happy for me, but because this would be the longest time we would ever spend apart.

"There you are, girls," Dad chimed as he rushed toward us.

My mother was hot on his heels, as were Joanne's parents. They were all bleary-eyed after shedding proud tears of joy during the ceremony.

"Let's get a decent photo of you to commemorate this occasion," Joanne's dad, Gordon, urged.

"Just the girls first, then we'll do one with the mums, then the dads, and then finish with a group photo," Gordon directed, organizing things.

I posed beside Joanne, both giving our best smiles before our mothers ambushed us.

After taking lots of photos, Gordon passed around the camera, allowing us all to view our pictures on the digital screen. My smile faltered as I witnessed the unfiltered reality of a standard image.

Where the hell was a Snapchat filter when you needed one?

"This is one of the proudest moments of my life,"

my dad, Arron, gushed with pride. "The other times were marrying you, Fiona, and of course, when you were born," he said as he pinched my flushed cheek.

I cringed, baring my teeth.

"Shall we go to the Smoke House for dinner?" I suggested.

That was mine and Joanna's favorite restaurant, and I wanted us to enjoy one last meal together before I leave for the summer. I would be gone for twelve weeks. That would mean three long months of missing everybody. I wasn't going to hold my breath that they would have sufficient Wi-Fi out in the sticks. It would be just my luck to be given a carrier pigeon to send messages back and forth.

"We've never been there, have we, Gordon?" Joanne's mum, Norah, asked.

Gordon pressed his lips together as he thought. "Isn't that the one that serves cowboy food?"

"That's the one," Joanne replied, rolling her eyes. "Honestly, Dad. *Cowboy food.*" She chortled.

"I bet our Izzy will get to experience the real deal over the pond," my dad added. "*Real cowboy food.*" He beamed.

Dad had always wanted to go to America and experience how cowboys lived. He loved watching old western films and often wondered what it would be like to ride on horseback. I didn't have the heart to tell him it wasn't all like that. Whenever he watched an old film on television, he would comment on how his lifelong dream was to sit and eat food that had been cooked on an open bonfire, ride through the Wild West, and sleep under the stars. *Sorry, Dad, but you're a few decades too late.* My grandparents' equestrian center a half a mile down the road from us didn't quite cut it in comparison. He would have to make do with an electric barbecue, and a walk, trot, and canter around the paddock.

"I will not be hanging around any cowboys, Dad. Where I'm going, there's nothing but forest and mountains for miles," I explained.

Not that the thought of strapping big countrymen wearing slack jeans and not much else didn't seem appealing to me, because it did. A girl could dream, and those were exactly the kind of thoughts I could pack in my spank bank and fantasize about during the twelve-hour flight.

My father's exuberant expression never faltered despite what I told him. "It's still going to be brilliant though, no matter what. It's a fabulous opportunity they have given you," he chirped happily.

"I couldn't agree more," I replied, still relishing the delicious imagery of me riding a ranch-hand named Hank like a bucking bronco. *Hank the hunk who was hung like a* —

"Earth to Izzy," Mum chuckled, snapping me out of my reverie.

I blushed furiously. I had been single for way too long, and my overactive imagination was reminding me of that.

Dad's upbringing was not as cushy as mine had been. He came from a life of poverty on a council estate in Bradford. Both his parents had died whilst he was little, and he went to live with his aunt. He shared a bedroom with five of his cousins, and each of them survived on one meal a day. Money was tight, and he left school to get a job so he could help his aunt the best he could. It was only after he turned twenty, he joined the police force, starting from the bottom, then spent years progressing through the ranks to become the Chief Inspector of the Metropolitan Police.

Mum came from a modest middle-class family in Warwickshire. Her life was a stark contrast to the way Dad lived. She had never experienced poverty and didn't understand how it felt to go hungry. My grandparents always made sure she was happy and never went without. They bred racehorses and enjoyed holidays abroad every year, whereas Dad was an adult when he visited the seaside. Mum studied to become a pediatric surgeon and currently worked at Great Ormond Street hospital in London. Both my parents came from opposite walks of life, yet their paths entwined together somewhere along the way. That's almost poetic if you think about it . . . like fate had brought them together.

My parents were supportive of me. I had always shown an interest in animal biology, so I knew it was my future vocation. The type of career that would enable me to travel the globe and take me to places that I could only read about in reference books. Those were my dreams, and I couldn't help but wonder whether fate had any plans in store for me too.

We arrived at the restaurant and were shown to a large oval table right in front of an open-plan kitchen. We could see the chefs cooking, turning the meat on the grills, and the yellow flames licking the sides of the steaks. The cowboy-themed décor and the aroma from the smokers made it feel as if we were in the real Wild West. After perusing the wooden-backed menu, I had decided on the chicken bucket special and a large glass of house red. A twenty-something guy wearing a red plaid shirt and jeans took our orders. We didn't have to wait too long before he worked his little butt off to bring the food to our table, earning his service charge as he worked those buns.

"Mmm, this brisket is to die for," Mum complimented as she tucked into her food.

Norah gave Mum a look which suggested that she was immensely satisfied. "It is. It just melts in your mouth . . . and this barbecue sauce is, *mmm*, heaven."

I flashed a grin at Joanne who was glowing crimson with shame, embarrassed by the orgasmic noises our mothers were making as they savored the food.

"I think we should bring our wives here more often, Gordon," Dad joked, looking at his friend with a wide-eyed expression on his face.

Gordon snorted with a nod. "I know. They seem to love the meat, all right."

At that point, Joanne nearly died of humiliation, and so did I. Her fork dropped from her fingers and clattered onto the table.

"Izzy, are you coming to spend a penny?" she asked hastily. It was a polite way to ask if I would accompany her to the women's restroom.

I followed her as she weaved past the tables filled with happy diners. The moment we were out of earshot, she rounded on me.

"Why are they like this? We can't bloody take

them anywhere," she whined in a mixture of amusement and embarrassment.

"They're having fun. It's cute. My parents work all the hours that God sends. It makes a change, seeing them spend time together like this," I replied with a shrug.

Joanne chewed on the inside of her cheek before answering. "Yeah, but they don't give a shit what they say and who hears them," she huffed with a half-laugh. "What am I going to do without you? I'll be all alone, wallowing in secondhand embarrassment."

Joanne was easy to embarrass. Just the mention of sex was enough to turn her a deep shade of red. I wasn't a prude by any means, but I kept my saucy thoughts to myself. I locked those in a vault in the back of my brain, never to be brought out into the open.

After a brief moment of respite, we returned to the table to finish our meals. The conversation flowed smoothly, and the alcohol lifted my spirits. Now wasn't the time to get all sentimental about leaving my family and friends behind. I was looking forward to whatever the future had in store for me.

Once the evening ended, we said our farewells. Three months would be over in a flash. I would be back before they knew it. My only concern was the lack of service my mobile phone was likely to receive high in the mountain range. It would make calling and texting difficult. But that was a problem I would have to face another day. Tonight, I was planning to dream about Hank and his extra-large plank.

CHAPTER
Two

The following morning

"**H**ave you got all of your travel documents and your visa?" Mum asked as she crossed off each item on the checklist.

Mum was a list maker. Not a single day went by when she didn't compile a list of things she needed to do or things she needed to buy. This time, she had put together a list of all the items I needed to take with me to America.

"Yes, Mum, they're in the travel wallet you bought for me," I replied, holding it up as evidence.

"See, Arron? Those things come in handy, don't they? They keep everything together all in one place. Everybody should have one," Mum suggested as she wagged her index finger at Dad. He had initially scoffed at the idea of owning one, back when she was ordering them from eBay the other week.

Mum began rhyming things off, using her fingers to count on. "Let's see, you've got your money. We packed your suitcases. Do you have a spare charger? Did you get one?" she questioned, her brows almost hitting her hairline as if we had forgotten a vital necessity.

"Yes, I picked one up the other day," I answered.

"Well, that's all then. Oh, wait. Here, I bought you some magazines to read on the plane," she remembered, then fished them out of a carrier bag.

"Thanks, Mum. I forgot to buy those," I replied with gratitude.

"She thinks of everything. She's sharp as a whip, this one," Dad praised, fawning over Mum in adoration.

She gave him a loving kiss on the lips before returning to fuss over me.

"I just thought, it's a twelve-hour flight. You'd get

bored to tears otherwise." Her eyes creased with concern. "You will be okay out there on your own, won't you?" Tears welled in her hazel eyes.

"Mum, I'll be fine. Even if I must communicate via smoke signal, you will hear from me one way or the other," I comforted her. "There will be loads of things to do when I'm not working. I'm sure that there will be plenty of people for me to make friends with. The university has rented me a car, so I can get from point A to B and not be destitute," I assured her, seeing her frown lines relax.

"Well, make sure you ring home, or else your father and I will be on the next flight over there," she warned in her warm, maternal tone.

My parents both accompanied me to Heathrow airport so they could give me a grand send-off. I promised myself I wouldn't cry, but my soft self was barely holding back the tears. I checked my luggage into baggage handling, then turned to bid my parents an emotional farewell.

Reality had kicked in by this point, and it took everything I had not to fling my arms around Dad's neck and beg him to take me home.

"Dad, Mum, I'm going to miss you," I bawled.

Dad's eyes reddened as he fought back the tears. He was such a gentle giant when it came to us, but to anyone else, he was an intimidating hulk. Mum's face already had tear tracks running down both cheeks.

"Oh, my baby . . . my only baby." Her shoulders bounced as she wept uncontrollably.

Even at twenty-one years of age, I would always be their little girl. I hugged them as if my life depended on it, and it took all my willpower to detach myself from them and walk away. As I turned around to give a final wave, I noticed them clinging to each other in a tight embrace. The sight almost broke me. Mum placed her fingertips against her lips as if to blow me a kiss, and Dad held one outstretched hand up in a somber wave.

Part of me welcomed the adventure, and part of me wanted to remain rooted in London. The moment I stepped foot on the plane, I had an ominous feeling that my life was going to change forever — or maybe that was Mum's apron strings snapping. It was a daunting feeling, the thought of fending for myself. Not only that, but I also hated flying. Just the thought of having a vast space between the ground and me made my ass cheeks twitch with trepidation. I resorted to occupying myself with magazines and perusing the duty-free brochure until my eyelids drooped. Not that I could sleep for long. It didn't help that they screened *Final Destination* as the in-flight movie. As soon as the landing gear hit the tarmac, my body relaxed, and I sighed with relief.

Then the second we were allowed to leave our seats, I scrambled to retrieve my belongings from the overhead storage compartment. I planned to make a run for the baggage conveyor before anybody else could get there. It was a British thing. We hated queueing. It was no different to a tourist getting up at the butt crack of dawn to claim dibs on a sun lounger. I was hoping to avoid the stampede of passengers and forego waiting in line.

My plan worked. I was the first to arrive at the baggage conveyor, smug as fuck. I waited and waited . . . and waited, glancing at my watch and tapping my foot with impatience, huffing and muttering my thoughts to anyone within earshot like a typical disgruntled Brit — complaining about the shit service and how they better not have lost my luggage or else there would be hell to pay. Then as the cases emerged, my luggage sporadically popped through the flaps as if they'd been to hell and back. I snatched the battered cases, tossed them onto a luggage cart, then made my way to the arrival area — and it was just my luck to have chosen the cart with a wobbly wheel, one that refused to turn the way I wanted it to.

There was barely anyone left in the foyer by the

time I got there. It was hard to miss the tall, bespectacled guy who was holding up a piece of A4 paper that had my name scribbled on it. I couldn't tell if he'd slicked his hair flat with gel or whether it was greasy because the light just seemed to bounce off all the moisture. The tweed suit jacket he had teamed with an Oxford shirt, jeans, and Converse made it look as if he couldn't decide between dressing like a professor or a student. He gave a surprised double-take as he noticed me approaching, blowing the stray hairs from my face, and swearing at the cart. I must have looked like a nutjob.

"Hi, you must be Isobelle?" he greeted me with a strong New York accent.

I caught the way his eyes ping-ponged from my eyes, down to my voluptuous cleavage, and back again as if they were having an involuntary spasm. I zipped up the jacket of my Juicy Couture tracksuit, cramming my ample bosoms inside.

"Yes, sir," I replied, unsure who I was addressing.

I smoothed down my hair and offered him my hand to shake.

Is he a student or a professor? I can't tell.

"Call me Peter. I'm a professor at the University of Michigan," he introduced himself, answering my unspoken question. "You're a real English rose, aren't

17

you? So pretty." Peter narrowed his eyes in a cheeky analysis. It didn't seem seedy, and he certainly didn't mean to intimidate me. It was a clumsy attempt at making chit-chat, and it made me cringe with embarrassment. I wasn't used to getting compliments from guys.

"You ought to be careful. The boys will trip over their tongues when they catch an eyeful of you," he remarked, chortling with amusement.

Instead of rolling my eyes at the cheesy line, I blushed awkwardly at his compliment. I pulled the cart out into the open air and over to where a blacked-out SUV was parked, the fucking wobbly wheel protesting like a dying mouse. Then Peter helped me to load my luggage onto the back seats. He jogged past me to open the passenger-side door, proving that chivalry wasn't dead. The polite gesture surprised me, and I flashed a thankful smile as I slid onto the cool leather seat and shut the door.

Apart from the few cringe-worthy comments at the airport, Peter wasn't the worst person to be stuck in a car with. The conversation maintained a steady flow, and we never ran out of things to talk about. I discovered that his age exceeded the mid-twenty benchmark, and he was in his mid-thirties, unmarried, and owned a short-haired Chihuahua named Derrick. He was single and was currently living in his grandmother's house. I had no room to judge because I still lived with my parents.

"How long is the drive to Lakewell?" I inquired, hoping it wasn't that far because I was getting a numb bum from all the sitting down. Not to mention the jetlag. All I wanted was to brush my teeth and collapse into bed.

Peter's lips twisted as he thought. "Uh . . . three, maybe four hours, tops. Depending on whether the roads are clear. There's a lot of traveling through woodland, and those roads aren't well lit," he explained.

My facial expression sank with fatigue.

Three or four hours. Great.

"Ugh," I groaned. "Where is Whitehaven, anyway?"

"It's off the beaten track so to speak. There aren't any road signs that'll lead you there, so there's no way to find it unless you know where to go. The guest house where you'll be staying is right by the forest. The owners are Chloe and Lincoln Anderson, and they have two little kids. They're mad tight," Peter mentioned, trying to put my mind at ease. "They'll make you feel at home."

"I'm grateful I don't have to make my own way

there. I could sleep for a week," I replied, fighting the urge to yawn.

He wasn't wrong about the drive. It took ages to reach the guest house. It was late into the night by the time we arrived. I could barely keep my eyes open. As Peter pulled the handbrake, it jolted me awake.

"Are we here?" I slurred, wiping the drool from my chin.

"This is it," Peter announced. "I got you here safe and sound, just as I promised I would."

I flashed an exhausted smile. "I didn't doubt you for a moment."

CHAPTER Three

I gazed out through the windscreen and up at the highlighted brickwork. The spotlights on the walls bathed the guesthouse in a pale-yellow hue, and a sun canopy stretched around the front of the building like a light and dark striped skirt. The inside was just as modern as the outside. Peter helped to bring my belongings to the reception desk. We had to be quiet so as not to wake the sleeping borders. Chloe and Lincoln were there to greet us, and what a fine-looking couple they were too. Chloe's summer dress clung to her voluptuous figure like she had been hand-stitched into it, and her blonde hair and tanned skin gave her a healthy glow. Her husband, Lincoln, stood around six-foot-five, rocking the hot mountain man look without really having to try. Either he was well-endowed, or a snake had slithered up the inside leg of his jeans, because fuck me, that was one impressive appendage. I turned my attention elsewhere.

Peter and Lincoln carried all my luggage to my room, allowing Chloe to give me a brief tour of the guest house.

"I hope you like your stay here at Whitehaven. If there's anything you need, just let me know," Chloe kindly offered.

"Thank you. I'm going to look around the town tomorrow to get a feel for the place. Maybe talk to a few of the locals, meet some people, and settle in," I replied, thinking that she was the luckiest woman I had ever met.

"You want some company? I was planning on taking the kids out for a few hours anyway," Chloe suggested.

"That would be great, but only if it's not too much trouble," I answered, not wanting to be a burden.

She gave me a look that implied *don't be silly* before responding in a hushed tone. "It's Linc's birthday this weekend, and the kids want to get him something special. So, trust me, honey, it's no bother at all."

"Oh. I'll tag along then. What time should I be ready for?" I asked.

"Oh, say nine-thirty after we sit down to breakfast. The kids usually have me up around six. They run into our room and bounce on the bed. They're natural alarm clocks." Chloe chuckled.

"Well, in that case, I'll let you get some rest. I know that I'll crash as soon as my head touches the pillow," I replied, struggling to contain a yawn.

Chloe escorted me to my room before saying goodnight. As the light filled the lavishly decorated suite, my jaw hit the floor. I considered my house to be a palace, but this place was stunning.

I let out a low whistle, wondering how much of the budget was being blown on my accommodation costs. Not that I was prepared to trade this in for a shitty truck-stop motel. No way.

They had crafted the bed from the same oak wood that flowed throughout the building. All the soft furnishings matched in cream-colored cotton with a country rose pattern. I took a seat on the bed to peel off my clothes, then pulled on a pair of pajamas, yawning and in need of some rest. As I cocooned myself in the feather-soft sheets, I sent a quick text to my parents and Joanne, just to let them know I arrived here safely. I didn't expect an immediate reply from them because of the time difference.

Drifting off to sleep was easy. I would have had a full, peaceful night if it weren't for the loud, harrowing sound that tore me from the land of slumber. I knew it was late because it was still dark outside. I looked around for my phone and pressed the home button to illuminate the screen.

"It's four o'clock in the morning for fuck's sake," I grumbled after reading the time.

I was too sleep-drunk to get up and peer through the open window. So, I just lay there and suffered through the commotion. Another loud chorus of keening howls filtered into the night. I recognized it as a wolfs' song. I had barely managed to grab two hours' worth of sleep, and as the sound grew louder, I groaned with annoyance. Fair enough, this is what I came here for, but for God's sake, I was exhausted. On clumsy feet, I stumbled out of bed and staggered to the window. The curtains were swaying gently in the cool night breeze, and I made a mental note not to leave it open the following night.

"Oh, bugger off and howl somewhere else," I complained sleepily. "I'll get revenge when I come and poke my nose into your habitat. If you disturb my sleep, I'll fuck up yours. Trust me, I have a box full of rectal thermometers and I'm not afraid to use them."

My fingers clutched the window frame and slammed it shut. That only made matters worse. It was as if the wolves were heckling me for their own amusement. My eyes strained through the darkness, but all I could make out were shadows. I yanked the curtains closed before shuffling back to bed. At least I knew my research was going to prove a success, especially if there was a pack of wolves living beyond Chloe and Lincoln's back garden. The insufferable noise continued into the early hours. Instead of letting it torture my eardrums, I plugged my headphones into my phone and listened to my playlist. With Adam Lavigne's dulcet tone crooning into my ears, I drifted back to sleep.

The annoying high-pitched sound of my phone alarm ripped me from a pleasant dream. My earphones only amplified the sound. I yanked them from my ears and rolled over, then grabbed my phone to turn off the alarm. A groan escaped my lips the second I saw it was already eight a.m. My eyes stung and my head felt foggy as if I was suffering from a hangover. The infernal racket from last night didn't help. I felt as if I hadn't even slept at all. After much deliberation, I forced myself out of bed and began my morning routine.

Having a shower helped to wake me up, scrubbing myself with the soapy sponge until I felt clean and refreshed. Clutching my damp towel around me, I shuffled over to the window, scanning the clear blue sky for any sign of a rain cloud. The sunny morning helped me to decide what clothes I should wear. I put on a vest top, jeans, and a comfortable pair of sneakers.

I had a good feeling about today. This place felt like a home away from home, although I wasn't sure why. New places were supposed to feel different. Whitehaven didn't. Before leaving my room, I grabbed my handbag and slumped off downstairs toward the communal dining area. Chloe was there, dressed and ready to start the day. She was busy fussing over her children who were arguing over who had the most cereal in their dishes. I watched as she tipped a few more grains into one bowl so that it evened them out.

"There, now you've got the same amount as your brother." She placed the bowl down in front of the little blonde-haired girl who had been giving her some attitude.

"I'm a big boy, aren't I, Mommy? I'm gonna grow

up big and strong just like Poppa Bear, won't I, Mommy?" The little dark-haired boy asked angelically.

"You sure will, Cameron," Chloe replied, then bowed down and kissed the top of his head.

"Will I be big like Poppa? Or will I be a princess like you, Mommy?" the little cute blonde girl inquired, scrunching her brows quizzically.

"Oh, Angelica, you're the only pretty princess around here," Chloe fawned, squeezing her daughter's cheeks. She chuckled, then leaned down to plant a kiss on the side of Angelica's face.

"Poppa calls you his princess," Angelica stated, her brown eyes flared wide with innocence.

"Yeah . . . and he's my big, cuddly teddy bear." Chloe noticed me standing in the doorway smiling and shot me a grin.

"Coffee?" she offered.

"That would be great, thank you," I replied politely. I would have preferred tea, but I doubted they drank Yorkshire Tea here. I didn't much care for alternative brands.

We ate a quick breakfast before we headed into town. It made more sense to take Chloe's car as it already had the kids' car seats installed in the back. After such an enchanting breakfast, listening to the children's tales, I was convinced that they were two of the most adorable children I had ever met.

Cameron and Angelica were four years old and were fraternal twins. Angelica loved to chat nonstop. Chloe often had to remind her to slow down while she was talking, whereas Cameron was the quiet one who hardly said a word. Chloe referred to them as her cubs. Maybe that was just a cute pet name that also meant kids, but they referred to their dad as Poppa Bear. So maybe that's where the nickname *cubs* came from.

CHAPTER Four

C hloe pulled into a free parking bay along
the edge of the town square. Lakewell was
a cute little place that had an ample
number of shops, despite being in such a small
populated area. I had an excellent view of White
Lake from this side of the town. There was a picnic
park along the water's edge with an adventure
playground for children. The harbor was bustling
with families all out enjoying the sunshine and
feeding the ducks clumps of bread. I could imagine
this place being great to raise a family. Chloe and
Lincoln certainly picked the nicest place to raise
Angelica and Cameron.

"I'm going to take the kids to choose a gift for Lincoln. We could meet up for lunch later if you don't want to be dragged from store to store by the kids," Chloe suggested.

"I'll meet up with you later," I decided, wanting to go off and explore on my own for a while. "I need to pick up a few essentials."

Chloe nodded, chuckling at the unusual term I used for browsing. "It's impossible to get lost around here. Whichever way you choose to walk around the stores, you'll end up right back here. It's laid out in one big circle. See that café over there, the one called Muffins?" She pointed to a quaint little café with a black and purple striped canopy that matched the signage. "Meet me there at eleven-thirty. We can all grab lunch together."

"Okay, see you later." I waved them off. Both children grabbed Chloe's hands as they pulled her off toward the shops.

My eyes glanced from left to right, deciding on which route to take. Chloe said it wouldn't matter as whichever way would bring me right back where I started. So, I went left and passed a pharmacy, a fishing tackle shop, and a suspicious-looking shop I guessed was a sex store. That shocked me in a quaint little town like this. The window display included scantily clad mannequins that had been arranged in compromising positions – which was rather amusing, but still quite scandalous. I shook my head, giggling to myself after seeing the outraged expressions splashed across other shoppers' faces.

One woman ushered her teenage son away after catching him stealing a glimpse through the window.

"Adam!" She swatted him with her shopping bag. "Don't stare. Especially at whatever that harlot sells in that filth store of hers. You'll find a nice feline of your own someday. You won't need to go looking at the likes of that trash," she chastised her son who was now glowing a bright shade of red with embarrassment.

Feline?

Her eyes flicked up to mine, and I smiled politely.

"That's the curious youth of today," I excused, seeing how flustered she was. "I think you're onto a winner by distracting him with a kitten."

She huffed with outrage, then scurried away. There was nothing to be ashamed about. Sex was natural, but some people were so prudish they made others feel embarrassed about it. It reminded me of back home, how Ann Summers was located directly in front of my nana's favorite café. My nan and all the little old dears in her knitting club congregated there on a Tuesday morning, casting disdainful glances at anyone who dared to enter the Den of Sin as they liked to call it.

"It's all that book's fault," my nan would claim. "Ever since that novel came out, everyone has gone sex mad. There was none of that back in my day," she would add, crossing her arms. "That book should be burned." Her eyes blazed with fierce determination. "Don't ever let me catch you reading it," she would warn while wagging her finger at me. "I'll disinherit you."

After my eventful shopping trip, I ended up back where I started. With my bags clutched in one hand, I waved to Chloe and the kids with the other, seeing them standing outside waiting for me.

"Isobelle!" Both children rushed toward me.

"Are you hungry?" Angelica asked.

"I'm starving," I replied, hearing my stomach give a growl in agreement.

We had to wait a short while for a table, but as soon as one became free, we grabbed a seat. The kids already knew the children's menu by heart and rhymed off their order as the server approached.

"Hey, Chloe, who's your new friend? She's not from around here, is she?" she asked cheerfully, but in the same way, her voice had a subtle, prying edge to it. At a guess, I'd say she was around her mid-to-late sixties underneath the inches of makeup, but I couldn't be certain. I smiled a humored tight-lipped smile, knowing that she was likely the type to gossip. Her grey eyes raked over my appearance, analyzing every tiny detail.

"Teresa, this is Isobelle. She'll be staying with us at the guest house for the next three months," Chloe introduced. "Isobelle is an environmental scientist. She came here to study the wolves," she added.

Teresa's intrigued smile fell from her heavily made-up face. "What?" Her eyes rounded with shock. "You're studying wolves?" There was a hint of hysteria in her voice.

She turned to Chloe and whisper-shouted, "Are you crazy?"

Chloe shook her head in confusion. "What? The university sent her with Alec White's consent. You've met Professor Peter Munroe, the guy who keeps visiting these parts. He's conducting a study on wolves in their natural habitat. It could help us get government backing to protect the forest." She turned to her children. "Kids, why don't you go fetch some crayons from the drawer? Go on, you know where they keep them." She smiled, waiting until they were clearly out of earshot before continuing the conversation. "Lincoln said more hunters have been encroaching onto the land. The Rangers have been going nuts over it," she finished, exchanging a worried look with Teresa.

"It's not just that, Chloe. You know what it is tomorrow, don't you?" Teresa mentioned in a whispered tone.

Chloe made a face as if to say, "Huh?"

Teresa huffed and rolled her eyes. "It's that time of the month," she spoke quietly, eye-signaling to her again and adding in a few winks.

I automatically thought of a woman's menstrual cycle when she said that and wondered what relevance it had regarding me conducting my investigation.

Chloe's eyes darted between the two of us as she must have interpreted the same thing as I did. Then her expression flooded with realization. "Oh . . . the full moon." Chloe chuckled.

I scrunched my face with sheer incomprehension, not having the slightest idea what they were talking about.

Teresa huffed, placing a hand on her hip. "It's the wrong time of the month to go searching for certain wolves in the woods." She turned toward me. "If you knew what was good for you, honey, you would go back to where you came from," she cautioned. "Nothing good ever comes from snooping around."

Chloe snapped back, appalled. "Don't go scaring away my guests, Teresa." She placed a palm on top of my wrist. "It's stupid urban folklore. Ignore her," she muttered.

"It's not bullshit when it's a fact," Teresa interjected, raising her finger in the air. Her fingernails were curved like cat claws. "Our sheriff warns visitors not to go into the woods during a full moon, and for their own darn good, too." She began telling the story using expressions, just to give it that chilling campfire-tale effect. "There's a hut, deep in the thickest part of the forest that's home to four men who like to keep to themselves. They come out once every full moon to hunt for a woman to sate their pleasures upon, if you know what I mean," she uttered in a lowered tone. "Not a woman for each of them. No. One they would share," Teresa finished, sounding horrified as if she disapproved of any such habits.

"Oh, come on, Teresa. Maybe if people weren't so judgmental about polygamy, certain people wouldn't need to go into the woods to fuck," Chloe raised a valid point. "It's no different than the naturist reserve up on The Hills. People go there for one thing, and they tend to share the love if you know what I'm saying."

"Seriously?" I was shocked, then I glanced over my shoulders to make sure no little kids were in earshot. Angelica and Cameron were still ambushing the drawers, filling their pockets with crayons.

"Yup," Teresa answered as a matter of fact. "You can ask anybody from Whitehaven. It's a free-for-all fuck-a-thon up on the summit of Forest Hills, but it's even worse in the forest with those horndogs running loose. You've got to lock up your daughters during the full moon. Especially if you hear the call of the wolf outside your door on the eve of one. That's a bad omen. So, you keep out of those trees for the next four nights, honey." She raised an over-plucked eyebrow. "If you know what's good for you."

"Oh, Teresa, that's ridiculous." Chloe rolled her eyes.

The thought of four big mountain men swam into my mind's eye, ravishing a poor defenseless woman, taking all their pleasures out on her helpless, fragile body. I shuddered, but not with fear. I suppressed a smirk. That sounded like a dirty sexual fantasy from one of my romance novels.

"What happens to all the women they take?" I asked, forgetting how to breathe for a second as my laughter stuck in my throat. I wasn't sure I could contain myself for much longer.

Chloe waved her hand to catch my attention. "Nothing because it's a load of baloney. According to the stories, they returned them to the edge of the woods, untouched. They said they weren't the ones they were looking for. I don't believe in it personally. It's nothing more than a scare tactic to deter tourists from roaming around the forest. If girls were getting snatched, the authorities would be all over it."

"Do you get many tourists?" I asked, wondering how people knew to come here if it wasn't on the map.

Chloe and Teresa shared a puzzled glance then both blurted mixed answers. "Occasionally," Chloe replied.

"Are you kidding?" Teresa spluttered, then rubbed her elbow gingerly. "I mean, not really. This is a nature reserve. We want to keep it that way."

I thought for a moment. "And this legend . . . about the men in the woods. Can you tell me anything more about that? If I'm going to be working in the woods, I want to know what to look out for."

Chloe rolled her eyes. "It's horse shit."

Teresa made a face as if to say, "Nah, not really. I've told you everything I know."

"Oh." My shoulders dropped with disappointment after such an anti-climax. "That's not much of a legend, even if it is bollocks. I would have thought there would be more to it than that." *And there I was, hoping for a bit of smut.*

CHAPTER
Five

"**S**o that's it? They just returned unscathed?" I asked disappointedly.

Call me wicked, but I hoped there would be a raunchy tale to tell. Something to fantasize about when I go to sleep at night.

"I can only repeat what I know." Teresa shrugged. "The girls weren't harmed in any way; they came back with the same excuses. That the men were searching for the ideal woman, but they never found the right one," she finished. "Personally, I think that most of them went looking for trouble. Most seemed disheartened when they came back unfulfilled." She scrunched her face in revulsion.

Chloe giggled and even Teresa relaxed and saw the funny side. The scientist in me was rolling my eyes, calling this out for the bullshit that it was, but after the night I had, something Teresa had just said resonated with me. Like an itch I just had to scratch or else it would bug me.

"I thought I heard wolves howling outside the guest house last night," I told them.

Chloe frowned. "Kids love to pull pranks this time of year. The local boys do it to scare the girls. So, if you hear a commotion tonight, that's what it'll be," she reassured me as if it was nothing more than a juvenile prank.

Teresa's eyes widened in surprise at Chloe's news, then turned to face me.

"Make sure you keep your window closed, honey. It isn't kids you ought to worry about. Wolves can pick up a scent from miles away. You don't want that poor, sweet girl going missing now, do you?" She eyed Chloe accusingly. "Isobelle is fresh meat, and you know what they all say about that. Fresh meat, new target."

"What do the wolves have to do with the story, anyway? What's the connection between the men and the wolves?" I asked with interest, wanting to learn more about the local folklore. "Do they impersonate them? Are they civilized, or are they wild men of the forest?"

Both Chloe and Teresa shared a furtive look, then Chloe attempted to ease the tension.

"It's like I said, it's just a story to put off tourists from going into the forest and stumbling across something they shouldn't. But don't worry about that. Sure, we are right on the border of the forest, but not a man nor beast would dare come near the house because of Lincoln," Chloe spoke with pride in her voice. "It's his territory."

Teresa chuckled. "Ahh, Lincoln Anderson, now there's a fine piece of man meat if I ever saw one. Nothing will come to get you with that grizzly standing guard, you mark my words."

Our conversation was interrupted suddenly by one of the waitresses dropping a plateful of food. The sound of shattering crockery startled us. Diners left their seats and rushed toward the windows, desperate to see what was going on outside. I made it just in time to witness a young man streaking buck naked past the windows, his flaccid dick slapping against his thighs. My mouth fell open with shock.

"See?" Chloe chuckled. "What did I tell you?"

"Oh, those darn teenagers," Teresa muttered, shaking her head, "always playing pranks on the eve of the full moon, scaring the poor girls like that. Why, they ought to be flogged raw," she seethed.

Chloe's shoulders vibrated in silent laughter. "Oh, Teresa, weren't you ever young once?"

I couldn't help but join in, seeing the funny side. A few of the locals found it amusing too. Watching the girls clinging to their fathers and boyfriends, seeking protection just in case it was one of the men from the woods coming to take them away.

"But why run around naked?" I asked out of sheer curiosity.

When Chloe finished her giggle fit, she explained. "Well, as the story goes, the men in the woods are always nude when they hunt. So, the resident boys dare one another to strip and run through the town, scaring girls. It's become quite a tradition. Don't worry though, the local sheriff will chase them off and tell their parents all about it."

I rolled my eyes, thinking how typical it was of boys to behave that way. It was a funny prank, I had to admit, and it lightened the mood. But where there was smoke, there had to be fire. There must be some shred of truth hidden within the stories, even if Chloe thought they were bullshit. Teresa believed them. We finished our lunches and headed back to the guest house. There were things I needed to discuss with Peter before he returned to Michigan.

We took a drive around the area so that Chloe could give me a brief tour of the place. A fleet of luxury boats lines the harbor. Chloe explained that if I went on one of the guided boat tours, I would sail down White Lake, which would take me past Whitevale, the oldest town in Whitehaven. Apparently, there was an island at the center of the lake that was home to the landowner, Mr. Alec White. Dense woodland kept his castle hidden from view, which was such a shame. I would have liked to have seen it. Something so magnificent shouldn't be concealed from the world — it should be appreciated. He should make it the town's focal point if it stands for something important. Chloe explained that Mr. White's fiancée was arriving shortly, and it was why the neighboring towns were having a huge makeover. The work was almost complete, and I was glad I would be here to see it finished. The hopeless romantic in me was impressed by the amount of effort Mr. White put into making everything perfect for the love of his life. He seemed like a true gentleman, but Chloe assured me that people weren't always what they seemed to be, and not to be blindsided by how much money they threw around.

She told me that Mr. White had his reasons for living in seclusion, cut off from the rest of civilization. We all harbored our demons. Even those who seemed perfect to everyone else may feel differently about themselves. I knew how that felt. My love life left a lot to be desired. Men found me attractive, but they complained that I talked too much. I bored them with my interests. Joanne used to say it was because they felt emasculated by me, and it was their problem, not mine. I didn't have guys beating down my door to ask me out. My five-foot-eleven height acted as a boyfriend deterrent, especially when I added heels to the mix.

Peter was waiting for us when we returned to the guest house. His tweed jacket was draped over his arm as if he was waiting to leave. Chloe and the kids collected their purchases and hurried inside to hide their gifts for Lincoln. I hung back, hoping to have a private word with Peter.

"Hi, Isobelle. I trust you've settled in well. I just wanted to say on behalf of the university how happy we are that you decided to take us up on the offer here. Your input will be invaluable to our cause."

He seemed to mean what he was saying. I appreciated that. At least he wasn't trying to bullshit me by blowing smoke up my ass. "It's an honor,

Peter, I'm grateful for the opportunity," I replied humbly.

His friendly eyes creased behind the lenses of his glasses as he smiled. "I just wanted you to know that you were chosen specifically for your academic achievements. Once my colleagues read your profile, they knew that you would be the perfect woman for the job. I'm confident they won't be disappointed with their choice."

"If you don't mind me asking, who are your colleagues? Who will I need to send my weekly reports to?" I hadn't thought to ask before.

"Oh, shoot," he said, swatting the air as if he'd accidentally left out a vital piece of information. "I should've mentioned this to you earlier. You should report your findings to me. The investors are not interested in scientific jargon. They only want facts. Your job is to prove that rare wolves can be found at Whitehaven," he explained. "It's the vital proof we need to secure the conservation project. I moved the research equipment to your room. I hope you don't mind."

I blinked and shook my head in a silent apology. "No, of course not. Sorry if I seemed abrupt with you, Peter. I assumed the university provided the grant. No one told me about the investors. Silly me, not doing my homework first." I tried to make a light-hearted joke to conceal my embarrassment. "But this will mean the pressure is on for me to provide substantial evidence within a set timeline, or else they'll cut my funding. That's generally how it works."

The last thing I wanted was to have the funds pulled suddenly from beneath me. And they could easily do that if they were dissatisfied with my work. It wouldn't go down too well on my resume, and my whole career could take a huge nosedive. This industry would never take me seriously again, that much I was certain. I could kiss goodbye to everything I've worked hard to achieve. No, failure wasn't an option. My job was to study wolves in their natural habitat, prove they needed protecting, and that stringent measures should be put in place to safeguard the forest. So that was exactly what I intended to do.

"I'm sure anything you report will suffice. You come with such high recommendations. Maybe I could even learn a thing or two from you." He tapped my shoulder in a friendly gesture.

"Well, thank you," I replied, flattered by that. It meant a lot to me.

Peter glanced at his watch. "Jeez, is that the time,

already?" He blew out a forced breath. "I should get going. I'm giving a talk at a seminar tomorrow morning, and I really ought to prepare. Goodbye, Isobelle, and good luck."

I returned his warm smile with one of my own. "Thank you, Peter." I stood aside as he plodded down the front steps to get to his car.

It wasn't luck I needed. I know what I heard last night. There were wolves in the forest. I just needed to show Peter the proof and prove they were worth saving.

CHAPTER
Six

All was quiet in the guesthouse as I returned. I wondered if any other guests had checked in since my arrival. There wasn't any sign of Chloe and the children. They must have gone into their living quarters to relax. I returned to my room, noticing the maids had made the bed and left clean towels on the comforter.

They hadn't touched my recording equipment. It was stacked in the corner of the room where Peter said it was. A large brown envelope caught my eye. Someone had propped it up on my pillow. It looked important. I emptied the contents onto the crisp white sheets, finding the keys to the car, Peter's email address on a piece of folded notepaper, and the log-in information I needed. As if the universe thought I needed a break, my phone rang. It was my mother.

I swiped my finger across the touchscreen to answer the call. "Hi, Mum. How are things at home?"

"Great," Mum replied. "I'm just checking in with you to see how you're settling in."

"Everything's fine. I went into Lakewell town today and picked up a couple of bits and pieces. You know me, I love to shop."

Dad muttered something about me being a spend-a-holic, poking fun at me. "What was that?" I asked, grinning.

"Oh, ignore him. You can indulge as much as you like. You've earned it," she defended me in a soft-humored tone.

We chatted for another few minutes before saying goodnight.

I was missing them tremendously, and I hadn't been gone for long. I was such an overthinker, second-guessing everything and panicking over trivial things. That resulted in a headache. I took some pain meds to sleep it off. Then I woke around ten p.m., drenched with sweat, so I took a shower to freshen up. My mind flitted from one thought to the next, overthinking everything as the soap sluiced down my legs and then down the drain hole. I decided that if the wolves were to howl again tonight, I would sneak outside to take a few photos.

After I dried off and changed into a simple nightdress, I checked that my camera had sufficient charge. The humid night air was too hot and muggy. I could barely stand it as I used my hairdryer, so I opened the window, thinking that would help. My room is filled with the scent of fresh forest pine. I found it calming. I loved the smell of the outdoors, providing it didn't smell of cow shit. As I glanced at my phone, I saw it was almost midnight. My eyes were dropping, but suddenly I heard the sound that I'd been hoping for.

I pressed the remote to turn off the television, plunging the room into a darkened silence. Then I grabbed my camera and crept toward the window, hoping that if I peered out of it, I would see wolves roaming around the grounds. It would be amazing if I caught evidence on my second night here. I struggled to see a thing in the pale moonlight. The trees cast eerie shadows on the lawn, making the scene below seem almost ghostly. Just as I was about to give up the search, another ear-splitting howl came from the edge of the forest. It sounded closer this time.

My keen eyes scanned the tree line, searching for any sign of life. Wolves tended to hunt at night rather than in daylight. The thought of spotting one so soon made me buzz with excitement. I had to be careful when encroaching on their territory, not wanting to disturb the natural order of things. This was amazing.

I just wanted to see a wolf . . . just one, and I could sleep comfortably tonight. Last night exhausted me, but tonight it pumped me full of adrenaline. I couldn't tell if it was a trick of the light, but I could make out eight glowing orbs among the foliage. I blinked for a second, letting my eyes adjust to the dark, then I leaned out of the window to get a better look. Just as I suspected, wolves were prowling around down there. One of them stepped onto the lawn, then bowed his head low. I could hardly believe what I was seeing. It was a huge black wolf – bigger than any wolf I had ever seen before. I watched with intrigue as it cautiously sniffed the air, then looked up at my window.

There was no way I could miss this. I pulled my backpack from the hook on the door and snatched my sneakers from beneath the bed. It wasn't like wolves to encroach onto human territory, and it was my job to find out why they were here. Maybe they were being forced from their natural habitat, or maybe their food source was depleting. Whatever the circumstances, the university would want to hear about it. I darted downstairs in a hurry, only stopping to pull on my footwear. It wouldn't do me any good to go traipsing through the garden in my bare feet. I flung the camera strap over my head, then tiptoed to the back door, which had one of those safety locks that didn't need a key to unlock it from the inside, so I was able to open it and slip away as quietly as I possibly could. I pulled the lens cap off the camera and altered the settings to night-vision mode.

This had nothing to do with the stupid urban legend. No idiotic kids were streaking across the green with their dicks flopping about. No naked men waiting in the wings to drag me into the forest. Just me and the wolves, who probably came here searching for food.

The black wolf seemed a lot bigger than he looked from my bedroom window. I could hardly believe it was a wolf at all, but I could tell it was a "*he*" by the size of his bollocks. Everything about him was big. He stood as tall as a horse and as wide as a bear. I clicked away with my camera as I walked around the edge of the garden, careful to maintain a safe distance between the enormous wolf and me.

"That's it, I'm not going to hurt you," I murmured, getting some great close-up shots.

The wind rustled through the trees, whirling my nightdress around my thighs. It was enough to raise the hairs on the back of my neck, making me shudder. I zoomed in, focusing all my attention on the wolf through the lens, and that's when I saw it too little too late – in the reflection of the silvery wolf's eyes, I saw a guy sneaking up on me. But before I could react, he fucking grabbed me and clamped his hand over my mouth.

CHAPTER
Seven

I bucked and thrashed to break free of my kidnapper's iron grip, but it was useless. Whoever he was, his strength exceeded my own. All I could do was scream bloody murder as he dragged me deep into the forest.

No one would know where I was. I dropped my backpack on the lawn. My camera was still dangling from the cord around my neck, weighing me down and biting into my nape. My terrified screams turned to desperate sobs. At one point, a hand pressed down so hard over my mouth that I thought I might pass out. I could scarcely see a thing as he pulled me through the thicket. All I could hear was ragged breathing and the sound of heavy footsteps beating on the ground — until the bickering started.

"What part of *'let me handle it'* did not sink into your thick skull?" an angry voice roared.

"Can we not discuss this now? I'm kind of busy here, in case you haven't noticed," the guy holding me answered him.

"Go easy on her, she still needs to breathe," a raspy voice snapped.

There are three of them.

"Careful. You're gonna hurt her," a softer voice spoke.

Okay, so that makes four.

He seemed concerned about my welfare. That surprised me. *No, wait! What if they need me alive for whatever horrors they have in store for me? On second thought, let him suffocate me now.*

I thrashed around on his shoulder, making as much noise as I could.

"She's a screamer. They'll hear her for miles around. You don't want the bear on our tails," another man spoke, his voice laced with humor.

Bear? There are bears here too.

My cry for help came out like a garbled noise. I

struggled against my captor, but he was built like a mountain of muscle.

"Here, use this to gag her with." I heard fabric tearing, then they shoved cloth between my lips.

The material bit into the corners of my mouth as they tied a knot at the back of my head.

"Mmph." I tried to shout out for help again, but the gag muffled my cries.

"Give her to me. I'll carry her for a while. I don't trust that you won't injure her any more than you already have," the guy with the raspy voice muttered sarcastically.

"I won't hurt her," my kidnapper protested, obviously offended by the remark.

"I said give her to me; it's my turn!" He swapped me into the other guy's arms, and my stomach collided with another rock-hard shoulder.

We gathered speed, and I bounced around like a rag doll. He hopped, skipped, and jumped along the forest floor. Every rough jolt felt like a punch in the stomach. I made another attempt to scream and wriggle free, only to feel a gigantic hand slap down across my backside, stinging my skin.

"Stop it. You'll fall and hurt yourself," the man with the stern tone berated me. "Hold her steady or give her to me."

"She's high-spirited. Just what we need to keep us in check," a guy with a softer voice spoke. He seemed more benign than the others.

"Speak for yourself. She *will* obey us, or I *will* punish her," the dominant guy threatened.

"Can you smell that? She enjoyed having her ass slapped. I may have to put her over my knee later," my kidnapper mentioned. He ran alongside us at my right, but all I could make out were his muscular legs and bare feet.

"Not before I do, you won't," the guy with the raspy tone replied.

My kidnapper chortled. "Do you hear that, Isobelle? Your ass is ours."

My mind was filled with dread at the threat of being punished. Did they mean tortured? I knew I was in serious trouble. They were dragging me farther into the forest with no way of calling for help.

The men squabble about sharing me, transferring me from one pair of arms to the other. All sense of time evaporated from my mind, and I wondered how long it would take for someone to notice I was missing. They were men, not boys, and they were taking me somewhere in the forest. I didn't catch any of their names, but they seemed to know mine. The way they were talking, it was as if they had been expecting me for a while.

"I hope she likes how we've decorated the cabin," the guy with the softer tone commented.

What? Cabin? Oh no. My mind flooded with dread.

"We know she likes green, so she'll love it. I don't know about you guys, but I can't get enough of her scent — honey and vanilla. It's driving me insane … I can feel the sparks running down to my —" my kidnapper remarked.

"For once, can you not think about *that* and focus on plan B considering you screwed up plan A?" the assertive guy snapped. "Thanks to your idiocy, we now have to improvise."

My heart sank as I realized what was happening to me. I was being kidnapped by the four men in the woods. My blood ran cold as I recalled the story Teresa told me earlier today. The part where the men in the woods were supposed to hunt naked. I slid my palm against my captive's lower back, and I felt nothing but naked skin. A little lower and I made a full-on smack against his bare backside.

"Careful or I'll return the favor," he warned me.

"Hmmm." The muffled words left my mouth. What I tried to say was, "Let me go, you fucking perverts." This was not the sexy fantasy I had in mind. Who in their right mind would get off on being kidnapped by a bunch of naked guys?

What if Teresa is right? They might bring me back unscathed.

Yeah, and pigs might fly.

With any luck, they would realize their mistake and would take me back to the guest house. I tried to mumble a coherent plea, but the taut rag hampered my speech. If they would just stop bickering like a flock of seagulls fighting over scraps and allow me to speak, I could beg them for mercy. I wasn't a complete twat. I could be reasonable. If they would just turn around and bring me back, I wouldn't press charges. We could brush this off as a prank and laugh about this over drinks. My treat.

"Here we are, Isobelle, home sweet home," the one holding me announced as he carried me over the threshold of a wooden hut.

It was too dark to see inside it. I couldn't tell what the room looked like, especially from my upside-down angle.

The one time I traveled alone, I was kidnapped on my second night.

I waited with trepidation in the pitch-black

darkness as they all bickered among themselves. It was some ridiculous rant over whose responsibility it was to have kept the fire burning. I felt myself being pulled into a tight embrace before finding myself sitting on someone's bare lap.

Didn't they own any rope so that they could tie me to a chair like regular kidnappers? Was it necessary for me to have to sit on a stranger's lap and feel his cock swelling beneath me?

The first flicker of firelight brought the cabin into view, and I could finally see the faces of my captors. I had to blink twice for my eyes to adjust, but as soon as I could see clearly, my eyes darted all over the place. It was a real log cabin, not some dingy hut in the woods. The wooden furniture matched, and the sage green sofa complimented the curtains. As I glanced around, I didn't spot anything I didn't like. But that didn't ease my anxiety. These guys still kidnapped me, no matter how impressive my prison was.

I glanced up into the faces of three hot men with more muscles than I could count, their skin naturally tanned from working outdoors in the sun or living like naturists — who knows? I'm guessing they spent their days chopping wood, logging, and hiking up mountains because no one could look that fit and not work out. I spared a hesitant glance over my shoulder, seeing the fourth bloke cringing sheepishly. He was just as handsome as the others. Four glorious sights to behold, and all stark-bollock naked. Now that I could move my arms, I tugged the gag from my mouth and let it drop around my neck. My lips mashed together to wet my withered tongue.

I scrunch my eyes shut. "Please, for the love of God, can you put on some pants?" I begged, hating how my eyes were being drawn to their swinging appendages.

I don't want to go straight to Hell when they murder me.

"As the lady wishes," I heard one of them say. "Promise that you won't try to run away if I let go of you?" the guy sitting beneath me asked.

My nostrils flared with indignation. "I promise," I lied.

The second he released me, I bolted for the door. My fingertips grazed the handle before the guy who first kidnapped me, pounced on me.

"You just told a straight-up lie. You're just asking for trouble," he rasped into my ear in a warning tone.

I tried to butt-bounce him in the dick to make him release me, but that didn't work. If anything, he seemed to like it rough.

"Just let me go!" I cried at this point. "I promise I won't tell anyone about this. I don't want any trouble.

I just want to go home." And by *"home"* I meant back to London.

"Shh! It's okay. Don't cry. Nobody's going to hurt you, I promise," he reassured me for all the good it did.

I bet they say that to all their victims.

CHAPTER Eight

He turned me around and pulled me to the couch, the soles of my sneakers squeaking against the varnished floor. The men darted back from the adjoining room wearing shorts and nothing else. One guy flung a pair through the air, and my captor caught it with one hand, then whirled me into the arms of a blond guy. He wasn't as rough, but he showed no signs of letting me go, pulling me back on the couch and onto his lap. The guy who dragged me from the door put on his shorts, then went to join the others.

They huddled together and muttered between

them, "Why don't you say something? You're the eldest."

Two of them shoved the nominee forward — a strapping guy with dark hair, a cropped beard, and silvery-grey eyes. He seemed like such a bad-tempered bastard, turning to snap at them like a rabid dog. But then he dragged his gaze to me and held it there as if he was contemplating what to say.

"I'm Alex Bennett," he introduced himself; his tone remained firm. "On behalf of my brothers and myself, I can only apologize for our impulsive behavior. This was *not* how I intended our first meeting to go." He dragged his gaze to my kidnapper, giving him a death glare to suggest this was all his fault.

The second guy spoke next, running his fingers through his dark brown hair to rake out the snags and pieces of twig. His hazel eyes softened as he smiled, like he was trying to seem less threatening than his brother. "Hi, I'm Grayson, the better-looking brother," he spoke modestly. "You might hate me right now, but you'll thank me later."

Alex released an exasperated huff and dragged a hand down his face. He jerked his head to the guy with dark blond hair and green eyes, prompting him to introduce himself to me.

"Lucas," he replied in the same raspy voice I remembered from the forest. I waited for more, but he was done talking. Something told me he was a man of few words, not one to let his guard down to those he didn't trust.

That only left my human armchair. I turned around to lock eyes with him, and my God, he was handsome. His bright blue eyes brimmed with kindness and had a face that could make angels weep. His hair was almost as light as mine, honey blond.

"I'm Mason, and you must be Isobelle?" His voice was as smooth as melted chocolate and sounded just as sweet.

I bounced my shocked gaze between them. "How do you know my name?" I asked, removing my camera strap from around my neck. The chafed skin felt sore when I touched it, but that was the least of my problems.

"We'll explain everything," Alex promised. "Just hear us out."

"Here, let me get that," Mason uttered as he untied the knot and pulled the gag from around my throat.

"What the fuck do you want with me?" I asked, my voice strained with emotion.

Crying made me feel weak, even though it

shouldn't. But that's how I felt. I couldn't fight them off, outrun them, or use tactics to trick them. They were holding me here against my will, and I was powerless to do anything about it.

"To get to know you," Mason answered.

"If you wanted to know me, why didn't you try talking to me? Ask for my number or invite me to dinner? Not kidnap me like a fucking psycho." I glared at them all.

Alex shot Grayson a mordacious look. "That was the plan."

Grayson cringed. "Can we maybe . . . start again?"

My jaw dropped with a mixture of shock and outrage.

Alex glanced at the others for reassurance, then came to crouch beside me. He tried to take both my hands in his, but I pulled them back.

"Don't touch me," I warned him.

He sighed and dropped his gaze. "You're ours, Isobelle. We've been waiting a lifetime for you."

"What?" I wheezed, my mind flooding with panic.

"You belong to us," Alex reinforced.

The others nodded their heads in agreement.

"That's right," Mason spoke as he held me against him. "You are the one that we've been looking for."

I couldn't suck in enough oxygen to breathe. I hyperventilated, my body shaking, my mind whirling. *What?! Me?* Mason pulled me into a reverent embrace, hushing me as if to calm me down. And it was working. *How can this stranger comfort me?* I squeezed my eyes shut until I stopped shaking.

"Give her a minute, Alex," Mason spoke in a hushed tone.

Moments passed, but it felt like forever as I processed what they said. They were the four men in the woods, that much was clear. It wasn't bullshit. The rumors were true. They existed. And they thought I was the one they had been waiting for. So, in a nutshell, they were never letting me go. I'd be trapped here forever.

Mason tapped me on the shoulder from behind. "Would you like a mug of tea, Isobelle?" he asked in a reverent tone. "You prefer tea, don't you?"

Whipping my head around, I narrowed my eyes in a thunderous glare. They kidnapped me, and he dared to ask me if I wanted a brew . . . like this was a cozy little tea party in Covent Garden. Had he fallen over in the forest and bashed his skull? It inclined me to demand a jam and cream scone and some ham sandwiches to go with it, but I somehow doubted the hospitality would stretch that far.

"A cup of tea? Are you joking?" I asked, eyeing him disdainfully.

"Are you sure I couldn't tempt you? I bet you're parched." Mason's eyes sparkled with adoration.

I didn't quite know what to make of this behavior. Mason seemed like a nice guy. But for all I knew, I could be gazing into the eyes of a psychopath. Accept a brew or decline the offer. I desperately needed a drink. That dirty rag had chaffed the corners of my lips raw.

"Fine . . . I'd love a cup of tea, thank you," I replied, reluctantly accepting the offer. "I take it with a dash of milk and two sugars. You can leave out the poison."

Alex snapped his head up in shock at my sudden change in mood, hurrying away, muttering that he would make the tea. The other two men, Lucas and Grayson, were standing a few feet away, watching me suspiciously. They dragged their eyes over my scantily clad body now that my nightdress had ridden halfway up my legs, exposing my thick thighs. I pulled down the material to give me an extra inch of modesty, but the elasticity made it spring back higher.

"Sit the fuck down. You're making her nervous,"

Mason berated his siblings — if they *were* his siblings. They could just be saying that.

Grayson huffed as though we had banished him to the other side of the room. He took a seat on a single armchair, brooding like a scolded puppy. Lucas backed away with a crooked smirk, not taking his eyes from mine. The crackling firelight illuminated his handsome features, *and God strike me dead*, but I couldn't help but admire the way his muscles flexed and rolled as he sat. Lustful images swam into my head, and I shoved them away, hating the way my body reacted to them. This should not — *could not* — be happening.

"Something smells good," Lucas murmured, his voice nothing more than a dark rasp on the edge of breathlessness. I watched him fidget on the chair and pluck at the front of his shorts.

"Are we turning you on, baby?" Grayson remarked amusedly.

"Don't call me baby. I'm not your baby, okay . . .," I snapped back at him, putting him straight.

"Sexy, then," he corrected himself.

Grayson shamelessly gawked at my breasts, and when I glanced down, I saw why — my nipples poked at my nightdress, leaving nothing to the imagination. Shame blasted through me and colored me red. They could see everything through the thin fabric . . . it was like they had x-ray vision that could melt it away. Not even my last partner had seen me naked in the cold light of day. Being rather curvy had made me body-conscious. A pretty face and a well-thought-out outfit could hide a multitude of sins. It didn't warrant how these guys were staring at me as if I was their last meal on earth. No one had ever called me *sexy* before. As much as I had dabbled in the art of seduction, it just didn't come naturally to me. But with these guys, I didn't need to try. For some fucked-up reason, the universe had tossed together everything I ever fantasized about in men and presented me with four different flavors. And they were not asking me to pick one – they were a package deal.

"You have the time it takes me to drink the tea to explain what the fuck you want with me," I reasoned with them. "You wanted me to hear you out. I'm listening. So, start talking."

CHAPTER
Nine

They wanted to wait until Alex came back from the kitchen, which was fair enough. This concerned him too. He carried a red mug by the handle, treading carefully so as not to spill a drop onto the floor.

So, he's houseproud — noted.

I could tell a lot from someone by their actions. The way they respected their living space and the people around them.

"Here, I hope I've made it right," Alex handed me a mug of steaming hot tea, then put a coaster onto the coffee table in front of me.

I took in every detail, making a mental note of

their behavior patterns. It would help me to figure out what made them tick. After inspecting the tea, I risked a sip. It wasn't too milky, and it wasn't too strong . . . it won my seal of approval. We were off to an impressive start.

Alex watched me, cringing to see whether the drink was to my liking. *He wanted to impress me, but why would he care?* Kidnappers were supposed to be wretched, horrid, despicable human beings with agendas. They don't offer their hostages tea and then bother to check if they like it. *What would he do if I spit it out onto his nice clean floor and spattered his coffee table? Would he offer to fetch a replacement? Would that be a step too far to make him lose his temper?* Who was I kidding? They had me cornered from all angles. Being stubborn would get me nowhere.

"Mm, thank you, it's a lovely cup of tea," I told him honestly.

There was no need to lie. He could tell I enjoyed it by my satisfied sigh. I hadn't started foaming at the mouth, so I knew it hadn't been poisoned.

"Glad my tea-making skills, or lack thereof, haven't repulsed you." Alex chuckled; his laughter was genuine.

I sipped in silence, not knowing what to make of this weird situation. Was I a prisoner or not?

"So, Isobelle," Alex added, after clearing his throat, "I bet you're wondering why you're here, and why I said those things before," he said, adopting a sympathetic approach.

"It had crossed my mind," I admitted rather sarcastically.

Lucas fidgeted in his seat, eyeing me like prey. I liked the way he was looking at me . . . more than I should, so I tried to avoid the urge to look at him. Well, that was the plan. I couldn't help myself. It was the same with Grayson, Alex, and Mason, too.

"I'm going to cut straight to the chase," Alex started. "We decided that we would explain everything to you from the start because we don't want to begin our relationship with any secrets or lies." His unfaltering gaze remained upon me, waiting for my response.

My left eyebrow quirked up at the word *relationship*.

"My brothers and I are wolf shifters," he continued, making my eyes bulge – just when he gained my attention, that one line blew my fragile trust to smithereens.

I choked on my tea with a snort. Mason patted my back to assist me.

Alex flinched but then chose to continue, "We are

the wolves you heard last night, and the same wolves you met with tonight. We're the investors funding your research project. I first spotted you at a seminar in London. You might not remember me, but I was giving a speech on conservation of our forest." He shifted nervously, rubbing the back of his neck.

I waited for the punchline . . . but it never came. Then I wriggled out of Mason's grasp. He didn't stop me from getting up to stand.

"Wolf shifters?" I scoffed, still stuck on that joke. "Now I know you're fucking deluded." I set my mug down on the table; the contents sloshed over the rim and made a mess. Not that I cared. Then I snatched my camera from beside Mason's leg and wrapped the cord around my hand. "Point me to the guest house and I can find my way back from here."

Alex scrubbed a hand over his face in agitation. "Do you need me to prove it?" he offered; he used a clipped tone as if he had run out of patience. "We're sharing a personal secret with you . . . the least you can do is listen to what I've got to say."

I scowled with disgust, crossing my arms under my tits. "You won't get away with this," I retorted, trying to take back control.

Alex moved like the wind, snatching my wrists in his shovel-sized hands, and forcing me to feel his heartbeat. "Do you feel the energy between us?" he asserted. "Open your mind and feel our shared connection. It works both ways. You must feel something."

Without thinking of the consequences, I shoved my knee hard into his groin and watched him drop to the floor, the room erupting into the sound of brash laughter. "How do you like that energy, fuck face?" I grunted the words out, because if the pain in his balls were half as bad as the pain that shot through my leg, then I was proud of my achievement.

"Alex," Grayson called out, giggling. "Let her rest. This can wait until the morning."

The pointed glare in Alex's eyes subsided. He dragged himself up from the floor and then staggered to the kitchen. I assumed to get an ice pack for his bruised balls, but he returned with paper towels to clean up the tea spill. He glowered at me, and I glowered back. We both refused to concede.

"You should rest," Grayson mentioned, holding his hand out to me. "You can take the bed. We'll sleep out here."

I didn't accept his hand, and he didn't seem offended by that. He let me follow him into the bedroom of my own accord. He didn't attempt to join me, keeping hold of the door handle as if he intended to close it on his way out.

"You have nothing to fear from us, Isobelle. We would never hurt you," he reassured me.

"Says the wolf shifter," I retorted cynically.

Of all the men to kidnap me, I got the hottest fucking nutjobs on the planet.

Grayson huffed with amusement as he closed the door. I noticed there wasn't a key lock beneath the handle, just a simple lock on the inside which I locked to keep unwanted creepers out. Pressing my ear against the varnished wood, I could hear their hushed whispers as they talked amongst themselves. I couldn't make out what they were saying exactly, but they were obviously talking about me. After an hour or two of lying on the bed, nursing my knee, and straining to listen, their conversation fizzled into silence. It was at that moment I seized the opportunity to escape. I weighed up my limited options. Any attempt I made to try and sneak out through the front door would be thwarted. I knew that. Only sheer stupidity would inspire me to try it. The only feasible means of escape was to climb through the window. We were on the ground floor, so I wouldn't have to worry about falling from a great height and breaking both my legs. My bruised knee be damned; it didn't hurt too badly. I could walk on it. Maybe even run if I had to.

Every movement I made was slow and stealthy as I crept to the window. To my astonishment, the window wasn't locked, and it opened easily enough. Cool air blew into the room, fanning my flustered face. I established a landing point, then eased myself out through the square gap and onto the ground. Armed with nothing but my camera, I ambled to the tree line, sparing a last-minute glance behind me to make sure I wasn't being followed. The coast was clear. My labored steps turned into an awkward run, but as the taste of freedom became ever so sweeter, I chased it with everything I had. My lungs burned as if they had been doused with fuel and set alight, struggling to keep up with the supply and demand for oxygen. Everywhere I turned, my breath turned to white smoke. I made it. I got away.

A foreboding howl tore through the forest, turning my blood ice cold.

Oh shit.

The sound of the chase consumed me – twigs snapping, foliage rustling, paws thundering across the ground. Pain shot through my legs in several places as something sharp scored my skin. Blood pounded behind my ears. Adrenaline raced through my veins like a spark chasing gunpowder. My limbs pumped harder, burning with protest, and my fingers curled into tight fists of fury, slicing through the air to increase my velocity. Howls reverberated every which way, seeming to come from all around me. The inky cloak of nightfall covered everything it touched, hampering my sight. I couldn't see anything, reliant on touch and sound like a blind person stumbling around in the dark. The scent of thick vegetation ravished my throat, flooding my lungs with an icy burn and filling my mouth like a lake. I didn't want to die. Not like this. Not torn to shreds by a bloodthirsty pack of wolves. A bittersweet thought taunted me that I got what I came for. I was here to learn everything there was about wolves and their natural habitat, and here I was, hunted as their prey.

My brain tried to rationalize all the reasons why a wolf would want to hunt and kill a human. It wasn't normal behavior. Wolves preferred to eat bison, rabbits, and deer. They only killed to survive, and the chase was usually over quickly. There was no question that I was being herded. It was a skillful technique to capture their prey. Each warning growl was meant to deter me from going this way or that. The wind rushed overhead, and a forceful impact hit the ground with a thump. My feet skidded through the loose chipping to stop myself colliding nose to nose with the snarling beast. Tearing my camera strap from around my neck, I held the expensive item like a lance, whirling it above my head as a warning that I would beat the living crap out of anything that came toward me.

The sound of branches snapping accompanied the sounds of men grunting, but with little to no natural light, it was difficult to see anything but shadows. I was surrounded. The chase was over. I expected to feel the wrath of sharp teeth and claws. I braced myself ready for it.

CHAPTER Ten

"**I**sobelle, stop!" Alex's commanding voice sent a jolt through my heart.

My startled scream rang through my ears before a rough hand covered my mouth.

"You're bleeding." Lucas's raspy voice accompanied a hot gust against my ear.

He was behind me. Alex was in front of me. My fingers attempted to peel away Lucas's grip as I wrestled against him. Then two wet snouts nudged against my elbows, causing me to whimper helplessly.

"Are you trying to get yourself killed?" Alex berated. "The forest isn't safe during the day, let alone at night."

"Hey!" Lucas barked back, "Lay off her. Can't you see that she's scared?"

Lucas curled his arm around my waist, pulling me against him. The heat from his skin seeped through the thin cotton of my nightdress, permeating through to my heart. Warmth. Protection. Safety. Those feelings surfaced, instilling somewhere within my inner core, enabling me to relax. There was no way they would let me get ripped apart by wolves. Alex stepped forward and brought his hands to rest on either side of my face; his warm breath tickled my skin, so close our noses almost touched.

"Look at me," Alex commanded.

I obeyed and saw that his irises were glowing silvery white. My startled gasp skipped in my throat, wondering how it was possible. Lucas dropped his hand, allowing me a moment to breathe.

"Your eyes . . . what's wrong with them?" I stammered.

I flicked my gaze around and discovered that Lucas's eyes seemed different too. His were the same color as smoldering embers, wild and intense. Either they were wearing some fucked-up contacts, or Alex slipped LSD into my tea.

"And the wolves." My voice held a hint of

hysteria as I glanced at either side of me. "Whose are they?" I asked, stepping back cautiously.

I had been around wolves before, but those had been bred in a sanctuary. They were used to human contact. These were wild, abnormally huge, and yet they acted more like domestic pets who craved my attention. I didn't want to risk petting them in case they bit my fucking hand off. They could smell fear and use it to their advantage.

"They're yours." Lucas's husky chortle tickled my neck, causing my spine to arch.

My skin prickled with tension, needing to get the fuck out of here and fast.

Alex cleared his throat. "Let's get you home."

Home?

"Then you'll bring me back to the guest house?" I asked hopefully. "It'll soon be morning, and Chloe will notice that I'm missing. She'll call the police, and then it'll be out of my hands."

Lucas scooped me up to carry me. "We're not taking you back there, princess. By the time the night is over, you won't want to leave us; you'll want to stay."

"Now look who's scaring her," Alex muttered from behind us.

Both wolves loped at our sides, and I wondered

whether they were the same wolves I saw earlier tonight. My insides twisted at the concept of Alex's words ringing true. Werewolves? What utter nonsense. I bet he just said that to scare me into submission. Bloody sadist.

Lucas carried me through the forest in no time. As we stepped back into the pale moonlight, I could finally see all the angry welts on my skin. It made the pain increase tenfold. Like seeing was believing. Even the cool night air did nothing to ease me. It just made it worse.

"I bet you're sorry you ran away," Alex commented briskly. "Maybe you'll think twice before disobeying us next time."

Was he always this bossy? The snappy tone of his voice made it sound as if he was in a constant mood. Someone who liked things to run smoothly and orderly, his way or no way. Perhaps he would be better suited in the military. That way someone could shove a marching baton up his ass for being a colossal prick. So, why did I find his dominance arousing?

I wriggled against Lucas. "Put me down."

He did as I asked, and I winced with pain as my feet touched the ground.

"Mason . . . Grayson," Alex boomed without so much as removing his steely gaze from me.

The two wolves padded around me in circles.

"Show her. She needs to see for herself before she can learn to trust us," Alex spoke to the wolves.

"Show me what?" I half-whined. I was in too much discomfort to care. "Are you seriously going to pretend that those wolves are your brothers?" I chuckled a pained laugh, hobbling on the spot.

The wolves hunched to the ground, my eyes widening with terror as they began a metamorphosis like that of a horror film. I was almost sick as their bones moved beneath their fur like mechanical snakes. The hairs on their limbs receded, revealing unblemished skin over firm muscle, and their snouts shrank back inside their skulls to reveal two familiar faces. They grunted and groaned as they worked through their shift, gasping for breath as it ended.

"Oh my God!" I shrieked, backing into Lucas, then I recoiled away and bumped into Alex, bouncing between them like a pinball.

Alex grasped my jaw, not forcibly but gently, and made me watch until Mason and Grayson rose to their feet like men. I witnessed firsthand that werewolves existed, and the research I was here to carry out would amount to nothing. No one would believe this. These guys would never let me go. Not after witnessing this. I was stuck here forever, never to see my loved ones again.

"You . . ." I dragged my finger through the air, pointing at each of them. "You're werewolves."

Alex bristled, and he snatched my wrists in case I tried to run again. "Oh, come on, Isobelle. You should know by now that we're not going to hurt you, but if you take off again you *will* be disciplined," he growled a warning.

Mason's eyes flashed with guilt as he took in the sight of my fearful expression. "Come here," he spoke soothingly, holding out his arms.

"But you're nude," I pointed out the obvious.

If this was going to be a regular occurrence around here, then I needed to get used to the nudity. As the saying goes, *"if you've seen one dick, you've seen them all,"* but that wasn't true. The Bennett brothers put all my exes to shame in the dick department.

"And you're complaining because . . ." Grayson narrowed his eyes as he delivered his cheeky retort.

"Because I hardly fucking know you, that's why!" I spat back, mortified.

Alex raised his hands at his sides. "So, give us a chance to change that." He bounced his shoulders in a simple shrug. "I know you feel our connection, so there's no use trying to deny it."

"Oh yeah, and what makes you an expert on my feelings?" I argued, refusing to admit it.

His eyes locked with mine in a battle for dominance, sending my arousal into overdrive. My pussy clenched with the thirsty need to feast, but I would be damned if I was going to stroke his ego and submit to him. It thrilled me to see his nostrils flare with annoyance.

Alex stalked closer and sucked in a lungful of air through his nostrils, doing the very thing that made my stomach flutter. "Deny it all you want, but your body is betraying you, sweetheart."

Shit . . . how can he tell?

The husky rumble of his voice made love to my ears, quickening my pulse, and melting my insides. I was consciously aware of the warm gush seeping into my knickers, proving the smug fucker right.

"There will be time for all of that when we've tended to her wounds?" Mason suggested, easing the tension between us.

Then Mason engulfed me in a comforting hug, sending pleasurable sparks skittering through my body to eliminate the pain I was in. How could that be? They defied medical science in all ways possible.

Grayson took over from Mason, slapping his arms

away from me. "Give her to me," he commanded, swatting him away like a fly. "I'll take it from here."

Mason scowled at him. "Fine, but don't blow it. I'll make her some chamomile tea." He sprinted back in the direction of the cabin.

Lucas and Alex held back to talk as Grayson carried me. I didn't put up a fight this time. It hurt too much to walk.

"It's all right," Grayson soothed. "Daddy has got you."

Did he really just say that?

As much as that comment made the hairs on the back of my neck bristle with *what the fuckery* vibes, he sounded tender and sweet. Not creepy. There was a loving edge to his voice that wasn't there before. And in all honesty, I liked it. But as much as I tried to forget what I saw and pretend they were men, I couldn't. They were not regular men, but mythical creatures who had pledged themselves to me. It hardly seemed real. Something wasn't quite right. There had to be a catch.

CHAPTER Eleven

Isobelle

G rayson put on some shorts, then finished cleaning my wounds, wrapping bandages around the nasty ones. The cabin was quiet. Nobody else came into the bedroom while he was tending to me. They got the hint I needed some space. Grayson grinned, holding a fistful of colorful Band-Aids for me to choose from.

I cocked my head to one side. "Seriously?! I'm not five," I muttered sarcastically.

He was taking the whole "Daddy" thing to the

extreme. If I misbehaved, would he put me on the naughty step or force me to stand in a corner and face the wall, or worse . . . would he put me over his knee and spank me? God, why did I secretly want that?

His brows jumped a few millimeters. "Humor me."

I sucked in a languid breath through my nose, then tapped a pink one with sparkly princess crowns on it.

"Give me that one," I replied with an exhausted sigh.

Grayson coughed to clear the back of his throat as if he was prompting a further response from me. I waited for a couple of seconds before adding an exasperated, "Please."

This seemed to satisfy him, and he removed the outer packaging and secured the childish Band-Aid on my knee. Then he kissed it. He pressed his lips against my knee as if he was kissing it better. My nostrils flared, and my eyes rounded, not knowing what to make of that.

"Do you hurt anywhere else?" he asked, using a gentle tone with me.

I let my gaze trail to my side, wondering if I should mention the gigantic bruise that was forming on my hip bone. But no. It was probably best not to. If he started kissing me all over, there was no telling where this might end up. I could hardly deny how handsome he was. He was gorgeous. They all were.

"No, I'm fine," I told him, playing it safe.

Grayson's brown eyes flinched as he thought. "Do you feel something happening between us yet?"

"Like what?" I replied, needing him to be more specific.

If he wanted to know whether I fancied him, then the answer was yes. Did I fancy his brothers? Yes. Did I believe in werewolves? Well, I sure as shit did now. They must have tipped the scales of my sanity because I was feeling rather calm about it. Either that or I was on the verge of having a nervous breakdown.

Grayson's shoulders plummeted as he sighed. "It doesn't matter. You should get some rest."

As he stood to leave, I instinctively reached out and curled my fingers around his forearm. "Wait. Tell me what you meant. I want to know."

He crouched back into a squatting position and took my hands into his. My skin tingled all over, giving me a warm and fuzzy feeling inside. I looked him directly in the eyes, not wanting to miss the flicker of truth or lies. My trust was balanced upon a knife's edge. I wanted to believe he had the best intentions.

"You're supposed to feel safe around us. It's supposed to feel like you are home; that we're the center of your universe, like you are to us. That kind of feeling," he explained, then waited for my reaction.

Grayson's words left me speechless, wondering how on earth I was supposed to respond to that. It was the nicest thing that anyone had ever said to me – a guy, I mean. My heart skipped several beats.

My nose brushed against his as I leaned forward, pressing my mouth to his. He gasped with surprise, having not expected me to react in this way. I felt his smile curl against my lips in a mixture of relief and joy. But as quickly as the kiss began, I pulled back, embarrassed with myself.

"I'm sorry. I shouldn't have done that. I don't know what came over me, I just . . . it just . . ." I shook my head, struggling to make sense of my tangled thoughts.

"It felt right," Grayson finished my sentence.

Yes.

He stood this time, and I didn't stop him. I didn't correct him, either. As I crawled into bed and snuggled between the cool satin sheets, those words rang true to me. It did feel right, and I was wicked, filthy, and disgusting for wanting it.

Grayson

I knew she could sense something, even if she didn't understand what it was. The need to be cherished was ever-present in her eyes. I could give her the world if she'd let me. The urge to be her caregiver, and her lover, boiled deep within my loins. I'm a dirty-minded bastard for thinking this way, but I can't help how I felt. Alex could somewhat relate to this.

I closed the door and heard the soft whimpers leaving her lips. It took every ounce of restraint not to charge in there and comfort her. But it wasn't what she wanted. She still needed time. If she were a shifter like us, she would have jumped our bones within the first five minutes of meeting us, but not Isobelle. She was human, and we had to respect that. Just like now in the bedroom, when she kissed me, I swore as she leaned in and pressed her lips to mine, my heart exploded. She had to have felt something to make her react that way. As I replayed that moment inside my head, my cock kicked in my shorts. The fucker was reminding me of his presence, threatening to rear his one-eyed frisky head and let my brothers in on our little rendezvous with our girl. I found them sitting on the front porch, knocking back cold beers, and talking about the night so far. It was quite an occasion. Our plan worked. But only just, no thanks to me.

"Sit your ass down and explain to me why the fuck you smell of pussy?" Lucas growled as he looked my way, green-eyed with envy.

I held my hands out in front of me, offering him a whiff. The lack of Izzy's sweet nectar was enough to vindicate me, but they still cast me the stink-eye, thinking the worst of me as always.

"She kissed me. I didn't kiss her," I spoke defensively. "It's not my fault if her sex hormones are going haywire."

That wasn't true. It *was* our fault. It was her body's way of reacting to the mate bond. Sex was a huge part of it.

"Shit," Lucas hissed, raking his fingers through his tousled hair. "She kissed you?" He frowned with disbelief.

Mason threw me a can of beer. "Here, dude. Take a load off."

"Thanks," I uttered, catching a cold can single-handedly, my fingers sliding through the condensation.

"How is she?" Mason asked.

"Confused," I replied, the gassy hiss filling the air as I opened the can. "And overwhelmed. I think she's had enough excitement for one night."

Mason had always been the shy, sensitive one. Maybe she would respond better to him instead of being freaked the fuck out by either mine or Alex's kinks. Alex thrived on order and precision and had the emotional capacity of a teaspoon. Lucas was a dark horse who spent most of his time in his wolf form, and that affected his vocal cords. Our parents warned him time and time again to shift regularly but not to overdo things, but Lucas preferred the primal life. Mason could articulate his feelings better than any one of us could. The man spoke, and it was like he was reciting a fucking sonnet. I opened my mouth and spouted filth dressed as humor.

Pick a fucking Band-Aid.

The cold beer helped to ease my inward cringe-fest. I might as well have handed her the keys to my car and pointed her to the guest house. She probably thought I was the world's biggest pervert.

If she knew I had visions of her looking up at me

through those luscious lashes, cooing, "Yes, Daddy," she would run away screaming. The thought of her needing me in that way turned me the fuck on. *Not that I'm into any sketchy, underage shit because I'm not!* That was just sick and wrong, and I wasn't into that. I just have the urge to nurture her. To care for her, and for her to need me in that way. It's my ultimate fantasy, kink, or whatever you want to call it. Either she would accept me for who I was, or she'd run for the hills. I hid my feelings behind sarcasm and dirty jokes to mask how I truly felt when all I ever wanted was to find my mate and for her to love me – to love us all.

Fuck! I'm so screwed. The little lady has me by the balls, and she doesn't even realize it.

Mason

I've never seen Grayson give a shit about anything other than his Porsche before. *Holy crap, maybe the guy has depth after all.* I can tell by the way he avoided my gaze that he was stressing about something. Grayson was usually so laid back he was horizontal. The fact that he hadn't locked himself in the bathroom to jerk off meant that our girl occupied his thoughts.

Isobelle Harding, you are something else, young lady.

"I think we should fetch her belongings from the guest house. It'll help her to settle in," I suggested.

My brothers nodded their heads in agreement.

"I'll go," Grayson volunteered. "I'll take Alex's SUV."

"No, you won't!" Alex never let anyone else drive his car. There was a momentary pause before he piped up, "I'll drive."

His response was right on cue, making me chuckle. We were all so damned set in our ways it was comical. Our girl was going to shake things up in our little quartet, that was for sure.

"You better wait until daybreak. I wouldn't go hammering down Lincoln Anderson's front door at this ungodly hour. Not unless you have a death wish," I reasoned with them.

Grayson opened his second beer after draining the first in a few chugs. Alex didn't touch another drop, honoring his offer to drive. One perk of being a shifter meant that we have a fast metabolism. Alcohol doesn't stay in our systems for long, but that doesn't matter to a guy like Alex. He's so fucking rigid he's stick-straight.

"Hey, Lincoln is just as guilty as we are," Lucas mentioned in a sleep-deprived rasp. "I hope Izzy doesn't take it to heart. Chloe and Linc are good people. I was hoping she'd made a friend."

Lucas must have been bone-tired after fulfilling twelve hours of ranger duties before all the shit kicked off. The guy looked like he was about ready to crash.

"If Isobelle wakes up before we return, do you think you can handle it?" Alex cast Lucas and me a pointed look.

"We'll be just dandy," I answered, seeing the way Lucas scowled back at him, outraged.

There was no way I could deal with breaking up a scuffle between those two hotheads. The last time it happened, I had to use the garden hose as a water cannon.

"Yeah," Lucas growled. "At least you won't be here to yell at her again. She is allowed to get upset, you know?" He hauled himself up from the porch stairs. "And anyway, I don't remember kidnapping being part of the plan. Weren't we supposed to get her to trust us? That plan just sailed down Wolf Creek without a paddle."

Yikes.

Alex bristled as Lucas hit back with the truth.

"Don't look at me," Alex retorted snappily. "I wasn't the one who grabbed her from behind."

Grayson flinched with remorse. "I panicked." He paced across the creaky decking. "You were prancing around in front of the camera as if you were posing for Whitehaven's *Next Top Model*, so I improvised. How many times do I need to apologize?"

Alex huffed through his nostrils. "I wasn't prancing. It was all part of the three-month plan to gain her trust, but now we're fucked. We might as well confess to Alpha Alec that we screwed up and hope he'll spare our hides, but don't hold your breath."

I felt a sudden rush of panic.

"We can't do that. If Isobelle doesn't agree to mate with us, he will never let her live. She knows our secret," I reminded him, my heart pounding with dread.

I loved my Alpha like a father, but I didn't always agree with his rules despite having to follow them. And Alex could make flippant remarks about coming clean to him about Isobelle, but Alec would not show leniency. The rules were there for a reason, and all pack members must respect them or face the Alpha's wrath. No exceptions. It was all or nothing.

"He's right," Grayson commented. "And I'll be damned if I'll let anyone lay a hand on her, even if it means committing treason."

Silence stilled the air, filling the forest with a somber vibe. We all felt the same invested feeling for Isobelle, and the choices we had made. She was ours, and we would die to protect her whether she wanted to be with us or not.

CHAPTER Twelve

Alex

"Jesus, how much does one woman need?" I stared at Isobelle's luggage with disbelief.

My car was on its ass, fully loaded with all her *essentials*.

Fuck me, where are we going to put it all?

Lincoln Anderson lent me a bungee cable to secure the trunk after I fought to keep the door closed.

"Do you think it's a good sign that she has pink

Playboy bunny symbols all over her luggage?" Grayson mentioned.

I envisioned an illuminated light bulb hovering above his head as his mind whirled with possibilities. *Is she kinky? Or does she just like pink?* Lincoln cast him a puzzled look, probably wondering what the fuck he was talking about. That brand wasn't well known here in Whitehaven. Only Grayson had an outside subscription.

"There . . . that should hold it," I announced, flustered, sleep-deprived, and agitated. This business with Isobelle tied my stomach in knots.

Grayson let out a low whistle. "Holy cow, that's a serious amount of stuff. Where is it gonna go? We clearly didn't think this through."

He was right. We would need to build an extension to accommodate all her belongings. I was guessing this was only the tip of the iceberg to what she had back home. *Oh, boy.* Then there was the prospect of having pups someday. I told those assholes we'd be better suited to a mansion in Whitevale, but oh no, they wanted to be closer to nature. More like they were sick of getting looked at like trash. Our entire family had always been the topic of gossip, fated to lead a harem lifestyle over a straight-up monogamous one. My brothers and I were no different. That was why they were so keen to leave town. It still didn't stop people from talking shit about us hunting for women on a full moon. We never did any of that. The thought of last night's antics brought a slight smile to my face. It was enough to drive all the gossips crazy.

"We better get going before Sleeping Beauty awakes," Grayson mentioned to Lincoln. "Thanks for all your help, man. We appreciate it."

"No problem," Lincoln replied gruffly. "Just remember what I said about human women. They need their independence. She'll probably want to call her mother every day, sometimes more than once. When I first moved in with Chloe, she was on the phone several times a day to Molly. It's a female thing." He shrugged his shoulders with a baffled expression.

Grayson and I exchanged a furtive look. "Yeah, speaking of *mothers*," Grayson rubbed the back of his neck sheepishly.

"Don't even go there," I warned flatly. "Not yet. I want us to mark and mate with her before we drop that bombshell on her head."

Lincoln chortled. "Good luck with that."

I grunted a *hmph* noise, to show my indignation. When our mom got her paws on Isobelle, she would recruit a powerful ally. The last thing we needed was for Izzy to learn all about our family legacy. That was sure to scare the bejesus out of anyone.

Grayson clambered in through the passenger side as I climbed into the driver's seat. The moment I started the engine, the operatic symphony resumed playing from exactly where it left off. Grayson winced with displeasure, preferring new-age metal over my orchestral classics.

"Do you have any gum?" Grayson asked as I studied the road ahead.

My fingers gripped the steering wheel tight enough to make the leather creak. "You're not chewing gum while I'm driving. The incessant sound of lip-smacking drives me crazy."

He blew out a forced breath, then began tapping his fingers against his knee in time to the music he so blatantly hated. After about thirty seconds, I couldn't stand it any longer.

"What the fuck are you doing?" I cast him a fleeting glance.

"Oh, will you lighten up?" he retorted.

My posture stiffened, and my jaw pulsed, causing my teeth to grind together. *Lighten up.* I was doing just fine until he started irritating me. *Why does everybody assume I have a grievance against everything because I'm particular?*

"You know . . . I think you ought to apologize to Isobelle for yelling in her face last night. Even if it was to stop her from running into danger. The least you can do is clarify that you only did it because you care. She probably thinks you don't like her or something," Grayson pointed out.

Am I really so uptight? I don't mean to be. I just like everything to run like clockwork. And when it doesn't, I don't feel as if I'm in control. Too many people depended on me to step up and take charge. Being the eldest of the family, even if it was only by minutes, made me feel like I must set an example to the other three. I was also the lead ranger. It fell to me if hunters crept past our western outpost. It was my responsibility if anyone got hurt on my watch. It was me who found our mate first, and it was me who thought of a plan to lure her here. Sometimes the pressure of leadership was unbearable. I had so much pent-up frustration and nowhere to relinquish it. And it made me rather irritable.

"Was I really that harsh?" I asked, maintaining an impartial tone.

I didn't demonstrate remorse because that would mean admitting I was wrong. Although, Grayson's words stung, and an unexplainable sensation churned my stomach. *What is this feeling I'm experiencing? Is it guilt? How do I make it stop?*

"I'd say you were," Grayson concluded. "You know, you can instill discipline and show affection at the same time."

His words hit close to the bone, making me bristle. I ached to claim her from the moment I saw her at the conference. There were other darker ways I'd like to reprimand her, unleashing unbridled savagery I kept locked away deep inside me. Not even my brothers knew the full extent of my yearning to dominate. My need for a submissive. Isobelle's sassy mouth and feisty attitude awakened the beast within me. It was biding its time, thinking up ways in which it could make her kneel.

"I'll make it up to her and apologize," I decided.

And just like that, the tension in my chest subsided.

Lucas

"Listen . . ." I held my finger against my lips as Mason approached the bedroom door.

We both grinned as the sound of loud, rumbling snores rattled around the cabin.

"No way." Mason chuckled. "Alex is going to need earplugs when he hears her snoring."

Speaking of Alex, he was due back at any minute. One of the perks of being a werewolf was that we shared a pack link, but because we were quadruplets, we had a unique psychic link that even the other pack members couldn't tap into.

"We better wake her up before he gets home. You know how much he hates people lazing in bed past breakfast," I mentioned.

If it was down to me, I would let her sleep in all day. I wasn't exactly the world's most sociable wolf when it came to initiating a conversation. Shove a wrench in my hand and leave me out in the yard and I would service your car free of charge. I was a man of little needs. If I was fed, watered, and exercised, I would be happy. Just like any regular wolf, I was as wild as they came.

I knocked briskly on the door and waited for a response. Nothing. I knocked again, but this time a little louder. Nothing. I could see that Mason was deliberating whether to peek inside, but I beat him to it and barged my way in. The mug of tea was burning my fucking knuckles, and I needed to deliver it before I dropped it on the floor.

The sight of Isobelle twisted up in the sheets with her ass hanging out made me wolf-whistle loudly. Izzy woke up in a state of startling disarray, then looked around as if she had forgotten where the hell she was. Her eyes bounced back and forth between Mason and me as if she thought she was still dreaming. It was cute how she pulled her nightdress down to cover her modesty, and it was so fucking adorable how she swiped the back of her hand across her mouth to check for drool. Now I wish I had slapped that ass while I still had the chance.

Bummer.

"Good morning," I announced in a bright sing-song voice that was better suited to Mason.

Mason turned to me, detecting my sarcasm, and narrowed his eyes with disdain. I placed the scalding mug of tea down on the nightstand and took a step back in case she decided to throw it over me. She needed a few moments to process things, then checked around the room.

"Where are the other two?" she asked. "Grayson and Alex?"

It shocked me that she remembered their names, and it also spiked my jealousy that they'd made a strong enough impression on her. I'm always last in the pecking order of things. Always the forgotten one. Mason may be the youngest, but he was known for his intellect and artistic flair. I was the strong silent one who nobody ever found interesting. At least, not enough to get to know me.

"You're Mason," Isobelle pointed at my brother, and my heart sank.

Of course, she knew who Golden Boy was. He was probably in the running to be her favorite.

Mason flashed a million-megawatt smile that made him look every inch a GQ model. I wasn't going to stick around to be asked to introduce myself. What was the point? I had plenty to do outside, like reorganizing my tool shed, and feeling sorry for myself.

"Lucas, wait," Isobelle called out just as I turned to leave.

The sound of my name leaving her lips stopped me dead in my tracks, and I turned my head, my lips parting with surprise.

"Thank you for the tea," she mentioned gingerly.

She picked up the mug, brought it to her lips, and took a grateful slurp. "It's a good brew. Ten out of ten for effort."

My heart fluttered in my chest, and I let out a

genuine chuckle. She fucking marked me ten out of ten for my tea-making skills. For the first time in my life, I shied away from a woman, flattered by the compliment.

Clearing my throat, I muttered, "Thanks."

I was no good at making small talk. So, I stalked out of the cabin, needing to occupy myself with manly tasks and take my mind off the growing tent in my shorts.

Mason followed a couple of moments later, finding me elbow deep in engine grease.

"The lady is taking a bath," he pre-warned me in case I wanted to use the bathroom.

"If nature calls, there's no better place than out here in the wide open," I reminded him, watching his nose wrinkling with disgust.

"You need to stop doing that. I would've thought you'd be potty-trained by now," he reprimanded, casting me an admonishing look to match.

Just as I was about to come back with a snarky comment, the rumble of Alex's SUV saved him. The tires crunched through loose chippings before coming to a stop at the front porch.

Grayson grinned as he exited the passenger side, then jerked his head as a signal that we should check out what Alex was doing. Our sophisticated sibling emerged with an impressive bouquet of colorful flowers and a bag full of groceries.

Grayson waited until Alex disappeared through the door before rounding on us with an explanation.

"He's bringing out the big guns to show her that he's sorry," he revealed. "He's hoping to impress her with his culinary skills."

Both mine and Mason's faces flooded with shock.

"Alex is apologizing?" The disbelief was clear in my voice. "Where's the fucking camera?"

Mason's brows hit his hairline. "This I've got to see," he uttered, just as stunned as I was.

CHAPTER Thirteen

Isobelle

I had the most amazing soak in the world's largest bathtub, then emerged from the room in a cloud of steam. Holding a fluffy white towel around my body, I crept back to the bedroom, tiptoeing past Alex in the kitchen. He was busy scrubbing a pan in the sink, and the heavenly smell of pancakes wafted past my nose.

"Good morning," he muttered over his shoulder. "I hope you slept well?"

"I . . . uh, yes, thank you," I replied, surprised by his pleasant tone.

"We brought all your belongings from the guest house, and I charged your cell phone while you were taking a bath," he mentioned, up to his forearms in soap suds.

What?! He'd gone to the guest house, and Chloe and Lincoln had just let him take my things without asking questions. I had a pile of dirty laundry on the floor by my bed. Did he get that too? My cheeks flushed with embarrassment, but I could sense the repentant tone of his voice and figured he was only trying to be helpful. There were still so many questions that needed answers, but until I got them, I was going to get dressed, and then eat some of those delicious pancakes.

Someone had stacked my cases in the bedroom while I was taking a bath. As far as I could tell, they'd neither tampered with nor mishandled my things. They placed the research equipment behind the sofa, out of harm's way. Someone had washed my dirty laundry because it was hanging on a washing line at the back of the cabin. I peered through the window and saw Mason hanging my knickers on the line.

Just as Alex had promised, my phone was plugged into the charger and now had a full battery. They weren't cutting me off from the outside world like I thought they were. If that was their intention, then why give me my phone so I could call for help? Dad could have the authorities here within hours. All it would take was for me to contact him, and he could track my phone's GPS. If they knew this, then why not just confiscate my phone and eliminate the risk?

I took my phone off charge and swiped my thumb against the screen, then I typed in my four-digit passcode. No one had tried to text me since last night. London's time zone was five hours ahead. It wouldn't be long before someone reached out to me to ask how my day was going.

"Oh sorry, I didn't realize that you were making a call," Mason excused, turning to leave me in privacy.

"I wasn't," I replied, shrugging. "I'm just checking my messages, but there are none." I tossed my phone onto the bed covers. "Nobody loves me," I muttered breezily.

"We . . . uh," Mason stammered awkwardly. "I came to tell you that breakfast is ready."

Was he about to say that they loved me? Nah . . . surely not.

At the mention of food, I left the confines of the room and followed the smell of food into the open-plan living space. They'd been meticulous when designing this place, with no expense spared. It seemed far too grand for a group of forest rangers . . . I meant to say, werewolves. It would take a while to get my head around that.

As I emerged from the bedroom, Alex greeted me with a bouquet of pretty flowers.

"I hope you're not allergic," he spluttered, his eyes bulging as if this only just occurred to him.

A grin spread across my face, finding his awkwardness amusing. "No, I'm not allergic to anything."

"I wanted to apologize for giving you a hard time last night." His eyes flinched regretfully, and I saw how sincere he was.

"These are beautiful. Thank you," I replied, not expecting him to take back the way he snapped at me last night. He seemed like the type of guy who stood by his word until the bitter end.

The flowers injected some color into the room besides green and brown. They came in their own presentation box filled with water. I didn't have to do anything, just admire them. I set them down on top of the kitchen counter, not knowing where else to put them. This wasn't my home. It was theirs.

The boys gathered around the table, chair legs scraping across the floor, and cutlery clattering together. I took a seat between Lucas and Grayson. Mason was sitting diagonally from me, and Alex faced me. I kept flicking my gaze across the table and would catch Alex staring. Darkness shaded his eyes, making it hard to tell what he was thinking. It mattered what he thought of me. I can't explain why. It was like I needed his guidance and approval, and that only left me feeling guilty and ashamed. This wasn't normal behavior for me. I shouldn't be sitting here enjoying breakfast with these men. So, why was I?

"Isobelle." Alex's assertive voice captured my attention. "I think we should talk about last night. Especially now we're all sitting here calmly."

I snorted with amusement, witnessing him controlling the situation as if we were his subordinates and that he was the boss. Biting my lip with subtlety, I suppressed a snarky retort.

"You're owed an explanation," Mason added. "It wasn't supposed to go down like this. You must think that we're a bunch of Neanderthals."

I finished swallowing the last morsel of pancake and syrup and washed it down with some freshly squeezed orange juice. They were so fluffy and light it was like eating a delicious cloud smothered with sugar.

"All right. I want to know why you chose me. You said that you saw me at a conference in London. Is that when you came up with the project?" I asked, not so much in an accusatory tone, but one that showed that I deserved the truth.

If they were going to stay true to their word, it would do me no good to slap away the olive branch and spit back with contempt.

It was Alex who explained his reasons. "Our meeting was purely coincidental. I didn't know I was going to meet my soulmate halfway across the world. My Alpha sent me to the seminar to find out what I could about a new forestry project. We have a major problem with hunters claiming to be environmentalists. They are using the excuse of wanting to research the natural order of things here in our forest, but they are hunting down shifters to extract their blood. I don't want to turn you off your breakfast, but that's the harsh reality of what we're facing here. We keep our state secret from the rest of humanity. Hunters appreciate the value of shifter blood. Its healing properties mean it's worth more than gold. We don't know what would happen if people learned of our existence. It's not a risk we're willing to take. Seeing you sitting there across the conference room took me by surprise. I couldn't think of a better way to invite you over here. I saw an opportunity, and I seized it. I can't apologize for that."

Fair enough. I could understand that. My job as a biologist was to help conserve life and to study it. The thought of parasites like those hunters he just mentioned, using my role as a smokescreen, made me feel sick to my stomach.

"So, what am I here for exactly? I wanted to further my career," I expressed, trying to get him to see things from my point of view. "You lured me here under false pretenses. I'm supposed to be studying a rare species of wolf. I need to keep busy, or I'll go insane."

"We are a rare species of wolf," Lucas interjected, his mouth full of pancake.

I half-snorted. "What? I'm expected to study *you?*" I rolled my eyes at his comment. "And here I was thinking you wanted to be kept secret."

Alex practically choked on fresh air. "We do. That's not what my brother is implying."

Grayson released a sigh. "We want you to stay here and get to know us better. That was the master plan, was it not?"

Alex pursed his lips as he glared across the table at Grayson. "Yes," he hissed. He flicked his languid gaze to me, and in a considerate tone, he added, "We would like that very much. But it must be your choice." I detected a hint of fear in his eyes that suggested it was something I seriously ought to consider.

It seemed unlikely their Alpha would just let me go home, knowing what I know. Especially if they were battling with hunters.

"What about my parents?" I asked, and the second that I did, they took it as a sign of acceptance. That wasn't what I meant, and I needed to clarify that. "I mean, if I stay here with you, will you at least allow me to see them?" If they responded with a stern "no," then I would be leaving, and I would take my fucking chances.

"Yes," they all reacted at once, as if they had already decided.

That surprised me, and the hairs along my arms raised as goosebumps erupted across my skin. *What is happening to me? Where did this sudden burst of joy come from? Do I really want this? To stay here with these gorgeous men, and to have my cake and eat it too? What will my parents say about me being shacked up in a cabin with four strapping young brothers for company?*

"You won't want to leave us now the mate bond has taken hold. You'll get halfway across the Atlantic and have a full-on anxiety attack," Alex mentioned, and there wasn't a hint of deceit in Alex's eyes as he told me that. I had no reason to disbelieve him.

"We can invite your parents here, and we can accompany you when you visit them," Mason added, not seeing the bigger picture. I hated to be a Debbie Downer, but we just didn't do things like that where I came from. How would I explain this to any of my friends, let alone my parents?

Alex's brows furrowed into a deep analyzing frown as he gazed back at me expectantly. "You're embarrassed at the thought of being with the four of us, aren't you?"

Is he serious? Of course, I am! Society spits in the eyes of promiscuity. How can they expect me to sleep with all four of them? Individually, or all at once?

"We're quadruplets," Alex mentioned. "Sharing is second nature to us."

My words just wouldn't come out, not quite knowing how to respond to that.

"Don't knock it until you've tried it," Lucas rasped as if he knew what I was thinking.

His comment made me blanch. "Have you tried it?" I asked, surprised by the bitter taste of jealousy that tore through me. The thought of any other woman touching them conjured an ugliness within me that made me want to find out who she was and then claw out her eyes.

"No," Lucas answered straight-faced. "We have never shared a woman before, but because we're quadruplets, fate connects us. As we suspected, we are destined to share a female between us. It isn't uncommon for multiple shifters to share a mate if their souls are linked like ours are," he replied honestly.

Fuck me, that was the most I'd heard him speak. I couldn't see any deceit in his eyes, so I knew he believed in what he was saying.

"Will you accept us?" Mason asked. His voice had a saddened edge to it as if he expected me to decline.

All the moisture evaporated in my mouth, leaving my withered tongue as dry as a prune.

"Tick tock, Isobelle," Alex teased dryly. "Time is running out. You can give us a chance to show you how great it could be, or you can walk out that door right now. What's it going to be?"

I shook my head incredulously. "You're talking about a reverse harem. *Me* . . . and the four of you as my boyfriends." I flung my hands up dramatically.

I couldn't hold down one boyfriend. What made them think I could handle four?

"Husbands," they blurted out together.

"Once we take a mate, it's for life," Grayson stated.

"We offer you security and a sense of belonging," Lucas uttered.

"Love and companionship," Mason included.

"Passionate sex, whenever you want it," Grayson added with a cheeky wink.

"Forever and always," Alex finished.

I squeezed my thighs together as I considered that. Now I knew exactly how Adam felt when Eve offered him a bite of the forbidden apple. The sweet taste would be good while it lasted, but then what? I knew my heart and how fragile it was. Just one taste and I would be invested. I knew I would. *But if I don't try it, how would I know if I like it or not?*

Their eyes pinned me into place as I took a deep breath and sealed my fate. I must have dislodged a screw loose in my brain during the five-mile stint in the forest because all sense and reason seemed to elude me in making this decision. I should have said "thank you very much but point me back to the guest house" but I didn't. Instead, I gave this some thought, weighing up the pros and cons, and developing a fucked-up pornographic flow chart in my head. The kind of thoughts that would send Nana and all her avid knitting enthusiasts running to take shelter at the nearest convent.

"Okay . . ." My pulse elevated as I face-palmed myself. "God, strike me down dead for even thinking about this, but I'm curious to see where this goes."

CHAPTER Fourteen

Isobelle

"**Y**ou are?" Grayson spluttered with disbelief.

Alex collapsed with relief. Lucas slurped his coffee as if he hadn't been worried at all. His cockiness was cute, and I could see straight through it.

Mason looked as if all his Christmases had come at once. "You won't regret it," he gushed, sounding ecstatic.

"Can I just ask you something? If everyone

around here is a shifter, does that include Chloe and Lincoln?" I inquired, dodging the subject of sex.

It was bound to crop up next, and I was stalling for time. Sue me. My body was trembling with nerves, terrified of what it would feel like to be shared between them.

"Lincoln is a bear shifter from Forest Hills," Alex informed me. "Chloe is human, like you."

"And she didn't mind Lincoln being a . . . *you know?* A" — I cringed as I use the word — "bear shifter?"

Alex flashed a tight-lipped smile to mask his amusement. "Apparently not."

I bobbed my head in an awkward nod. "That'll explain the *'cub'* remark."

"Does that scare you?" Lucas asked, letting his hand rest on my bouncing knee.

It stilled instantly. The warmth of his palm seeped into my skin, stoking the furnace of my desire. I dragged in a ragged breath, clearly affected by the contact. As he circled his thumb against my outer thigh, I almost came on the spot.

If this was what it felt like to be stroked on the leg, what might it feel like to be touched elsewhere? I shuddered with anticipation.

"We are still just guys, Isobelle," Grayson rasped, adding his hand on my opposite thigh.

My pussy fluttered and pulsed as if it knew what it needed. Something only a man could deliver, and four brothers were offering me more than I ever dared to imagine.

"I should be," I confessed breathlessly. "I should be afraid of you, but I'm not anymore. If you wanted to hurt me, you would have done that already."

"Can you smell that?" Lucas mentioned. "She's so turned on I can almost taste it."

A deep rumbling growl came from within Alex, and his eyes flashed a bright shade of silver. "Not until she says so."

What are they doing to me?

The temperature in the room was stifling. My summer dress clung to my body as if it was molded to my skin. Even plucking at the front of it did nothing to cool me down. Perspiration formed across my brow and upper lip, and my skin flushed a blotchy shade of pink. Lucas edged closer to me. Close enough to brush his lips against my cheek. The sensation arched my spine, thrusting my tits out toward Alex.

"I can't wait to taste you. You smell good enough

to eat." His husky whisper ghosted against my skin, making my nipples pebble against the lace of my bra.

"Hmm," I moaned, much to my astonishment.

Dirty. Sinful. Incredible.

I should say no, but my body craved to cut loose of its inhibitions. I'd do anything to be free – to let go of all my insecurities and fear of what others would think of me if they could see me now. Would it be so terrible if I let them do all those wonderful things that they promised to do to me? I wished to feel loved, cherished, and all the things and more.

"Don't push her," Mason berated him. "Give her some space to breathe."

The moment their hands left my skin, all the warmth was sucked from the room like a cold rush of air had blown through. I shivered with disappointment.

"What is happening to me?" My tremulous voice sounded broken and fragile.

"It's the mate bond strengthening," Alex explained. "There's nothing dirty or depraved about this way of life. You're the center of our universe. The only opinions that matter are ours."

I swallow thickly. "I'm a little nervous," I admitted, even though it was blatantly obvious to them.

Alex's expression warmed, and the heat in his eyes ignited. "You won't have to do anything you're not comfortable with. If ever you want us to stop, just say so, and we'll respect your wishes."

I turned my gaze to Grayson, seeking reassurance. Fuck knows why I did that. It just felt right. His brown eyes met mine full of adoration as if I were one of the world's greatest treasures.

"I'm not in any fit state to be manhandled just yet. Last night's escapades left me covered in bruises," I uttered sheepishly. "It felt as if a herd of elephants trampled all over me."

I saw the flare in his eyes the second I agreed to any kind of intimacy.

"But going back to what you said about this being perfectly fine. We're all consenting adults, aren't we?" I justified my decision. "So, it's none of anybody else's business what goes on behind closed doors," I emphasized the latter part of the statement as a hint that I wanted this to remain as private as possible. There was no way I could explain this situation to my parents and expect them to understand. Few people would.

Grayson held my hand and pressed a kiss to my knuckles. "Let us take care of you."

"Okay," I replied, blocking all negative thoughts from my mind.

From the very beginning, I had felt a little spark of attraction toward them, so slipping into a romantic relationship seemed like a dream come true. No cheating. No jealousy. And there could be no favoritism if this was going to work. I became overcome with a carnal desire to let them ravish me salaciously, and all those feelings were beyond my control, surpassing all feasible explanations. I no longer had the urge to run. Grayson was right. I wanted to stay.

"When you say 'okay' does that mean you accept us?" Alex met my gaze with a look of fierce determination.

I knew he would want to instill some level of authority over me, and by accepting him, it would mean relinquishing my control. He was the master, and I would be under his command. Even though some dark, depraved part of me wanted that and to have him bend me to his will, I wondered what it might be like to penetrate his tough exterior and find a way into his soul. What would it be like to have a man like Alex eating from the palm of my hand?

"Yes," I agreed. "All of you." As soon as the words left my lips, tension permeated through the room, pushing at the corners as if it was trapped inside. The air grew thin, making it difficult to breathe. I glanced around into each pair of eyes, noticing the same dark storm brewing within them.

"Good." Alex wriggled in his seat.

Was he adjusting his lower region? My gaze followed his hands south, watching them disappear beneath the tabletop. He seemed to rethink his posture, and he stood abruptly. The corners of my lips twitched with amusement, loving the effect I was having on him. Wrapping him around my little finger might be easier than I thought.

"It's warm in here," I mentioned, fanning my face and neck with my hand. "Is there anywhere to sit outside?"

The boys were already finished eating, and Alex had collected all the empty plates to take them to the sink.

"Yeah, there's a bench on the porch," Lucas informed me. "Do you want some company?"

"Don't you trust me?" I asked, assuming he wanted to play *guard dog* in case I tried to run away again.

"Actually, it's me I don't trust," he rasped under his breath. "How about you come and take a walk with me instead?"

I pretended I only heard the last part. So, he couldn't trust himself. Well, that was useful to know. It meant I held the upper hand over him, too.

"Sounds great. Should I change?" I gestured at my outfit choice, wondering if a yellow summer dress and flat jeweled sandals were suitable enough for what he had in mind.

But then again, he wasn't dressed for a woodland hike, wearing jeans that were ripped at the knees and a gray muscle top shirt with an unfamiliar logo emblazoned across the front. Even his leather boots had steel toecaps, making him look every inch a bad boy biker who liked to crush skulls beneath his feet.

As if reading my thoughts, he replied, "I would put on some sensible footwear if I were you."

I made a move to stand.

"You're not taking her rock-climbing up the mountains of Forest Hills," Grayson chastised his brother, scrunching his face. "Stick to the nature trail."

Grayson was hot on my heels as I left to rummage through my luggage, looking for my hiking boots. They were brand new, never worn. I was likely to end up with blisters after my first time wearing them.

"Wait there," he said, darting toward a chest of drawers. "I have some thick socks you can wear." He produced a rolled-up pair and handed them to me. "Put those on while I adjust the laces in these boots. They're all wrong," he fussed like a tentative parent.

I took a seat on the mattress as I pulled on the socks. When Grayson was finished sorting out my boots, he even slipped them onto my feet and tied my laces like I was a clueless five-year-old.

"That's better, isn't it?" he cooed reverently. "Now they won't rub at your heels."

"Thanks, Daddy," I joked, chuckling at the situation.

Grayson froze in the crouched position, his features turning from relaxed to tense in a millisecond. His brown eyes took their time to lock with mine, but when they did, they were the color of smoldering embers. *Was it something I said?*

"I'm sorry . . . you were only trying to help, and that came out rude." I tried to retract my sarcastic comment and paper over the awkward cracks.

"Don't be," he replied in a dark rasp. "I like it."

I reached out and cupped his face, brushing my fingers against the grain of his stubble. I remembered how soft his lips felt in contrast to the coarse texture and dared to dip down for a second taste.

Grayson leaned up to meet me halfway, placing one hand at the small of my back and the other cradling my nape. My fingers raked through his silky brown hair that was long enough to grasp hold of; our mouths moving in perfect synchronization, warm, soft, perfect. Butterflies fluttered inside my stomach like a schoolgirl who'd just kissed a boy for the very first time. Only this wasn't a boy, he was a man. A man who was blowing my mind with his amazing kissing technique, flicking his tongue against mine as if he was eating my pussy, and oh my God, I wished he was. I bet if I were to lift my skirt and slide my underwear down, he would feast upon me like a starving man.

"Baby girl," Grayson cooed against my lips, alternating between kissing, and grazing his teeth against my bottom lip.

If the fire in my eyes was anything like his, it was enough to spark a flame. My pussy pulsed with need . . . my heartbeat matching the tempo of my throbbing clit with wild and erratic thumps. This kiss made up for the almost kiss we shared. The way his tongue was making love to mine was like a promise of more to come, and I couldn't wait to find out what that felt like. Grayson peppered my face with tender kisses, finishing with one against the tip of my nose and the last on my forehead.

"That was pretty spectacular," he gushed, sounding mind blown.

Grayson evoked a passion inside me that had been lying dormant. The way he acted around me, taking care of me like I was small, gave me a warm, fuzzy feeling inside. It made me want to climb onto his lap, curl up like a little schoolgirl, and go to sleep. When he held me, I felt safe. I felt loved, or at least I got a taste of what being loved was supposed to feel like.

"Have fun on your walk with Lucas." He wagged his finger playfully. "But don't wander off the trail. Stay where he can see you. Do you understand?"

I nodded. "Yes."

"Yes, what?" He arched an eyebrow, prompting a further response from me.

At first, I wasn't sure what he was waiting for, but his persistence meant I had to come up with an answer fast. It couldn't be please or thank you. So, it could only be —

"Yes, Daddy," I figured that was the word he was waiting for.

The satisfied glimmer in his eyes meant I was right.

CHAPTER
Fifteen

Lucas

I sobelle walked out onto the front porch, looking flustered to hell. My God, she looked good when she'd just been roughly kissed. Her lips were still swollen; her blue eyes searched for me as her golden hair danced around her shoulders in the summer breeze. I took my time to admire how beautiful she was, standing there shielding her eyes from the harsh glare of the sun. I wanted to remember the imagery, cataloging every detail so I could drag out my sketchbook and let my pencil work its magic. She was my muse, a vision of perfection, and I needed to immortalize her onto a canvas, turning her into one of those sempiternal paintings that never alters, never fades.

That's how I felt about love. I wasn't a man of many words, but what I lacked in etiquette I made up for with skills. Whether it be fixing up cars, building a motorcycle from scratch, or painting something that inspired me, I donated my time and effort, leaving a piece of me behind. That was how I breathed life into my work, whether it was a finely tuned engine or a brushstroke on a canvas, it derived from love. But Isobelle — she was a masterpiece in her own right. She complemented us, not the other way around. I took care of what belonged to me. Things that mattered most.

I might not find the right way to explain how I feel, but actions speak louder than words.

Isobelle's eyes locked with mine and narrowed into an amused scowl. "There you are." She swatted the air and made her way toward me.

She thought I was hiding on purpose, not standing there mesmerized like a lovesick pup. Moments later, she joined me under the shady forest canopy, and my eyes flicked down to her footwear.

"Nice walking boots," I complimented her.

Izzy flung her eyes up and down and clicked her tongue. "Oh, these . . . they're practical. I think I picked up men's boots by mistake. I wanted a pair with pink laces, but they didn't have my size."

Isobelle's words died on her lips as if she was worried that she was babbling. I didn't mind listening to her talk because her voice sounded heavenly. It made me wonder whether a guy had knocked her confidence about blabbering too much, and the thought twisted my gut with rage.

"So . . ." She came up with a little icebreaker.

It was cute because it meant she was interested in getting to know me. That was the concerning part. I could tell her everything there was to know about me in one sentence and have nothing left to talk about. I wasn't as alluring as Alex, nor as witty as Grayson, nor am I as gallant as Mason. I was just *me*, and I was hoping that it would be enough.

"You're a mystery," she continued, curling her fingers around the crease of my elbow. "Tell me something about yourself."

We took a slow walk, breathing in the warm alpine scent, our boots kicking through the loose chippings as if time didn't exist.

"Why don't you figure me out for yourself?" I dared her.

What else could I say? She wouldn't be interested in talking about bikes, shock-absorbers, becoming one with my wolf, and I was sure as hell not ready to let her check out my sketchbook. That would be as intrusive as reading my diary — if I kept one, which I didn't. I sketched. I painted. I fixed things. And I preferred the simplicity of nature. That was all there was to learn about me. I didn't want to bore her with that.

"There's something sexy about a strong, silent, mysterious man," she commented, bumping my side playfully. "One who spends half the night brooding in his shed, doing goodness knows what. I heard your brothers muttering about you. Alex thinks it's your way of wriggling out of chores."

I flashed a grin, knowing differently.

"What about you?" I diverted the question. "Aside from being a hot science chick, what do you do for fun?"

I cast my eyes diagonally and witnessed her shy away. "You think I'm pretty?" she murmured diffidently.

The doubt in her voice felt like a shock to my skull.

Has she never looked in a mirror? Seriously?

I brought us to an abrupt stop and tilted her chin up to face me.

"You're more than pretty. Look at you. You're gorgeous," I told her, even though I could see that she didn't believe me.

I made a mental note to punch the guy or guys who made her feel otherwise.

She bit her lip as she looked up at me, and my heart melted. "You've got four deadly wolf shifters who'll beat the crap out of anyone who tells you you're not."

I didn't know what I did to earn what happened next, but at that moment, she kissed me. And in return, I poured my heart and soul into showing her just how beautiful she truly was.

Alex

I huffed in annoyance as Grayson entered the kitchen and dumped his dirty laundry beside the washing machine. The laundry basket was tucked neatly in its space beneath the countertop — but no, Grayson neglected to acknowledge it. A lone sock skidded away, threatening to abscond beneath the vegetable rack. It was lucky I saw where it went because now I could reunite it with its twin. We could've had an odd sock situation, and that was one of my all-time pet peeves.

I had just finished cleaning the breakfast dishes and wiped the kitchen surfaces with antibacterial spray. With five people living in a small cabin, standards could easily slip into pandemonium. An organized home was a happy one. I refused to let our mate live in a pigsty.

Grayson was glossing through a magazine and stopped on a page displaying adult pacifiers.

Whatever floats his boat, I suppose.

My eyes zoned in on his abandoned coffee mug and saw he had failed to use a coaster.

Fuck my life. I'm living with a bunch of slobs.

I stalked across the open-plan living space to retrieve his empty mug. He was lucky it hadn't left a ring mark on the surface. For the next ten minutes, I busied myself sprucing the place up, plumping the pillows so they looked plush. If everything had its space, there would never be a thing out of place.

As I finished, Lucas sauntered through the front door, stopping only to toe off his boots, abandoning them beside the coat rack.

"Mason is just showing Izzy his Mustang," he mentioned.

"Hey, that is not the designated area for footwear," I pointed out.

Lucas rolled his eyes. "Hold on a sec while I count all the fucks I give." He paused for a moment, pretending to count on his fingers, then balled his hands into fists. "That's right . . . none."

Grayson slouched on the couch and placed his feet on top of the freshly polished coffee table. He pointed the TV remote at the fifty-inch flat screen and began flicking through the channels.

"Who's rattled your cage?" Grayson grumbled.

"I'll tell you who." I point directly at him. "Since when has the floor become the laundry basket?"

I knew I sounded like an agitated mother who was admonishing her offspring, but I was the carbon copy of my biological father. We thrived on structure, routine, and conducting our lives in an orderly fashion.

Grayson cast an indignant scowl. "The laundry basket is full," he retorted. "That was Mason's job. He was supposed to have taken care of that this morning, but he must have forgotten because *he has* a life. Anyway, I did my chores. I took the trash bags to the garbage site, changed the bedsheets, and I even washed your car because I'm considerate like that. Do I get a 'thank you'?" He cupped his hand around his ear, waiting for me to say thanks.

Pressure throbbed in my temples. I couldn't argue with him. It *was* Mason's turn to do the laundry, and he *had* gone AWOL right after breakfast. What was the point of me making a chore chart if no one was going to adhere to it? I might be the eldest, but I was not here to be a wet nurse for my brothers.

"Thanks," I mumbled begrudgingly. "I appreciate you washing my car, but it is basic common sense that if a job needs doing, you should do it. Leaving your laundry next to the washer will not ensure it gets washed. If I leave our dinner next to the stove, would it cook by itself?" I continued my rant, hitting him with logic.

"You just need to get laid, dude. You're beginning to piss me off," Grayson retaliated. "There's a tube of lubricant in the nightstand drawer. Take it and this magazine into the bathroom and rub one out."

I immediately saw red. "You disgusting little shit," I hissed, my expression twisting with outrage.

"What's going on here?" Isobelle's voice chimed around the cabin walls.

I straightened my posture, turning to greet our

mate with a civil smile. "Isobelle, did you enjoy your walk?"

Grayson's jaw dropped at my change in demeanor. Isobelle blushed, and Lucas cast her a flirtatious wink. I rolled my eyes, huffing my chest and crossing my arms. *They've kissed*. The scent of arousal still lingered between them like a guilty secret. Two of my brothers had gotten to taste her, and I was frustrated as fuck.

"Can I talk to you alone, please?" I didn't know why it came out as a question when I meant it as a command.

Isobelle's brows raised with surprise. "Of course. What's the matter?" she asked, sounding sweet and innocent.

That would change when we took her to bed. She was going to be taken in so many ways, cum so many times, she would forget her name because she would be far too busy screaming our names.

Lucas and Grayson grabbed a couple of beers and headed outside to talk to Mason. They took that as a subtle hint I wanted a moment of privacy and would advise Mason to tread with caution.

"I want to know if you're okay or if there's something you need," I prompted. "If you don't like the décor, we can change it. If there's something that you prefer to eat, I can cook it for you. I just want to help you feel at home here. The last thing I want is for you to be unhappy." I shrugged my shoulders, aware that I was scowling at the rug and not maintaining direct eye contact like I was accustomed to.

I corrected my mistake, pinning her on the spot with a penetrating glare. I was either calm or intense, zero to one hundred within a millisecond. I didn't have an in-between or an emotional filter so it seemed.

"Alex," Isobelle cooed my name, smiling up at me.

The corners of my eyes twitched as I wondered what was so amusing about that statement.

"Everything is fine," she assured me, glancing around. "You have a beautiful home."

"*We do,*" I corrected her. "This is *your* place too."

Okay, so her visa would run out in three months, but we could work around that. Our Alpha would smooth over the finer details when she became part of our pack. Speaking of Alpha White, he would want an update about how things were going with Isobelle. We would need to solidify the mate bond soon. The urge to fuck was driving me insane. It was partly the reason I had been walking around like a tornado, cleaning the cabin like a lunatic.

Isobelle stroked her fingers around my jaw, raking them through my short, groomed beard. I couldn't help but mirror her smile as she chuckled softly.

"You look even more handsome when you smile," she mentioned.

I grabbed her hand in a swift swoop and held her wrist between my finger and thumb.

"You know . . . women hate it when men say that to them." I let my gaze drift down to her mouth as I used an example. *"You look so pretty when you smile, you should do it more often."* I flicked my gaze back to catch the flare in her eyes as she realized her mistake.

"I was just trying to be nice." She chuckled.

I seized her other wrist as she tried to pull away. She gasped, her pupils enlarged, and I dipped low enough to feel her breath against my lips, deliberating whether to kiss her now or make her beg me for it.

"You drive me crazy; do you know that?" I told her the understatement of the century.

The way she leaned on her tiptoes and tried to steal a kiss from me made my cock kick with arousal, but I refused to grant her wish. Isobelle stilled, unsure whether it was a command to wait or a flat-out rejection. I couldn't bear to see the disappointment in her eyes, so I gave her what she wanted, devouring her mouth the way *I* wanted to taste her. Dominating, commanding, unyielding. She struggled against my grasp, so I released her wrists, allowing her the freedom to slide her palms against my chest, her fingers mapping out a route to my neck, reaching their destination as they drove through my hair to hold me there.

"Mm, don't stop," she whimpered as I pulled back, breaking the kiss.

She was not supposed to be calling the shots, but she demanded, and I obeyed. I drank my fill like I was dying of thirst. She was my oasis in the desert, and I would crawl on my hands and knees just to get a taste of her.

"I promise to smile for you every single day if you're going to kiss me like that," I uttered breathlessly.

"Promises, promises," she murmured like the sultry little minx she was.

CHAPTER
Sixteen

Mason

"**W**hat's taking them so long?" I directed my question at Grayson.

There was no point talking to Lucas because he came back from their walk like he swung the world's biggest dick between his legs.

It must have been some walk in the woods.

"So, where have you been all morning?" Grayson quizzed me.

I tapped my finger against my nose, signaling him to mind his own business.

"Dude, don't make me drag it out of you," he threatened, in a "stop fucking around" tone.

He could easily pry into my thoughts if he wanted to. When you have a bond as close as ours, there can be no secrets between us. Every thought, every feeling, every fear was shared evenly. And considering I had spent my morning doing something beneficial for our girl, it was only fair that I shared all the details with my brothers.

"I've been to see the Alpha," I revealed, sparking Grayson's intrigue.

"How come?" he asked, his brows furrowing with concern.

My minor detour proved to be rather eventful. Alpha Alec had some grim news he wanted to share with us.

"Do you want the good news or the bad news first?" I warned, baring my teeth with a cringe.

Grayson scrubbed a hand over his face as he considered that. "That depends. How bad is the bad news?"

At that exact moment, Lucas emerged from his shed. "What's this about *bad news?*" He tossed his wrench into the toolbox with a loud metallic clatter.

"Like I just said," I started to clarify. "I went to see the Alpha to ask him for a favor. He told me that his mate's apartment had been trashed by rogues. Not only do we have a hunter problem on our hands, but we have rogues to contend with too."

Our Alpha had his own problems to deal with. His mate was still underage and didn't know that she was his mate — didn't even know she was a hybrid — nor had she and the Alpha been introduced for this exact reason. His problems made ours seem mediocre in comparison.

"He needs us to mate Isobelle within the next few days so she can become part of the pack. It's for her safety," I explained. "He's expecting a raid and needs us to be ready."

My brothers nodded solemnly, understanding the implications of her being cut off from the pack link if anything was to go awry during a strike. If she became "pack", she would have the protection of the entire community. It would be unwise to drag this out any longer than it needed to be. We could appreciate that, but could Isobelle?

"What about the good news?" Lucas flared his eyes with sarcasm.

"Good news?" Isobelle's cheerful voice chimed from the porch.

Shit! Is anywhere private anymore?

She flounced down the wooden stairs and made her way over to us.

"What are you celebrating?" she inquired, bouncing her gaze between us and the beer cans in our hands.

"Gray, come give me a hand with this," Lucas insisted, jerking his head toward his shed.

Grayson took the hint and left me alone with Isobelle. She looked up at me expectantly, holding her bottom lip between her teeth in such a jovial expression. I didn't have the heart to tell her the truth just yet.

"Well," I began, having some good news to share. "I went to see our Alpha this morning."

"Was it a good meeting?" Isobelle replied, urging me to continue.

"It was a promising one. He's a scientist, quite like yourself," I revealed, much to her astonishment.

"He is?" she gushed.

I nodded my head in affirmation. "Yes, and he is looking to recruit a lab assistant. When I told him about your work, he seemed very impressed. He said to run this by you first, but he has a job for you if you're interested."

I expected her to take offense to my meddling and insisted I butted out of her business. Instead, she seemed overwhelmed with excitement and wanted to know more.

"Really? What does it entail?" She was quick off the mark, firing a barrage of questions at me. "Does he need to see my resume? Is it a permanent position?"

"You can ask him yourself when we introduce you to him. There's nothing for you to worry about because he seems keen to have you onboard. We are responsible for taking care of the local wildlife, but sometimes things happen that are out of our control. As Alex explained, we don't want anyone snooping around here causing us problems. We'd rather keep it 'in-house'."

Isobelle nodded to show that she understood.

"That makes sense," she agreed.

"I thought about what you said about your career." I bounced my shoulders in a shrug. "Why should you sacrifice everything you've worked for just to stay here with us? I want you to keep doing what you love."

"Thank you," she expressed, her eyes glazing with happy tears.

"You don't have to thank me. I just want you to be . . ." I was about to say "happy", but I didn't get to finish that sentence because her lips crashed against mine.

The sound of wolf-whistling and boyish chortling came from the shed. Any other time, I might have flipped them the bird, but not today. Instead, I put on a show that would leave them both green with envy.

Isobelle

The rest of the afternoon dragged by at a leisurely pace, and the boys and I spent most of it watching back-to-back episodes of a shifter drama called *Shifter Valley*. There were plenty of covert scandals, breaking pack laws, illicit affairs, rejecting mates for the rogue next door, a wolf shifter trying to explain to her mate that she was pregnant with a bear shifter's cub. They even did the thousand-yard stare right before the ending credits rolled. After I watched the first episode, I was hooked. I was sure the boys regretted giving me dominion of the TV remote.

As it edged closer to dinner time, Alex and Grayson began preparing our evening meal. None of my previous boyfriends knew how to cook, so our nights in front of the television included a takeaway or something simple like a ready meal. I couldn't compete with Mary Berry's cooking skills but was more than capable of navigating my way around a kitchen and preparing something simple to eat. Cooking was an activity that my mother and my grandmother had involved me in from a young age.

"Something smells amazing," I mentioned.

The neurons in my brain were going crazy, readying themselves for a treat. My mouth salivated, and I couldn't wait to sink my teeth into all that tasty deliciousness.

And the food . . . I was thinking about food. Okay, so I wasn't. I was drunk and giddy on the heady scent of cologne, the sight of four sexy Adonis gods walking around wearing tight shirts that clung to their muscles, slim-fitted jeans that enhanced every asset. I make no exaggeration that they were all hung like stallions. Each time one of them walked past me, my gaze migrated south.

Bad girl.

"It's ready; come and get it," Grayson called out.

I took a second to pause at that comment and a wry smile curled my lips.

Come and get it? Dear Lord, if only you knew what I was thinking.

We settled around the table and dug into the

steak, potatoes, and salad. We had wine with our meal tonight, and it added a little sophistication to the evening. But it did nothing to quell the sexual tension, and if anything, it fueled me with liquid courage.

"How long do I have until your Alpha needs an answer?" I asked, referring to the job offer.

Mason took a sip from his wine glass. "You can take a few days to think about it," he replied.

"That's a relief," I responded, dragging my knife back and forth through a medium-rare steak, "because I want to talk to my parents first."

The quads paused mid-chew, their expressions freezing with alarm.

Grayson forced his food down his gullet so he could speak. "Everything is okay though, isn't it? You're not thinking about changing your mind?"

"Of course, it's fine," I was quick to respond, earning four relieved sighs around me. "I just don't want to drop a bombshell on them, that's all. They will expect me home in three months. The sooner I tell them, the longer they will have to digest the news."

Lucas's brows remained furrowed, expressing his concern. "Do you think they'll get upset?"

"A little," I admitted, "but my dad will love an

excuse to visit. I'm expecting a few tears from Mum, but she'll come around eventually."

My upbeat attitude seemed to put them at ease. Maybe it had a lot to do with the wine. The full-bodied Malbec was going down like a treat, and I could feel it start to weave its magic as the alcohol took effect.

"Let's change the subject," Alex suggested.

He was in a better mood since we shared a kiss.

"I have a serious question to ask you," he mentioned.

I saw a glimmer of wicked humor dancing in his eyes, and I prepared to be put on the spot.

"Ask away," I insisted, waiting for it.

"Who's the better kisser?" he questioned, then chewed the inside of his cheek as he waited.

They all smirked, waiting for me to choose.

My innards squirmed as my cheeks burned with embarrassment.

"You all achieved ten out of ten," I replied fairly. "There can't be any favoritism."

"Ooh, that's such a brilliant answer, " Grayson chuckled.

"Still marking us out of ten, huh?" Lucas muttered.

I gave a simple shrug, then crammed another

piece of steak into my mouth. Normally, I hated being in the center spotlight, but I loved how sexy they made me feel. For once in my life, my insecurities were falling away like invisible restraints that once held me down. The more they boosted my self-esteem, the higher my confidence soared.

"And you don't feel like it's cheating?" Mason double-checked.

In any other circumstance, kissing four brothers in under twelve hours was considered rather scandalous. In any other instance, there would be jealousy, uproar, and someone would likely get hurt. The harem lifestyle they were offering included none of that. I had shared an intimate moment with each of them, yet here we were, sitting around the dinner table, chatting, laughing, and wondering what would happen next.

"No, it doesn't feel like cheating. I thought it might, but it's not like that at all. I can see how close you all are, and it's endearing that you want me to become a part of that," I replied earnestly.

They seemed more than satisfied to hear that. A savage hunger emblazoned in their eyes, suggesting we would skip dessert and head straight to bed.

"We want you naked in our bed . . . right now," Alex asserted, his voice drenched with lust.

Those words would have terrified me a matter of hours ago, but not now. The swell of my clit left me pulsing with need, and pressing my thighs together made no difference at all.

"I want that too," I replied, giving in to temptation.

My men scraped back their chairs to encircle me, then they swept me up into their powerful arms and carried me to the bedchamber like an empress. And no sooner had my back hit the bed, sinking into the soft, comfortable mattress, my four-man line-up started to perform a slow, erotic striptease.

CHAPTER
Seventeen

Isobelle

Lucas gripped the back of his shirt and pulled it over his head using one hand. The way his muscles flexed and rolled screamed raw sex. I couldn't take my eyes off him. His nipple piercings glinted in the light, drawing my eyes to them. Grayson crossed his arms, grabbed the hem of his T-shirt, and peeled it up over his head. He flashed a grin as he swung the garment around above him, then sent it flying across the room. Mason took off his shirt slowly, his tattoos dancing with every fluid movement. Alex unbuttoned his cuffs first, then began unbuttoning his shirt one button at a time. It was a slow, tantalizing wait, but the show was well worth it.

For my twentieth birthday, Joanna and I enjoyed front-row seats at a male strip show, but that was nothing compared to this. I should have played some music and got them to dance for me. Instead, the jingling of belt buckles and zippers created a raunchy symphony as I feasted my eyes on an abundance of flesh. Holy fuckery! I felt overdressed. So, I shimmied out of my summer dress and toed off my sandals, not knowing whether to leave something on for them to remove. My white lacy underwear felt almost virginal, but that only made this scenario feel dirtier. This was going to be an experience I would never forget — nor would I want to.

Down went their jeans and Alex's black fitted slacks. Raging hard-ons bulged at the front of their boxers as if they concealed weapons of mass destruction. Their thumbs hooked beneath the elastic waistbands . . . and then *wham*! Four gargantuan-sized cocks sprang free.

Oscar. Mike. Foxtrot. Golf!

What can I say? I'm a police officer's daughter, and those are the biggest cocks I have ever seen in my life.

Alex was quick on his knees, pulling my legs apart to position himself between them. He stroked my inner thighs with his fingertips to tease me. Lucas and Grayson closed in at either side of me, each caressing one of my breasts in their hands. Off came my bra, and they tossed it across the bedroom. Mason leaned over me, and from an upside-down angle, began to kiss me in slow sensuous movements.

Alex's short beard tickled the insides of my thighs as he trailed open-mouth kisses along my skin. His lips skated closer and closer to my pussy. His nose nudged my underwear, and I felt a cool vacuum of air as he inhaled my scent. That embarrassed me. I think I can speak on behalf of all womankind, that when a man shoves his nose within proximity of our lady gardens, we want to smell of roses, not weed killer. Alex couldn't get enough of it, peeling my knickers down my hips as if he was removing the ribbon from his birthday present.

His warm breath gusted against my shaved pussy, making me arch off the bed and moan into Mason's mouth. Heat and wet suction caressed my nipples, courtesy of Lucas and Grayson as they sucked me. I writhed beneath them, snaking my hips, desperately seeking Alex's warm, wet tongue. They pinned my wrists to my sides, and Alex's broad shoulders kept my knees wide apart, splaying me out like a virgin sacrifice. I was their dirty human fuck toy, and they could take me however they pleased.

"Please," I mewled against Mason's lips, needing the friction on my pulsing bundle of nerves.

"You're ours . . . say it!" Alex commanded.

Mason eased up so I could reply.

"I'm yours," I cooed, undulating my body like a seductress.

The reward was incredible. Four mouths stoked the embers of my desire, delivering a maelstrom of pleasure and pain. Alex's taut, wet muscle slithered around my clit like a rampant creature.

"Uh, uh, that's so good!" I moaned breathlessly, letting Mason swallow my gasps.

Alex ate me for supper. My helpless pussy didn't stand a chance.

"I'm gonna . . . I . . . oh, my God!" I cried.

My muscles clenched, the building pressure in my stomach intensified. My men used their proficient oral skills to feast upon me, claiming me like one entity. Their combined growls charged the air with electric static. Rough, calloused hands roamed my body with sensuous dexterity. The contrast of cashmere lips versus coarse stubble engulfed me in a pleasant wave of nirvana. My mind emptied, and I was gone, blown away, floating.

So good . . . so right.

Lucas, Mason, and Grayson held me in place as Alex anchored my trembling thighs apart, leaving me with no other choice but to lie back and feel everything. Lights flashed behind my eyelids as my orgasm exploded. Alex lapped and sucked as if it was his last meal, tipping me over the precipice of pleasure and into an ocean of bliss.

Despite my sensitivity, Alex fluttered his tongue to coax every last drop from me. My climax tore through my body like a tsunami, splashing against his lips.

"Uh, fuck yes," Alex groaned, lapping up my cream.

My brain rebooted, fogged up to the eyeballs in a sex haze. Finally, a real orgasm. I could have just melted into the mattress and died a happy girl.

What a rush . . . what a ride.

"Don't think for one second that we're through with you," Alex rasped, "By the time we're done, you're going to struggle to walk straight."

Alex leaned over me, his chest heaving proudly. I had to appreciate how glorious he looked at that moment, his lips parted and still slick with my arousal. He positioned himself between my legs, caging me in with his strong arms. Mason, Lucas, and Grayson scooted back to give Alex some space. Each awaiting their turn to ravish me.

"Are you sure?" he asked, looking down at me through hooded eyes.

I nodded. "Yes . . . and uh . . . I'm on the pill."

That was all he needed to hear. Kissing me passionately, the head of his cock nudged through my slick folds as he eased himself inside me. Inch by glorious inch, stretching my pussy walls wide. My eyes watered at the intrusion. No one had ever filled me to maximum capacity like this before. I had always had to fake it, but there was no way I could fake an orgasm with this humongous cock. It was every inch a giver as much as it was a taker, and I was such a lucky bitch to experience four mouth-watering cocks.

"You're so fuckin' tight," he groaned in appreciation, pushing in farther, sheathing himself to the hilt. "Feels so good."

He rolled his hips against mine, finding a slow, torturous rhythm, coaxing soft mewls from me. His lovemaking was controlled and dominant, dragging his impressive length through my drenched inner walls, almost to the point of pulling out before slamming his hips back against mine.

All I could do was cling to him like a monkey and hold on tight. His hands cupped my ass, angling my hips, then he began pummeling into me with pure masculine abandon.

"I'm going to . . ." I reared my head, my eyes rolling into the back of my skull, seeing stars bursting in my vision.

"Not yet," he growled. "Look at me."

I locked onto gray piercing eyes that blazed with authority, ordering me to wait, and they wouldn't be denied.

Alex pinned me down by the throat, not enough to choke me but adequate enough to exert dominance. The head of his cock was pounding on the door to my cervix, letting it know that there was a new sheriff in town.

"Now come for me," he ordered.

The orchestra of flesh slapping against flesh and cries of unabashed passion soon reached its crescendo.

"Uh, uh, uh," I moaned, hitting an octave that rattled my eardrums.

Alex slammed inside me with a roar, his hot jets painting my womb with his seed.

"Isobelle!" Alex groaned my name, his hips

jerking as he emptied his balls. I reached between us and gave them a gentle squeeze for good measure.

Alex let out a vulnerable chuckle, wriggling out of my grasp. With his chest heaving with ragged pants, he moved aside to allow Grayson to take his place between my legs.

I watched lustfully as he took hold of his cock, lined himself up, then entered me with one swift motion.

"Fast or slow?" Grayson murmured against my lips.

I gazed up into his hazy brown eyes. "Hard," I insisted, wanting to chase after my third orgasm in minutes.

As promised, the sex was fast, rutting into me with wild vigor. A sheen of perspiration coated his skin as he kept his momentum, stopping once to suck my nipples into his mouth in turn, then letting them go with a pop.

"You want me deeper, babe?" Grayson chuckled darkly.

"Yes," I panted. "Give me everything."

A cunning smirk graced his lips as he started to fuck me like a professional porn star, flipping me onto my hands and knees.

His fingers dug into my hips as he fucked me like

a dog, slapping my ass as he drove in hard. His forceful thrusts rocked my body into oblivion, stealing my breath and rattling my teeth in my mouth.

"Yes, yes, yes!" I screamed, my mouth forming a silent O as my orgasm neared.

"You're so fucking beautiful," he growled, "I want to hear you scream."

He pulled out as I was close to my climax, leaving me empty for a fleeting moment. As my back slammed onto the bed, he drove himself inside me like a sex-starved maniac. My pussy clung to his cock, sucking him down to the balls. She was a needy, greedy bitch who developed a taste for thick, hot cum. Who was I to deny her more? Grayson canted his head to one side, admiring how my big breasts bounced as if he'd hit the jackpot.

He lifted one of my legs over his shoulder to penetrate me deeper.

Slap, slap, slap.

Grayson fucked hard and fast, picking up my other leg so that he had one draped over each shoulder. The feeling was too much, too full, and I was going to explode. Grunting through his gritted teeth, he drilled his hips into me, using his other hand to circle my sensitive clit. The sound of our cries and the musky scent of sex filled the air.

"Uh, uh, uh, Grayson!" I cried out his name like a filthy whore as I came all over his dick.

"Too good, babe, I'm gonna cum," he warned.

His expression scrunched with pleasure, and his lips parted in a silent cry, bucking his hips as he pumped me full of seed.

"That was mind-blowing," he praised, biting his bottom lip as he pulled himself out of me, his slick cock oozing gooey strands onto the sheets. Their combined essence trickled down my ass crack and cooled in the air. This was so filthy, fucking four men one after the other, but my god, I was loving it.

Grayson kissed me before getting up and backing away from the bed, giving Alex a satisfied grin. "Look how well her body responds to us," he commented. "I thought her pussy was going to chew off my cock, she came so hard."

Alex's lips twitched in agreement. Not wanting to be left out, Lucas and Mason crawled onto the bed with an air of dark predatory grace. Mason positioned himself on the mattress, pulling me on top of him. Lucas settled behind me, guiding my hips to his groin. His fiery breath trailed across my skin as he kissed the curve of my throat. Their rough, calloused hands fondled my breasts, pinching, rolling plucking at my nipples. Our breathing turned ragged with excitement. Mine especially. I'd never taken two lovers simultaneously. I had no idea what it would feel like, or if they would both fit.

"How are we doing this?" I asked, my voice a little shaky.

"I'm gonna fuck your ass as you ride Mason's cock," Lucas stated.

I was nervous to try it, having never experienced anal before. Lucas dipped two fingers into my swollen center, then spread the mixture of seed along my back passage to lubricate me. It wasn't enough. Grayson grabbed some lube he found in the nightstand and squeezed some onto Lucas's fingers. His thick digits toyed with my puckered star, rimming me for a while and then pressing, massaging, working their way inside me. He started slowly, pumping in and out, priming me ready. And my god, I would need to be ready. So far, the quad's cocks were destroying me.

Mason lifted me by my hips, guiding me onto his thick, meaty cock. Both of us groaned as he sheathed himself to the root.

"Oh, babe," Mason groaned as I began rocking my hips back and forth, gazing down at his inked, muscular torso with awe.

Lucas and Mason were the only ones with any

visible tattoos. Each design was a work of art. Mason's lips curled into a sinful smirk as he caught me staring and placed his hands on my hips. His blue eyes shimmered as if I was the love of his life.

I leaned forward to kiss him as Lucas stretched me ready to take him, pushing another one of his thick fingers inside my tight star. The burn was incredible — feelings I had never experienced before washed over me, and I mewled with ecstasy. Lucas removed his fingers, parting my cheeks as he pushed the fat head of his cock into my virgin hole.

"Ow, uh, oh, fuck," I whimpered as it burned.

"It's okay, we've got you. Ohh, fuck, baby, your ass is so tight," Lucas groaned.

As he sank to my depths, he let out a low guttural growl. So much more primal than his brothers, much more animalistic.

Mason held on to my hips as Lucas eased himself in and out. My limbs shook as the stretch and burn became too much to take.

"Oh, God," I moaned loudly.

Mason and Lucas worked in tandem, keeping me filled with long, thick cock. Both Alex's and Grayson's seed was now sliding down my legs as both men thrust into me, delivering a new kind of pleasure. Mason began stroking my aching clit, forcing me into another earth-shattering climax. I could tell by the pleasurable grimace on his face that he was close to cumming. Lucas's desperate grunts told me he was too. Mason's eyes clamped shut. His head reared back open-mouthed, loving the feel of my pussy clenching around him.

"I'm cumming, I'm cumming," I chanted breathlessly.

I shamelessly screamed as the heat of my pleasure flooded through me, my pussy walls tightening, tipping both men over the edge. Mason came straight after me, gripping my hips and crying out with ecstasy, his pulsing jets coating my womb.

"Oh, fuck, Isobelle, I'm so close," Lucas said, bending me forward so he could fuck me harder. His fingers dug into my hips as his heavy balls slapped against my folds, coaxing an encore. Our bodies shuddered as he came with a roar, milking my last resolve.

"Fuck, yeah." His thick, musky cum warmed me throughout.

We collapsed onto the bed, boneless and spent. A few moments passed, and then Lucas turned me around with a possessive growl.

"Come here, beautiful," he rasped, smashing his

lips onto mine as he devoured my mouth and then stung my ass with a slap.

"You're going to think of me when you sit tomorrow," he spoke with pride, looking at me through hooded eyes, his muscular torso glistening with beads of perspiration.

Mason pulled me over to him, his arms encasing me in a warm, sensual embrace as his tongue parted my lips. Our sweat-slickened bodies slid together, feeling the damp hair beneath our fingertips. Grayson and Alex rejoined us, each taking turns to kiss me.

So, this was harem sex?

After taking a bite from the forbidden fruit and savoring all that the Bennett brothers had to offer, I was hooked. There was no turning back. I had four hot men to worship me, all with an abundance of stamina — thanks to their werewolf genes — and enough testosterone to keep my hormones screaming for the rest of my life. Yes, I had my reservations at first, but who wouldn't want this? I had spent my adult life dating assholes. And now I had found the Bennett brothers, I wasn't about to look a gift horse in the mouth.

CHAPTER Eighteen

Isobelle

It was a strange feeling, waking up in a tangle of limbs and not knowing whose arms and legs belonged to whom. Mine could be determined by the lack of leg hair, not that I could feel them after last night's antics.

"I'm going to run a bath," Alex muttered hoarsely.

He rolled himself into a sitting position, then stretched his arms above his head with a yawn.

A long soak sounded wonderful right now. I was

sticky in places where I ought not to be, and I felt as if I'd been kicked in the twat by a donkey.

"Thanks," I croaked, my speech sounding groggy.

Lucas stirred, making a soft humming noise as he pulled me against him like a teddy bear. Grayson woke soon after and followed Alex out of the room. A moment or two later, the hissing sound of the kettle boiling was like music to my ears. I needed to get up and pee, but the Mason and Lucas sandwich was preventing me from moving. So, I stroked my finger along the length of Mason's nose, intending to wake him. His fair lashes were like golden crescents against his tan skin. When they fluttered open, it was like watching the sunrise over an ocean horizon.

"Good morning, " I cooed, my lips curving into a smile.

His tawny lips pulled into a shy grin, flashing a perfect set of pearly white teeth. Even his canines were visible. I hadn't noticed them before, but there they were, pointed like that of a wolf. It was hard to believe they were werewolves. They seemed so normal — like me, and everyone else.

"Last night was . . ." His eyes shied away, and he toyed with my hand in his.

It was cute seeing this big strong wolf act so bashful. It was only a matter of hours ago that he and his brothers had taken turns to fuck me, and now he was blushing as he gazed into my eyes.

"I know," I finished his words, flaring my eyes suggestively.

Lucas groaned behind me. "Ugh, what time is it?"

"It's time we took a bath," Mason muttered. "We reek of sweat and pussy."

Lucas chuckled mischievously. "I could get used to waking up like this every morning." He gave my breast a gentle squeeze. "Do you want some morning wood?"

I swatted his hand away, rolling my eyes. "No, I bloody well don't. I need to go to the loo before my bladder bursts."

"Aww, spoilsport," Lucas chortled.

I clambered over Mason, then staggered to the bathroom. Grayson was busy making some tea and didn't look up as I passed him. Alex took the hint that I desired some privacy to do my business and vacated the steamy bathroom to leave me to it. My ass touched the toilet seat, and oh my god, I almost screamed as I urinated. My poor pussy had taken a beating, and now they had ruined it for any other man.

Not that I could ever revert to dating a regular

guy after my night with the quads. Why would I settle for one dick when I could have four?

My eyes danced around the sauna-style bathroom, drinking in the craftsmanship that must have gone into building this house. Three steps led down to the sunken bathtub. It was four times the size of a large hot tub and had water jets around the sides I could lean against to massage my aching muscles. They sourced the water from the nearby spring and heated it in a tank beneath the cabin. The warmth seeped through the wooden floorboards and felt cozy underfoot. I imagined it would be toasty warm during the winter months. I did my business and pressed the flush lever.

"You can come in now," I called out, then turned to pour some bubble liquid into the tub.

I didn't care if the guys protested; I liked bubbles. Soon enough, the room was infused by the fruity-smelling aroma.

"The bath is ready," I bellowed.

Their timing was impeccable, arriving just in time to see the apprehension on my face as my ass touched the water.

"Ah, ah, ah, shit," I hissed, grimacing with discomfort.

"Are you sore, love?" Grayson asked as he stepped into the tub.

"Yeah, but I'll be okay. The warm water is helping," I replied.

Alex lowered himself into the water, followed by Lucas and Mason.

"Did we hurt you, baby?" Mason bunched his brows with concern as he leaned down to peck my lips.

I shook my head. "No, it's just been a while since I . . . you know . . . had sex with anyone," I admitted.

They didn't have to know exactly how long since I'd had any dick, and that they had done a fantastic job of knocking the cobwebs off my disused snatch. My drought days had ended. I would need to increase my caffeine intake to fuel my sexual escapades from now on.

Lucas lathered some soap between his hands and bathed me gently.

"The next time I fuck you, it'll be like nothing you've ever experienced before. I'm going to rock your world," he whispered in my ear. The sexy husk in his voice made my spine arch.

"We will each need to mark you, sweetheart. But we all require a private night with you to make each occasion special," Alex spoke from across the pool.

"I know how I want to do it." Mason blushed, gazing at me the way only lovers did. "There will be candles and silk sheets, and I want to take my time to worship you like the goddess you are."

Grayson leaned his head back, thinking out loud. "I'm gonna do it in here, I think. Here in the water, standing up with your legs wrapped around my waist. We can get clean and dirty at the same time."

Alex chuckled, shaking his head. "I'm planning on cooking for you first, then spoiling you with a massage. Then we are going to play my way, and only after then will I make love to you in front of the fire."

Lucas cupped my breasts with soapy hands as he pressed his muscled torso up against my back. "You know me. Go big or go home. I'll be naked as the day I was born. Then I'll take you from behind under the stars and on the forest floor while you're on your knees. That's how wolves do it. Then I'm gonna make you beg me to claim you as you come hard on my dick." He swiped his wet tongue across my ear as he spoke.

My body shuddered with delight. They were liberating me from the shackles of social norms. Every kiss, caress, and moment of intimacy uncovered a piece of me I never knew existed until now. Right here, in the arms of my four lovers, I felt free.

"Izzy, are you hungry? I've made some breakfast," Alex mentioned.

He sure had a spring in his step this morning. By the time I had dried my hair, put on a little eye makeup, and picked out an outfit, Alex had completed all his daily chores. I felt bad for not contributing anything.

"Thanks, that would be fantastic," I replied gratefully.

Alex was the embodiment of perfection, and not only did he look like everything I had ever wanted in a man, but he could also navigate his way around a kitchen.

I chose a seat at the table, and Alex placed a plateful of scrambled eggs, bacon, and sausages in front of me. When he leaned in for a kiss, I responded ardently.

"Mm, I love your English accent," he muttered against my lips. As he sat beside me, his woodsy cologne ignited my senses. My pussy should be punished for such gluttony. Instead, it throbbed for a repeat of last night.

"Eat up," Alex insisted, "You need to conserve your energy."

No sooner had I picked up my cutlery, Alex's palm came to rest on my thigh. His warmth seeped into my skin, and his thumb stroked me in small circles. It seemed like an affectionate gesture between lovers.

"How did you sleep?" he asked, making light conversation.

I finished swallowing a mouthful of food before answering, "I slept fine, although it was rather crowded in bed. I couldn't move."

Alex's palm migrated a little higher, but I ignored it.

"Agreed. We need a bigger bed," Grayson mumbled through mouthfuls of bacon and eggs.

"I don't mind sleeping on the sofa?" I offered, not wanting to put them out.

It was strange that they slept in one gigantic bed. If I had any siblings, I would demand my own room.

"Ah, why would you want to do that?" Mason whined.

Grayson and Lucas looked as if I had just slapped them both across the face, then took a massive shit in the middle of the kitchen table.

"Once we mark you, you won't choose to sleep apart from us. You'll see. I think Grayson is right . . .

we need a bigger bed." Alex's raspy whisper tickled my ear.

"I think we need to decide who will be the first to mark her," Grayson mentioned.

"It needs to be fair," Mason chipped in.

"Mark me?" I narrowed my eyes quizzically.

"It's where we make our mating bite," Grayson explained. He saw the whites of my eyes and continued. "It'll hurt for a couple of seconds, but after that, you'll feel nothing but pleasure. A mating mark symbolizes that you're our mate."

"Like a wedding band?" I asked, wondering if it was similar.

"Sure," Alex answered. "But mating is a *'till death do us part'* kind of deal. There is no backing out once we've committed."

I liked the sound of that.

"So, you'll be mine forever?" I clarified. "You'll never look at another woman?"

Four offended scowls glared back at me. "You're the one!" Mason reassured me. "There is no other woman for us. We belong to you and only you."

That was all I needed to hear. In the past, men had always made me feel inadequate. I had caught them side-eyeing women as we walked down the street. The fact that the Bennett brothers were pledging themselves to me meant everything. It was all that a girl could hope for.

"Well, why don't you all write your names on a piece of paper. That way, I can pick them out of a bag randomly. The first one can have tonight," I suggested fairly.

"All right," Alex replied, pushing back in his seat. He darted off to fetch something.

Moments passed before he came back with a black drawstring pouch, a notepad, and a pen. I watched as each one of them wrote their names down and folded the paper before passing it back to Alex. Alex opened the pouch and removed the contents. Nothing could have prepared me for what he took out. He pulled out a blindfold, silk ties, a paddle for spanking, and a strange string of beads.

"Uh-oh, Alex has pulled out some of his Dom tools. Watch out, Isobelle. That's just his mild stuff. He's been planning for you for years," Grayson teased me playfully.

I gulped, flaring my eyes at what he considered as *toys*.

Alex winked at me and shot me a killer grin before putting the folded paper inside the bag and gave it a shake.

Shit! He was a Dom. I should've known.

I sighed, frustrated with myself at having ignored all the obvious signs.

He held the bag open in front of me, and I dipped my hand inside. Closing my eyes, I rummaged around, feeling each folded piece of paper brush against my fingertips. I wondered whose name I would pull out first. I made my choice and withdrew my hand from the bag. All four of them watched and waited with anticipation as I unfolded the paper.

I hesitated on purpose, dragging out the torture. I could see how impatient they were getting and found it highly amusing. "The first to have their night with me is . . . Mason," I announced.

"Yes!" Mason gloated in triumph.

His smile spread across his handsome face. Whereas Lucas looked as if he'd just lost a million dollars at a casino. He swore under his breath, then leaned back in his chair, scowling like a sore loser.

I pulled out the second piece of paper and unfolded it, smirking as I read it. "Grayson, you get tomorrow," I announced.

"All right!" He punched the air, looking over toward Lucas with a cocky smirk on his face.

Lucas exhaled a forceful huff through his nose, then pressed his lips into a tight thin line as if he was all out of patience.

For the third time, I reached into the bag, pulling out another piece of paper to unroll it. My eyes darted between Alex and Lucas, who were both watching me intensively.

"Lucas," I announced. "You're getting the night after Grayson."

I giggled as he exhaled with relief.

"That means, Alex gets to go last," I said, looking toward him.

"Saving the best for last, huh?" Alex chuckled.

He placed his hand back on my leg and stroked farther up my thigh. Somehow, I remained impassive as I carried on eating, even though my clit was mimicking my pulse pattern between my legs.

Fuck! What was he trying to do to me?

Last night, I had more sex in one night than I had ever had in my lifetime, yet I craved more. Alex leaned close to me and whispered in my ear. It was barely audible, but the warmth of his breath raised the hairs on my skin, "I could make you cum right here, right now, just by using my fingers. All you've got to do is tell me where you want to be touched."

Well, fuck my life and my formerly disused pussy.

The thought of turning him down seemed inconceivable to me. My back arched as he brushed his fingertips over my thigh, teasing me with the faintest touch. I leaned back in the chair, allowing my knees to fall apart.

"I don't want you to make a sound. Not one, or else I'll stop, and you won't get your reward," he rasped.

I looked at Grayson, Lucas, and Mason. They seemed oblivious, or were they? I couldn't be sure. They were all chatting and eating, paying no attention to what Alex was doing. Alex moved his hand an inch, rubbing circles along my thigh with his thumb. I almost gave out a moan, which caused him to move back down to my knee again.

It was a game, and if I did as I was told, he would give me my reward as promised. I bit my lip as his hand advanced farther, inches away from my pussy. My body tensed, and my pulse quickened.

Another inch, and another. Every one of my nerve endings was on fire. I trembled, unable to move. Alex ran the tips of his fingers over my mound with a feather-light stroke. By this point, I was soaking wet, knowing that I would fall apart with only a few strokes of his fingers.

"Say it. Tell me where you want me to touch you," he ordered, keeping a lowered tone.

"I can't," I whispered back, feeling the heat of my embarrassment scorch my cheeks.

"If you don't say it, then you don't get it," he warned.

Fucking hell!

He needed to hear the words. Just the thought of speaking those filthy words out loud made me cringe with embarrassment. Who did he think I was? I rarely behaved like this, let alone vocalized how I preferred to be touched. "I want you to touch me there," I spoke in a tremulous whisper, trying to avoid saying the word *"pussy"* altogether.

"Where?" he demanded, his warm breath grazing my skin in a delicious prickle. My clit pulsed, swelling to double its size.

Ah, the fucker would not relent until I said it, and I was all out of self-restraint.

"My pussy . . . I want you to make me cum, Alex," I replied in a breathless whisper.

He brushed his fingertips along my labia, trailing down to my soaking channel, then dipped a single finger inside. My abused hole sucked him inside with no resistance. It stung at first, but the pain soon turned to enjoyment. Alex dragged his moistened finger between my parted folds and caressed my sensitive bud in slow, torturous circles.

My hips undulated, and I ground myself onto his fingertips, gripping the edge of the table as my pleasure consumed me. Alex seemed to thrive off the control he had over me, whereas I was still semi-conscious of the three other men who were sitting an arm stretch away from us.

My breathing became uneven. I tried to retain my composure so that we wouldn't be discovered. I knew he would stop the second I made a sound. If he did, I would die, I needed this release. Just as I felt the build-up of an orgasm, he stopped moving his finger and just held my clit between his forefinger and thumb. I snapped my gaze toward him with frustration. He had me right on the edge and was keeping me there.

His gray eyes bore into mine with a strong, dominant command festering within them. He wanted me to beg, he expected me to plead with him to give me what I needed. The moment I did that, they would all know. The scent of a new climax would overpower the sex smells from the previous night. I was convinced that they could smell me now, but they didn't show it.

Alex knew what he was doing, holding all the control. He was in charge, and he wanted my submission.

I gasped as he pinched down on my engorged

bud, rolling it between his fingers with such a brutal, yet delicious torture.

"Say it … tell me what you desire," he commanded in a firm husky voice.

My three other lovers stopped what they were doing as they looked toward us. Each one grinned at me as if they had known all along. He held me on the cusp of ecstasy, right there on the tipping point.

"Please, Alex, I need to cum," I groaned.

"It's about damn time," Grayson commented.

Mason and Lucas chuckled, seeming to agree with him.

Alex dipped two fingers inside my soaking wet channel and started pumping in and out of me, curling his fingers and massaging my textured inner wall. His thumb stroked mercilessly over my throbbing clit, blasting me straight through the stratosphere.

"Cum for me, but don't make a sound," he commanded in a dominant growl.

My erratic breathing quickened as he picked up the pace. Lights flashed behind my eyelids, legs quaking as my inner gush flowed through my pussy, the fleshy walls tightening around Alex's fingers. The evidence of my pleasure played out its wet symphony as he squelched in and out of me, letting me ride out my release. I came apart silently, just as he wanted, demanding my full submission, just how I gave it. My body relaxed, feeling fully content and shaking with the aftermath.

"Don't wear her out too much, Alex. She's mine tonight," Mason spoke, his voice drenched with lust.

CHAPTER Nineteen

Isobelle

The day dragged by at a snail's pace. There was nothing at all to do inside the cabin besides watch television. I had used all my mobile data playing Candy Crush. It bored me to death, having nothing left to occupy me.

As soon as I stepped foot on the porch, the hot rays of the sun licked my skin. It was a good thing I packed plenty of sunscreen, not wanting to get sunstroke. With the warm scent of forest pine filling my lungs, I took a slow stroll around the cabin and found my men taking advantage of the glorious weather.

Mason was sitting cross-legged on the grass with an acoustic guitar on his lap. I watched as he replaced a broken string and began to fine-tune it. My eyes drifted a little farther and saw Alex and Grayson practicing martial arts. Both were shirtless, their taut muscles dappled red and glistening with sweat from getting too hot. One brother was missing. I looked around but couldn't see Lucas anywhere.

Where could he be?

I could hear noises coming from the shed, and as I walked closer, I heard him rummaging around in there. So, the sleuth in me decided to investigate. I was close enough to peer through the crack in the door, hearing the noises stop suddenly as he caught my scent.

"Lucas? Can I come in?" I asked awkwardly.

The clattering sound of wooden sticks and rustling of paper told me he was busy stashing something. A moment later, Lucas emerged in the doorway, bracing his arms on the wooden frame to block me from seeing past him.

"What's up?" he replied, scrubbing a hand across his paint-splattered face.

"I'm bored," I admitted, peering over his shoulder

while I got the chance. "I wanted to ask if you'd take me on another walk, but I can see that you're busy."

He put his hand back on the frame to block my view again. I turned to leave and heard him exhale a weary sigh.

"Izzy, wait. There's something I want to show you," he mentioned, sparking my interest.

At first, I thought it was an invitation into his private domain. I was desperate to find out the reason for all the secrecy. What was he guarding in there that he didn't want me to see? Lucas was an enigma, and that only fueled my curiosity.

"Oh yeah?" I arched my brow. "Like what?"

Lucas locked his shed door behind him, then slipped the key into the pocket of his cargo shorts.

"Since you're going to be working with our Alpha, you ought to learn first-hand what you're up against," Lucas explained, somewhat ominously.

As we passed the others, Lucas gave a loud whistle to grab their attention. They stopped what they were doing, their eyes finding us in a heartbeat.

"I'm taking Isobelle to the edge of the red zone. Who wants to come with us?" Lucas asked them.

Without uttering a word, they followed us into the forest and beyond the nature trail. Sparse rays of sunlight penetrated the mosaic of branches above us.

My pale skin was glad of the shade, but the humidity in the air was almost suffocating me. I listened to their testosterone-fueled chatter, playful teasing, and their debate about who was better in bed. By the time we came to a stop at the edge of a small stream I was drenched from head to toe with sweat and misery. I regretted not bringing my Hydro Flask with me. It meant I had no choice but to consume the lake water, providing it was safe to drink.

"Is the water clean?" I asked, peering into the crystal-clear liquid.

It was better to ask to make sure since I didn't bring my test kit with me. I didn't want to get sick from any germs or parasites that lurked in there. A nasty dose of Giardia would give me the shits. I peered into the water. The stony bed was visible. I couldn't see any fish swimming around in it, which was why I thought it was best to check with the guys first.

"Sure," Grayson confirmed it was safe.

He hankered low with cupped palms and scooped up a sizable amount of water.

"It's nice and cold," he spoke, enticing me to take a sip.

I covered his hands with mine as I drank my fill,

providing my parched mouth with the vital nourishment it craved.

"Thanks," I responded gratefully.

Grayson wiped his palms against his shorts and placed his hands on his hips.

"We were going to wait a few days before springing this on you, but Lucas is right. You ought to see this," Grayson mentioned, adopting a serious tone.

"We're not in danger out here, are we?" I asked in a sudden rush of panic.

Mason shook his head gently. "No, we'd never place you at risk," he assured me, "but you're about to witness the atrocities of a hunter attack."

Alex and Lucas stepped carefully among the ferns, searching for something on the ground.

Grayson pointed above us. "Listen to the sounds of the forest," he instructed. "Can you hear how the birds are singing?"

I nodded. "Yeah."

"You can generally tell when a predator is close because the forest falls into an eerie silence. Our kind can communicate telepathically. This enables us to inform each other of any dangers nearby. Now listen because this is important," he mentioned, maintaining eye contact. "We can't mind-link anyone from outside our pack. If we want to warn our shifter cousins, we use a chorus howl. If a wolf is trapped out here alone, he or she will cry out in a high-pitched howl. When the roar of a bear or cat reverberates around the woodland, you don't hang around to find out why . . . you haul ass out of here. Do you understand?" His stern expression commanded a response from me.

"Yes," I answered quickly.

The rustling of twigs and foliage snatched our attention. "Found one," Alex muttered, his voice laced with disgust.

Grayson moved me back to a safer distance, and it was just as well. The moment Alex tugged on something, a net lifted from the ground, raining bark chippings and loam onto the area below.

"Oh my god," I spluttered with shock.

"That's nothing, " Lucas mentioned. "You should be more concerned about getting caught in one of these." He held up a rusty-looking bear trap that had been hidden amongst the ferns. The severed leg belonging to a wolf was proof that the poor thing had chewed its way out of it.

My eyes bulged with revulsion. Grayson wrapped his arms around me, holding me close against his chest. "This is just the tip of the iceberg. Part of your job will be to monitor the wellbeing of the local wildlife and check the lake for any sign of pollution. We have to discard this kind of shit from our forests and keep the hunters at bay."

"Do you think the person died?" I questioned them soberly.

It would be naïve of me to assume the quads had never been in harm's way before, but that was before I met them, before I started to care for them, dare I say it . . . before I started falling in love with them.

What if it was one of my men who had gotten hurt?

"He'll be in pretty bad shape, provided the hunters didn't get to him first. His scent is fresh." Alex's gaze drifted across the forest, then he pointed ahead. "His tracks lead back that way, back toward Whitevale." Alex sounded certain of that.

"Isn't there more we could do to stop the hunters?" I bleated. "What about the government?"

Alex answered this time. "The fox shifter community has a hand in politics, and they do all that they can to keep our state off the radar. You know as well as we do humans would have a hard time understanding that we're not a threat. They will assume that we would act to overpower them, then before we realize it, they would ambush Whitehaven."

"This was a sanctuary for all shifters. A peaceful

place where we could thrive and raise our young. If we go public, we'd be putting thousands of lives at risk," Mason spoke solemnly.

I relaxed into Grayson's protective embrace, knowing that they were right. This was my new home, my neighbors would become my friends, and my children would go to school with theirs. I had to help protect this place at all costs.

"Will you be all right walking back home with Mason?" Alex asked, the somber note still present in his voice. "You have your date night to prepare for, and we ought to see if we can locate the injured wolf."

Lucas dislodged the severed limb from the trap. "He'll be needing this back," he muttered, scrunching his nose.

My eyes bulged wide. "That's goosed," I uttered the polite phrase for *fucked*.

Lucas chortled.

"Honestly," Alex spoke. "If reattached, it'll mend itself. We have rapid healing abilities. He'll be right as rain in a few hours."

"It's just as well," I mumbled, "because anything could happen out here."

"Don't worry, we'll be home by dawn," Alex assured me.

"Make sure you are," I warned, then kissed each of them goodbye.

Mason laced his fingers with mine as we walked back home. I could tell by his hasty steps and the cagey looks he kept throwing from left to right that there was more to this than he was letting on.

By the time we reached the cabin, I desperately needed a shower. There was no way in hell that I was prepared to take a hot bath on an occasion like this, so I made Mason puncture holes into an old bucket and attach it to a hook at the back of the cabin. It worked like a charm, despite it needing to be filled several times while I rinsed the soap suds out of my hair. Even Mason had to agree that a shower would save time and help to conserve water. He promised to include one in the en-suite when they extended our home.

"A towel for milady," he offered, holding out a fluffy white towel.

"Thanks." I pulled it from his grasp and wrapped it around myself.

My hands were trembling, and my teeth were chattering. It wasn't down to the air swirling around my wet skin because it was a scorching afternoon. I was about to take a giant leap, like exchanging marriage vows. I felt like a blushing bride, standing at the altar, and trying to steady her last-minute wedding jitters.

"Don't overthink it," Mason reassured. "I promise to make it beautiful in every possible way."

That comment made my lips twist into a cute smile, completely awed by the man standing before me.

"How did I get so lucky?" The answer to that question baffled me.

Because if truth be told, I didn't quite know what I had done to deserve them.

CHAPTER Twenty

Isobelle

The dilemma of what I should wear ate up most of my hour. Should I dress nicely or casually? We weren't going anywhere. We were staying in. But as this was a special occasion. It was only fair that I made an effort. At least I packed the perfect outfit — a little black dress in case someone invited me to dinner. Not that I would be wearing it for long. I picked out some sexy black underwear to entice him to bed.

I applied light makeup and sprayed on a little

perfume. Mason knocked on the bedroom door, and my nerves tumbled about all over the place.

"Come in," I called out.

Mason stepped into the room and paused in the doorway. "Wow," he breathed, seeming mesmerized. "You look incredible."

I looked away and uttered a bashful, "Thanks."

There was an awkward pause until Mason spoke,

"I have a surprise for you in the kitchen. Why don't you wait in the living room while I get the bedroom ready?" His voice burst with excitement as if he couldn't wait for me to see what he was planning.

I felt one hundred percent safe with Mason, like I could talk to him about anything, and he wouldn't laugh at me or judge me no matter how stupid my question was. He could light up the room with his infectious smile, just like a beam of sunlight sent to chase away the rain clouds. Even now, I could see he was nervous and was trying to hide it behind an angel's bluff – and by that, I meant he remained calm to ease my nerves. It was all for my benefit; he put my needs before his own. I found a bottle of champagne on ice in the living room, a platter of strawberries, a tray of dainty little sandwiches, and cakes. I placed a hand over my heart, feeling it swell with affection.

He had recreated an English afternoon tea-style dinner for me.

How adorable is that?

"Enjoy the food and help yourself to some champagne. I promise I won't keep you waiting long," he said, closing the door.

He paid attention to detail, adding scented candles around the room, vases of flowers, and the tea set was gorgeous. The fine china teacup and saucer set reminded me of the ones in my nana's Welsh dresser, pink and chintzy, with a hand-painted flower design.

Don't cry, you'll ruin your mascara.

My eyes landed on a small white envelope that had been set upright against a champagne flute. Next to it was an open rectangular-shaped box containing a glittering diamond bracelet. It was beautiful. I picked it up to admire it, then opened the envelope to read the note.

"Isobelle, from the first moment I saw you, your beauty enchanted me. As I learned more about you, your intelligence captivated me. You are the epitome of perfection. My one and only love. I will spend the rest of my life showing you just how special you are. Forever yours, Mason."

Fireworks detonated inside my ovaries. My fingers trembled as I fastened the bracelet around my wrist. Gosh, it was gorgeous. It must've cost him a fortune. I reread the letter over and over until my tears blurred the words. This was the first time a man had bought me jewelry – not including my father, but he didn't count. I needed that glass of champagne like a vital organ. It was Veuve Clicquot. The bottle looked rather old like he had been saving it for his mating night. It was like he had thought of everything to make this night spectacular. I poured myself a drink, the effervescent liquid almost bubbled over the rim of the champagne flute. The fizz popped against my nose as I took a sip. Too many of those would go straight to my head. I needed to soak it up with something stodgy, so I decided to eat my way through the pyramid of dainty cakes before moving on to sweeter things. Chocolate was my weakness, and the bite-size double-chocolate fudge cakes were practically calling to me, begging to be eaten. As I crammed two tiny wedges into my mouth like a hamster, Mason chose this precise moment to walk back into the room.

"Ready," he announced.

Shit.

Lucky for him, I had my back to him. I spared his eyes from the horror of my chocolate munching massacre, chewing at the speed of light so I could answer him.

"Izzy?" he repeated inquisitively.

Bollocks!

I chewed so fast my jaw ached, then I swallowed it down, running my tongue around my teeth as I turned to face him.

"Izzy, are you all right, love?" he asked, sounding worried.

I dusted my lips for crumbs.

"Yes . . . Yes, I'm fine," I replied, attempting to mask my gluttony with a sugar-sweet smile.

My gosh. He looked like a dream in his stylish jeans and a light gray shirt that he rolled at the sleeves. His eyes flashed down to my wrist, noticing that I was wearing his gift. He didn't have to ask me whether I liked it. I couldn't stop myself from admiring it. And that told him all he needed to know.

"Thank you," I spoke fondly. "The bracelet, the letter, all this . . ." I threw a hand gesture at the cute little tea party. "I love it . . . all of it."

Mason cleared the distance between us in a heartbeat. Leaning down to speak in my ear, he uttered, "The night is still young, my love. More pleasures await beyond the bedroom door."

A tantalizing shudder raised the hairs along my

skin; my clit throbbed; my nipples pebbled beneath my bra. I couldn't wait to find out what more he had in store. With Mason, I bet he could make every day feel like Valentine's Day.

He held my hand as he led me into the bedroom. I saw he had placed candles all around the room, emitting a mellow amber glow from the dancing flames. A warm woodsy fragrance wafted from the incense sticks. Wisps of delicate white smoke unfurled in the air all around us.

"What scent is that?" I asked.

"Patchouli. It's an aphrodisiac," he spoke in a sweet seductive voice. "It heightens sexual pleasure by stimulating the hormone receptors."

I went to remove my heels, but he stopped me. "No . . . leave them on but take off everything else. I want to watch you as you strip," he instructed.

My fingers flew to work, unzipping the back of my dress. The material floated down my body and pooled around my feet. I stepped out of it, wearing only my black lace underwear and heels. He watched me through hooded eyes as I unclasped my bra, sucking in a breath as my breasts burst free before him. Mason removed his clothes, pulling off his boxers to release his iron-hard cock. He stroked his length slowly, not taking his eyes off me for a second.

I hooked my thumbs under the edge of my thong and dragged it down my thighs, letting it drop around my ankles. My pussy was already soaking wet, and I ached for him to touch me. Mason backed me up toward the bed, and I fell onto the mattress, then moved up to accommodate him. He crawled toward me, covering my quivering body with his tattooed work of art. In one fluid motion, he claimed my mouth in a passionate kiss.

"Hold still," he whispered as he kissed all the way down my body, peppering a feather-light touch all over my skin, creating a goosebump effect.

Mason settled between my legs, lifting them over his shoulders, his fingertips stroking from my ankles, my shins, his tongue tasting with a trail of kisses down to my knees, my inner thighs, the mattress dipping deeper the closer he got to my middle. A blast of hot breath caressed my mound, and I threw my head back with a loud, grateful moan, gripping the sheets as he parted my folds and dragged his tongue through my slick flesh. Mason was savoring me slowly, swirling his tongue over my engorged clit in lazy strokes, then he inserted a finger inside me, twisting it before adding another, stretching me wide. He alternated between pumping in and out and sucking on my clit, blowing me apart.

"Ah, fuck! Yes, Mason!" I mewled. He set a torturous pace, fluttering his tongue, and suckling me until all I could see was stars.

I was in heaven, bucking and thrashing on the bed. My stomach tightened, and my legs stretched rigidly, struggling to contain the pressure that was building. As if sensing the inevitable, Mason held me steady and tongued me like a brute.

"Mason!" I screamed his name, hearing my rapturous voice rattle the cabin walls as I climaxed.

All I could do was lie back, boneless, and pant like a parched puppy. Mason chuckled, crawled over me, and nudged my knees apart. My nipples stood like stiffened peaks, begging him to suck on them, and he did . . . God, he did. I tipped my head back, arching my spine as his teeth grazed against one, then the other. The tip of his cock nudged through my wet heat and drove my walls apart.

"Oh, oh, yes," I bleated raggedly.

"Tell me what you want, baby," Mason rasped against my ear.

"Please, Mason, make love to me. Please, I need you," I pleaded desperately.

His blue eyes locked with mine as he dragged his length through my aching wet channel. I could taste myself on his lips, my musk filling my airways. My walls clung to his cock, holding it hostage. My greedy girl was eager to fuck, thirsty to suck down all of Mason's cream. I locked my legs around his waist as our bodies rocked together, his mighty organ stroking my pussy into sweet submission. It was so intense. Nobody had ever made love to me like this before. I squeezed my thighs tighter around his hips, causing the tips of my heels to dig into his ass cheeks. Mason grunted his enjoyment, relishing the pleasure and pain it caused. Each firm hip roll made me mewl like a kitten. His hands found mine, pinned them above my head, and laced our fingers together. His quickening pace pounded into me with punishing thrusts.

"Yes, yes, yes," I groaned with each firm slam of his hips.

"You're mine, baby," he breathed out, changing his technique, and rotating his hips in slow circles.

"Yours . . . I'm yours," I uttered.

Mason's tattooed torso flexed and glistened with sweat as his pleasure consumed him, his breathing ragged as he chased his release.

"Oh, baby, you feel so good," he groaned.

"Harder . . . fuck me harder," I cried out with each firm slap of his hips. I was coming hard, and he knew it.

"Mark me," I begged.

Mason barked out a harsh cry, expelling himself inside me. I exposed my throat, inviting him to bite me, mark me, make me his. He didn't keep me waiting, piercing the skin between my neck and my shoulder blade. Pure agony flooded through me, worse than any sting, cut, or injury I'd ever felt before. My veins were ablaze with hellfire, a terrible kind of pain, but it soon manifested into pleasure. The sensation sent me over my tipping point, delivering me onto the verge of another earth-shattering orgasm. Mason collapsed on top of me, our bodies wrapped together, gasping for breath, and coated in the sweat of our effort. He tended to the wound on my neck, licking away the blood and blowing on it gently until it barely even hurt anymore.

"You're mine now, Isobelle," he whispered lovingly.

Our night was far from over. We continued to make love until the sun came up. Only then did we finally sleep, tangled together among the twisted bedsheets.

CHAPTER Twenty One

Grayson

After a long and eventful evening, all I wanted to do was to crawl into bed and sleep for a week. My brothers and I were in our wolf forms, patrolling the forest for any sign of hunters. We discovered the injured wolf three miles away from Whitevale. The eighteen-year-old scout was on his way home when he got caught in a trap. He was lucky we found him when we did. Rogue wolves were about to close in on him. We held them off until help arrived. Our Alpha and a team of pack soldiers helped us to fight them off and took our wounded comrade to safety.

"Is it me, or does Alpha Alec seem crankier than usual?" Lucas mentioned as we hurried home.

Our Alpha was as deadly on two legs as he was on four. The guy fought like a berserker, obliterating anything who was dumb enough to stand in his way. Rumors of his fragile state of mind had been gossip for decades. If I had to sum him up in a nutshell, he was the shifter version of Dr. Jekyll and Mr. Hyde.

Fortunately for us, our thoughts were private. Even in our wolf forms, we could communicate separately from the pack.

Alex stilled; his ears pricked at a squawking bird. Lucas and I followed suit, pausing until it was safe to move.

"It's hardly surprising his mood just lately. It's mating season," Alex muttered through the link. "I expect he'll be different when his mate comes of age."

"You bet, it's mating season," I remarked, feeling my heart somersault with excitement.

It was my mating night. Soon, my baby girl would be mine. But Alex was right. It was that time of year when the adults in our pack got a little amorous and shook the forest with their illicit debauchery. It always hit our Alpha the hardest, having spent an eternity alone.

A new day was upon us. The sun stretched and yawned over the mountain peaks of Forest Hills. A golden hue kissed all that it touched, heating the ground and dew-coated foliage with soft curls of vapor. Droplets of moisture fell from the sky like glittering diamonds, and insects chirped their morning chorus. Whitehaven had woken from its slumber and was astir with life.

"Stay vigilant," Alex communicated. "Follow my lead."

Our eldest brother created a pathway through the ferns. Lucas followed him, and I covered the tracks we made. A visible trail would invite danger to our door. None of us wanted to risk Isobelle's safety. Our cabin was pretty secluded out here in the forest. A lone wolf would find the isolation a struggle, cut off from their own kind. But we Bennetts served as a pack in our own right. We had each other. We were never alone.

"I could sure murder a hearty breakfast," Lucas mentioned as his stomach rumbled.

Alex huffed through his snout. "Is that a hint?"

Lucas responded by nipping Alex's tail.

"Ouch! Watch it, Fido," Alex growled in

annoyance. "Act like a feral animal, and I'll treat you like one."

We shifted at the tree line, arriving home to see that the curtains were still closed — usually a sign that the occupants were still sleeping, yet the combined groans and cries of passion left us exchanging shocked glances on the porch.

"Are they still at it?" Lucas asked incredulously.

Alex flared his eyes as he spoke. "So it would seem."

"They'll probably be hungry after all that . . ." I curled my finger and thumb, using my finger from my opposite hand to pump in and out of the circle. "You know?"

Alex rolled his eyes. "Hint taken," he grumbled. "Someone better check-in with the mated couple . . . pull them apart or throw a bucket of water over them or something."

Lucas flashed me a grin, and I knew exactly what that fucker had in mind.

Not happening, bro.

My reflexes were fast, holding him in a headlock so I could shuffle around and beat him to the bedroom. He collided with me, hissing a series of profanities. I raised a finger to my lips as I curled my hand around the doorknob. A hurricane could sweep through the house and suck out every item of furniture, but it would take a lot more than that to stop me from walking through the door.

"On the count of three," I whispered.

Lucas grinned mischievously.

"One . . . Two . . . "

I flung the door open so that it bounced off the opposite wall. My eyes homed in on the sight of Isobelle riding Mason like a bucking bronco.

"Whoa!" Lucas murmured, his eyes rounding like dinner plates.

"Is this a private party or can anyone join in?" I commented with dry humor.

"Dude, get the fuck out!" Mason roared, sending a pillow hurtling at us.

They continued to finish what they started as if we had never interrupted them.

Izzy's large breasts bounced as she fucked, her face scrunched with intense pleasure.

"Uh, uh, uh!" The pitch of her screams reached an octave that could have shattered glass.

Blood rushed straight to my cock, breathing life into the fucker. I turned to Lucas, who was already jerking off as he watched them.

"Fuck," he grunted, engrossed in the show.

My lust-filled gaze drifted back to Izzy. The urge

to fuck was boiling in my balls, but it turned on the voyeur in me from watching her pogoing on Mason's cock.

A silent dare blazed in her eyes, and a lewd smile curled her lips. She wanted us to watch them and was getting off on it.

"Holy shit!" Mason gasped as she began grinding her hips like a siren.

Lucas edged around the opposite side of the bed, pumping his cock as he enjoyed the show. If that's what my lady yearned for, then that's what she would get. I mirrored the actions, my cock giving her a standing ovation as I stroked.

"Come on me," she pleaded, throwing her head back to ride her pleasure wave.

I watched how she reached around and found Mason's balls with her fingertips. As she squeezed, Mason looked ready to blow. His face crumpled into a pained grimace.

"Uh," Mason dragged out a groan as he blew his load, his eyes bulging wide before rolling into his skull.

My climax burst through my balls, shooting hot strands through the tip of my cock. Lucas came soon after. Both of us splashing thick white jets onto Isobelle's tits.

"Yes, oh God, yes," she cried as she came undone, her body shaking as she rode it out.

A brisk tap on the door frame startled us.

Alex's stony expression suggested that our play session had been distracting him from cooking.

"Breakfast will be ready within the next fifteen minutes. You better be washed and dressed before the dishes hit the table."

Only I got to see the amused smirk on his face as he turned to leave.

Isobelle

Alex's threat held no validity whatsoever. I shuffled from the bedroom wearing my dressing gown and slippers to the sound of running water as it filled the bathtub.

"You read my mind," I mumbled with appreciation.

Alex threw me a devilish smirk. "Not yet, but in time, no secret will be safe around me."

That information daunted me. The lack of privacy was something I wasn't used to. Now I had to share my personal space, my body, and my brain with four sexy werewolves.

My thoughts raced around my head as I soaked in the tub. I was almost out of birth control pills. Any day now and my period would start. If I thought I was going to end up at a shag-fest, I would have come better prepared. During my brief excursion with Chloe, I spotted a pharmacy in town. Perhaps if I mentioned it to the guys, one of them could drive me there so I could purchase more. If all else failed, they would have to resort to using condoms. There was no way I could risk getting pregnant with a baby werewolf. I had visions of it clawing its way out of my uterus like a monster.

"I've got to say, Izzy. You've made me love mornings." Lucas grinned as he scrubbed shampoo into his hair.

Grayson nodded as if he agreed. Mason was busy washing. Now and then, he would cast a sinful smile that fluttered my lady garden.

"I'm going to see what Alex has cooked for breakfast. Are you staying in for a little while longer?" Mason asked.

"I'll be out in a minute." I closed my eyes, fully relaxing in the steamy water.

My aching muscles needed this to replenish

themselves for Grayson's turn tonight. Lucas and Grayson got out soon after Mason, wrapping towels around their hips and removing their sexiness from the room to give me a moment's peace. After taking care of my business, I dried and dressed, then styled my hair into a messy bun. They had all finished eating by the time I joined them.

"Oh, there you are. You're gracing us with your presence." Alex joked teasingly.

He tilted his head expectantly as if waiting for a kiss. A quick peck on the lips wasn't what Alex had in mind after missing out on our morning antics. I straddled his lap, my pussy rocking back and forth against his gargantuan bulge. The way he assaulted my tongue with his showed me just how much he wanted me. I craved nothing more than to unzip his fly, release his long, thick cock, and ride it until it erupted inside me. He must have smelled my arousal because he chuckled salaciously.

"What are you hungry for?" he rasped; his voice was drenched with lust.

You. All of you. Your monster cocks fucking me into oblivion.

"I'll take whatever's on offer," I replied flirtatiously.

Alex lifted me off his lap and placed me onto the seat beside him.

"We've saved you some bacon and eggs. You're going to need to eat a substantial breakfast to keep up your stamina." He winked suggestively.

Oh, so he doesn't plan to bang me over the kitchen table.

I picked up a piece of toast and folded it around a bacon rasher. Before I took my first bite, I asked, "Did you find the injured wolf?"

Alex nodded. "We found him safe and well. There's no reason he shouldn't make a full recovery," he explained, keeping it brief to spare me the gory details.

Grayson looked at him over the rim of his coffee mug. Something had happened out there that they didn't want me to worry about. And that bothered me.

"That's good news. Did you tell your Alpha about the hunter traps you found?" I asked, maintaining the conversation.

Lucas cleared his throat. "Uh, yeah. We discussed it."

I picked up my cutlery and nudged the bacon with my fork. The boys were acting suspiciously, and I wasn't sure why.

Alex and Mason shared a serious look between

them before Alex continued. "It's being taken care of; don't worry," he mentioned, downplaying it.

That only snowballed my anxiety.

Alex nudged my elbow, prompting me to focus on my breakfast. "You should eat to conserve your strength. You'll need it for that horny bastard." He pointed at Grayson.

"Damn straight," Grayson agreed, eyeing me like the red-blooded carnivorous male he was.

CHAPTER Twenty Two

Isobelle

fter an intense goodbye with Alex, Lucas, and Mason, I waved to them from the porch as they shifted and disappeared into the forest.

I hadn't told my parents about my new living arrangement. Not that I could keep this a secret forever. I tried to pluck up the courage, only to chicken out at the last minute. They would never understand this. The timing would never be right. I knew that. It would have to be done sooner rather than later though, because they were expecting me to return home in three months. The closer it came to the deadline, the harder it would be to explain things. I planned to rip off the Band-Aid after I mated with Alex, Lucas, and Grayson. This was special, and I didn't want a fallout with my parents to cast a dark cloud over it.

"Grayson?" I called out, wondering where he had gone.

He was busy preparing a bath and heard me calling to him.

"In here," he answered, sounding a little nervous. I peeked around the doorframe and saw him hide something behind his back. He side-stepped to the shelves and dropped something rubbery onto a towel bale.

"What's that?" I inquired, trying to see past him.

His eyes flashed wide, and he stepped forward to stop me from snooping. It was cute seeing him act this way. He was usually so cocky and self-assured. I could tell that he wanted this night to be perfect, and it made me wonder what else he had planned for us.

"It's ready now," he announced.

I glanced around and saw that he had brought more suspicious items into the bathroom.

"Grayson, what on earth are those?" I asked, afraid of the answer.

He shifted nervously, scrubbing a hand over his face. "Those? Ah . . . those are sex toys," he replied as if they were everyday household objects.

I couldn't stop gawking at them. It looked as if he had looted a sex shop and brought it back to the cabin. A friend of mine had once hosted an Ann Summers party at her house, and I was guilt-tripped into buying a vibrator. You can't exactly leave those parties empty-handed — it's rude. My silicone bad boy took three weeks to arrive. When he came, he needed six AA batteries to power up. So, I nicknamed him Buzz — the ten-inch pussy tornado who boasted six-speed settings, a rotating shaft, and a double-pronged clit tickler that looked like bunny ears. He looked terrifying. I kept him hidden inside my knicker drawer, concealed behind my tummy control pants. Buzz wasn't very discreet, which was why I never risked using him whenever my parents were home. Our walls were thin, and my dad could hear a pin drop.

"Sex toys?" I swallowed a gulp.

A lewd smirk curled across Grayson's lips. "Not just any sex toys. You're going to love them."

Grayson stripped at lightning speed. By the time I

had finished toeing off my shoes, he was already stark bollock naked. My eyes rounded with awe at his solid appendage.

"Anything else caught your eye, babe?" he asked, curling his fingers around his rock-hard cock.

Oh, the arrogance.

His tantalizing strokes pulled my gaze in like a tractor beam.

I made light work of unclasping my bra, then wriggled out of my knickers. My body shook with nerves, wondering where the toys would go.

"Do you need me to get into the bath?" I asked, pointing to the soapy water.

"Not yet," Grayson answered. "Do you see that towel I spread out? I want you to lie down and get into a relaxed position for me."

I did as he asked, unsure of what to expect. Grayson chuckled to himself, and that prompted me to have a sneaky look at what he was doing.

"Oh my God," I muttered when I saw what he had chosen.

"Lie back, lift your knees up, then let them fall apart," he instructed.

He should have been a gynecologist.

I did as he said, giving him a warning look as if to say, "This better not hurt me or else."

"Relax, you'll enjoy it . . . I promise," he soothed in a smooth, sexy voice.

He better be right, or else I'll be shoving a ten-inch length of latex where the sun doesn't shine.

Grayson crawled on top of me, his athletic body making me feel small in comparison. The heady scent of sandalwood and manliness swamped my senses. In my world, if Grayson wasn't a werewolf, and we didn't have a spiritual tether binding our souls, I would find it difficult to trust him because of his flippant attitude toward sex, his pleasure-seeking ways, and his unabashed flirtatious personality that made him so unapologetically himself. I didn't expect him to change, and to be honest, I wouldn't want him to. But him being a werewolf, and us having a soul-binding bond, knowing he would never cheat on me, that his eyes wouldn't roam where they shouldn't, or that he wouldn't be tempted, not even once, brought me a sense of peace that I didn't have with anyone else. Apart from Mason now that we had mated. It felt good to be the center of someone's universe. I was hoping that when I explained this to my parents, they would understand if I explained it from the heart.

"Have you been thinking about me?" he asked,

his words laced with desire. "I've been unable to think of anything else but you all day."

I would never get enough of hearing that, just knowing he had been thinking about me and only me.

"Yes, Daddy," I replied. A dark lust clung to those three syllables, letting him know just how much I had been thinking of him too.

The Daddy Dom role-play was cute, providing it stayed that way. I didn't want him to dress me like a toddler or force me to wear a diaper. Although, I could throw a monumental tantrum when things didn't go my way.

"Good girl," he replied in a husky rasp.

His thick, meaty cock presented hard against my stomach. My pussy throbbed with the promise of a good, hard fuck, and that was exactly what I would get from him. As much as Grayson loved to baby me, he had a filthy mind, and that was clear in the way he shamelessly eye-fucked my body. His eyes darted to my lips before covering my mouth with his. Warmth flooded through me, priming my slit ready to take him. The greedy bitch was begging to be filled. Her entrance was salivating, getting ready to suck him down to his ball sac and suck them dry.

Grayson's tongue danced with mine, and soft

growls escaped his throat as his pleasure consumed him. The musk of my arousal seemed to drive him crazy. He had me all to himself, completely at his mercy.

"Fuck, babe," he breathed against my lips. "I need to taste you."

He was so turned on. Pre-cum leaked from the slit of his cock, leaving a sticky patch on my stomach. I wriggled my hand between us, seizing his length, and rubbed my thumb over the crown. His cream served as a natural lubricant as I stroked him, moving his silky veined skin back and forth over his iron hard appendage. He liked that. His ragged breathing became more haphazard the faster I pumped.

"Baby, if you don't stop doing that, Daddy won't last long," he warned in a strangled groan.

"But I'm a bad girl, and I need to be taught a lesson," I tantalized him, pouting.

Grayson chortled, his eyes dancing with humor. "It's our mating night." He held my wrist to stop my movements. "What kind of a bad daddy do you think I am if I were to light your ass on fire on our special night? It's all about making *you* feel good tonight."

He let go of me and went to fetch a tube of lubricant. Then he squeezed some onto his fingers and spread it over my back passage. He did the same with a string of black beads until they glistened, all slick and ready. I guessed where they were going and grimaced as he pressed the first bead, the smallest, against my butthole. The beads got bigger the more he inserted.

"Does this feel okay?" he asked as he started shoving the bigger ones inside me.

The knotted muscle burned with resistance as each one stretched me wider. I bit down on my bottom lip and nodded.

"Yeah, it just feels strange," I replied.

A light buzzing sound filled the room, and then it ceased. He tested another one of his toys, a small egg-shaped vibrator, before driving it through my pussy walls. Once he had inserted it deep inside my cunt, he switched it on by the remote, tickling my inner walls with a sequence of soft, gentle pulses. The incredible sensation permeated through my body, hitting all the right places.

"Oh, that feels so good!" I aspirated, my eyes rolling into the back of my skull.

Grayson looked down at me through hooded eyes. "It feels good to have your kitty and ass filled with Daddy's toys?"

I nodded vigorously. "Oh yes. Yes, Daddy, that feels so good."

My body thrummed with pleasure, feeling it throb and pulse inside my drenched cavern. I wanted him to rip them all out and take me hard on the bathroom floor, but I knew I'd have to be patient. He intended on giving me everything I needed, all in good time.

"God, Daddy!" I moaned.

He chuckled. "I love my new nickname, but I'm a wolf, baby. And this Daddy wolf wants to lick your kitty like a dessert. Would you like that? Tell me how much you want me to feast on your kitty."

I almost came hearing those dirty words.

"I want your tongue, Daddy. Please, make me come."

Grayson leaned over me in a sixty-nine position. A filthy, greedy feeling came over me, and I wanted to swallow his cock down my throat.

My lips parted for him, taking him inside my mouth as he drove his tongue between my lower folds. I moaned out loud, feeling the intensity of being stuffed from behind, the vibration in my center, and now Grayson's proficient tongue fluttered over my clit. I massaged his balls as I sucked him, hearing his soft grunts of approval as I took the full length of his shaft into my willing mouth, swallowing him down to the root.

Grayson knew what he was doing with his tongue

— my god, his technique was perfect. I knew after tonight I would crave it again and again. My eyelids fluttered, my toes curled, the sound of my muffled cries was enough to raise the roof. My fingers grasped his ass as I sucked up and down his rod like I was drilling for oil. I chased my release, dragging him along for the ride, needing that warm salty gush to hit my tonsils as my come splashed him in the face. He held me still as I bucked and thrashed, reveling in the feel of his wet muscle lapping at my pleasure place. His hands gripped around my thighs as he devoured my swollen clit without an ounce of mercy. As his mouth clamped down around my pulsing bud, stars burst behind my eyelids, blowing my mind.

"Mm," I mumbled, between sucking and swallowing.

Grayson lapped me all up, then craned around to look at me amid his ecstasy, his face scrunched with pleasure, his pupils wild, his slick lips parted in a ragged groan.

"Babe, that was amazing," he expressed breathlessly.

"Mm, it was," I agreed, still sprawled out like a boneless mess.

"Hold still," Grayson advised as he pulled the egg-shaped vibrator from out of my center.

It still felt as if it was in there buzzing away inside my empty cavity. He left the anal beads in place as he scooped me up and carried me into the bathtub. My legs were like jelly, too weak to walk. The water was just the right temperature. Not too hot, but warm enough to relax my muscles. I wrapped my arms around Grayson's neck as he leaned in to kiss me. It felt different this time. This kiss was soft and gentle. Grayson's kisses usually screamed, "I want to fuck you hard, and the dirtier, the better," but not this one. It was the type of kiss that felt more like *Marry me,* and that alone sent my heart fluttering to the heavens above. I knew what he was about to do meant more than any traditional marriage ceremony. He was about to bind his soul to mine.

Grayson picked me up by my thighs, and instinctively, I wrapped my legs around his waist, our kiss heating into something raw and passionate. My nipples pointed toward him, aching to be sucked. Grayson obliged, French kissing them greedily, the crown of his cock forever teasing my pussy lips, ready to burst inside at any second.

"Are you ready, baby?" Grayson asked, his husky voice dripping with sin.

"Yes, Daddy," I murmured, gazing at him full of adoration as if he was my everything.

Grayson's sex-crazed eyes locked with mine as he impaled me onto his iron rod, splitting me wide. His fingers dug into the globes of my ass as he thrust inside me, filling me so full of cock I could burst. Our kissing was frantic, our bodies moving together in a voracious dance of limbs. I couldn't take it. The sensation was too much. I was overwhelmed and at the complete mercy of this beautiful sex demon. My pussy skyrocketed into another earth-shattering orgasm.

"Uh, uh, uh!" I bleated as Grayson dragged his cock through my convulsing cunt.

Tidal waves of water crashed all around us, sloshing over the sides of the tub.

Grayson sucked on the soft spot at the base of my neck, and I knew what was coming next. I waited for the sharp sting of his teeth, and Grayson didn't disappoint me. He bit down hard, breaking the skin, and staking his claim on me. Fire burst through my body, clouding my eyes with a white mist of pain. Seconds passed and his teeth were still there — it was too damn long, and I couldn't take it anymore. He pulled back with bloodstained lips, his eyes wide and ferocious as he drilled himself inside me, finishing our fucking until I lost all cognition. Thank God we were in the water because my pussy exploded like a fire hose, to the point I thought I peed. Grayson roared his climax, his cock pulsing with each rapid hip jerk.

"Fuck," he barked, scrunching his face.

We stayed entwined like that for a long while, unable to move, think, or speak until we caught our breath, and Grayson's lips stretched into a lazy smile. Then as I sagged in his arms, he pulled the beads from my asshole, prolonging my pleasure. My walls quivered around his softening member, milking him for all he was worth. No words could describe the orgasm I'd just had. We held on to each other for what felt like ages, enjoying the newfound closeness we shared.

After our mating, when we were dry, and we had put away the toys, Grayson lounged on the sofa in his boxer shorts as I heated some leftover lasagna. I was wearing his shirt, his manly scent flowing into my airways with every subtle inhalation. It felt like we were newlyweds, settled and content.

"Do you need some help, baby?" he asked, fussing like I might burn my hand on the dish.

I turned to face him, resting my hand on my hip.

"I'm a big girl. I can manage," I reminded him.

Grayson huffed a dissatisfied sigh. "But *I'm* supposed to be taking care of *you*," he complained.

I wagged my finger in the air. "Ah-ah," I

interjected. "The role-play stays in the bedroom." My firm expression showed him I meant business. "I'm quite capable of taking care of you too."

"All right, I can live with that," he replied, sounding a little downtrodden, but he appreciated the caregiving worked both ways.

"Sit up straight, or else you'll get red-hot lasagna down your front," I ordered, holding out his plate.

They told me that werewolves have fast healing abilities, but they still feel pain, no matter how severe. I imagined that hot cheese sauce would burn like a bitch, werewolf or not.

An amused smirk curved the edge of his lips at my bossy attitude. "Yes, Momma," he replied with sarcasm.

I chuckled. "You're asking for a spanking."

Humor ignited the light in his eyes. "Yes, please," he retorted. He took the plate and placed a pillow beneath it. Alex would throw a hissy fit if he knew we were eating dinner in front of the television.

"Grayson, can I ask you something?" I picked my moment tactfully.

"Sure, you can ask me anything you want," he replied in between shoveling forkfuls of food into his mouth.

"I want to know what happened in the forest

yesterday. How bad is it out there?" I maintained an even tone to show that I could handle the truth.

As I suspected, Grayson bristled.

"What's the point in hiding it?" He exhaled a sigh of defeat. "You are bound to find out sooner or later." His fork clattered to the side of his plate.

"By not telling me, you're making me worry more," I reasoned.

Grayson nodded in agreement. "We ran into a bunch of rogues who tracked the scent of the injured wolf. The fact that they were inside our territory is a major concern. The last time we had a breach like this the future Luna was their target. Alpha Alec thinks they were tracking something else."

My eyes twitched into two narrow slits. "Something? Or someone?" I asked.

Grayson shrugged as if he didn't know. "All we know is that it's not safe for you to be wandering around outside beyond the red zone. At least, not until you're fully mated. Our Alpha has given us a few days to complete the bond. Consider it an honor. Most people only get twenty-four hours. You'll be expected to accept him as your Alpha, then you'll be accepted into the pack. I hope you understand why we didn't tell you last night. You were shaken enough as it was."

"Thank you for being straight with me," I replied appreciatively.

My next question was gnawing away at my insides. I needed to know, no matter how ugly the truth was.

"Are the others in danger right now?" I paused, terrified of the answer.

Grayson's eyes seemed to glaze over as he thought. It was strange. He appeared to be here *physically* but not *mentally* — like his mind had gone somewhere else. A moment passed before his pupils refocused. He was back again.

"No, they're all fine." He blinked rapidly and pinched the corners of his eyes. "The Alpha has everyone out on patrol duties."

I puffed out a breath. "That's a relief."

I couldn't eat another morsel of food. Grayson had already finished his dinner, so he took our plates to the sink. As he was busy scrubbing them clean, I shuffled off to bed. The second my eyelids fluttered closed I felt a warm hand sliding across my bare hips.

"Izzy," Grayson whispered, shaking me awake.

"What?" I mumbled sleepily.

"I need you again," he murmured beside my ear.

"You're fucking insatiable," I groaned, still experiencing the dull ache in my limbs.

He rolled me onto my back and climbed on top of me, nudging my thighs apart with his knees. I gasped as his rock-solid cock speared through my bruised folds for the second time tonight.

"I can't believe you're hard again," I gasped at the massive intrusion.

"Always for you," he groaned as he slapped his hips against mine.

Grayson rutted me like a man crazed with need. The head of his cock knocked against the apex of my sex as we worked up a sweat, our skin clammy with perspiration, the headboard thumping against the wall like a jackhammer. Grayson's muscled ass pumped like a frantic piston, fucking, claiming, stroking me until lights flashed behind my eyelids, our bodies tensing, then relaxing as we climaxed together.

"Oh, God," I kept chanting until my breath ran out and my voice lost sound.

Three rounds later and I was a boneless mess, utterly wrung out and spent. Even Grayson seemed exhausted by this point.

"Grayson," I mumbled.

"Mhmm," he replied, his eyes closed.

I leaned over him, only to notice he had fallen asleep. He looked so peaceful. His dark prominent eyebrows were relaxed and devoid of any stress. My fingertips followed his angular jawline, feeling the coarse texture of his two-day-old stubble. He was handsome all right, but inside he was much more than that, more than the dirty, flirty joker that everyone knew. He was beautiful, perfect, and mine.

Spending time with each of the Bennett brothers made me realize something. Mason would provide me with an abundance of romance and would nurture my sensitive side. Grayson was like every woman's dirty-minded fantasy, someone who would make me laugh as well as act as a caregiver. Lucas had the element of danger about him that would never fail to thrill me in all ways sexual. He was always challenging me to be the best version of myself. And then there was Alex. He would worship me in and out of the bedroom, incorporating a functioning structure and routine into our relationship. I was his everything just as much as I was his submissive. They each brought something unique to the table. I was the luckiest woman alive.

CHAPTER
Twenty Three

Isobelle

I cradled a mug of steaming hot tea between my hands as I waited for the boys to come home. The early morning air bit my skin with its chilly teeth. Jets of white vapor billowed from my mouth like dragon's breath. If it weren't for the heat seeping into my palms from the tea, I would have darted back indoors and not tortured myself out here on the porch. Fast-moving clouds hid the sky from view, dragging a light shower of rain across the forest.

I blew the steam from my tea, creating a ripple effect across the light brown liquid.

Grayson came out to join me, holding a patchwork blanket over his arm. He shook it out, then draped it around my shoulders.

"I've changed the bedsheets again. I don't think they've ever been washed as much in a month as they have this week," he joked.

"Have you always slept in the same bed as your brothers?" I asked out of curiosity.

Grayson's brows dimpled in the middle. "Yeah, why? Don't human siblings do that?"

I swallowed another mouthful of tea.

"Yes, but just not all the time." I wasn't sure how to explain it to him without it sounding judgmental. "People tend to have a bed of their own nowadays. My grandparents used to tell me stories about when they were younger. My gran was the eldest out of eleven children, and they all shared one bedroom above a shop. They slept on a double mattress on the floor, and all huddled together for warmth. Times were a lot different back then. I'm an only child. I can't imagine having to share a room with a brother or sister, let alone a bed. I enjoy my own space."

It was common for children to share beds with

their siblings if they had no other choice, or if they were afraid of the dark. But if they had the option to choose, they would grow out of that habit eventually. It was uncommon for grown men to share a bed, even if they were brothers. Human adult brothers wouldn't necessarily choose to share a bed. They would want one of their own. I just didn't know how to mention this without making him feel awkward about it.

"I hope you don't enjoy it too much," Grayson was quick to respond. "My brothers and I have always shared one bed between us. Mom always used to say we behaved like a litter of pups. It's not uncommon for multiple-birth shifters to share a unique bond. Chances are they'll share a mate too. My brothers and I can't stand to be apart for too long. We get homesick. It affects our mood if we're separated for too long."

"That's so sweet," I fawned. "I wonder whether our kids will be as close." I mentioned without giving it much thought.

An awkward silence followed my comment, making me wish I could retract it.

Why did I have to mention babies?

Worried that I had just given him coronary heart failure, I was quick to recover. "Speaking of which, I need a ride to town. I'm almost out of birth control pills."

Grayson's eyes rolled, and his nostrils flared.

What's got him looking so worried?

"I wouldn't concern yourself with that." He winced as he spoke.

My confused frown prompted him to elaborate.

"If a shifter wanted to impregnate you, it wouldn't matter if you had swallowed a whole truckload of those pills. He could still sire offspring. Our sperm is stronger than any pharmaceutical contraceptive ever invented." He saw my startled expression and gave my knee a reassuring squeeze. "Don't worry. We'd never do that without your permission."

"Why didn't you mention this earlier?" I queried, sounding as baffled as I felt.

"Because we wanted you to let go and enjoy sex with us without worrying. For all you knew, we could've been spinning you any old bullshit just to get inside your pants," he reasoned.

"How do I know you're telling me the truth now?" I countered, making a valid point.

Grayson huffed a sigh. "What would I gain by lying?"

"Not a lot, I suppose," I muttered in agreement.

I took another sip of tea, noticing how it had cooled.

"What are your parents like?" I asked, taking an interest.

Grayson blew out a forced breath, flaring his eyes. "My parents . . ."

I chuckled at his reaction. "Oh, come on. They can't be that bad."

He made a face to suggest otherwise.

"You'll meet them eventually. Then you can make up your own mind." His line of sight shot to the tree line. "Here come the guys."

He was right. Alex, Mason, and Lucas loped out of the forest in their wolf forms. That was our cue to go back indoors for breakfast.

After they had washed and dressed, I assisted Alex with the cooking duties. Now and then, he flicked his grey gaze to me. There wasn't an obvious smile on his face, but his eyes shone with delight.

"What?" I finally asked.

Alex looked away, grinning. "I can't believe how lucky we are. I'm so glad that my Alpha sent me to London. Imagine if I passed it up. We might never have met," he contemplated.

"What was your first thought when you saw me?" I inquired, fishing for compliments.

Alex thought for a second. "I thought, *wow, what a knockout. This girl has a face that could stop traffic."*

He flattered me, making a smirk tug at the corner of my mouth.

"I must take after my nana then," I mentioned. "She has the ability to stop traffic too."

"I guess beauty runs through your entire gene pool," Alex spoke, using his charismatic charm to compliment me.

I chewed the inside of my cheek before answering, "Nah, she's a crossing guard," I joked, because she wasn't. My nan and grandad bred racehorses and owned an equestrian center. It was mostly Grandad's livelihood because Nan didn't do much besides gossiping and knitting.

A chorus of manly chortles rang out around the cabin, and Alex conceded, appreciating my joke. He turned to me, grinning wildly.

"You got me," he chuckled, wagging his finger. "You've spent way too much time alone with Grayson."

Grayson held his hands out in an exaggerated shrug. "The girl's got game. She was made to keep us on our toes."

"We better keep her sweet then," Alex noted, leaning down for a kiss.

Over a minute passed and our kiss was still in full swing. We almost burned the bacon if it wasn't for his keen sense of smell.

"Whoops," he mumbled against my lips, then turned to shut off the heat. "Take a seat and I'll serve breakfast."

The boys discussed plans to extend the cabin, and I used the spare few minutes to check my phone to see if I had any message alerts. Mum had replied to my last text. Dad had sent two texts. One was a selfie of him and Mum at my favorite restaurant, and a caption that didn't make any sense. In the next message, he apologized for his dyslexic predictive text and mentioned that he missed me. Joanne had also texted to say that she missed me too.

Wait, what's this?

There was another text message but this one was from Peter Munroe.

What could he want?

Frowning at the screen, I opened the text and scanned my eyes across the message.

Oh, God!

He wanted to know when I would be free to meet up for drinks. I assumed that he was in on the boys' plan to lure me here. After all, he had seemed so convincing when we first met. Then again, so did

Chloe. What was I supposed to do? Since I was going to permanently live here, it would be nice to keep the friends I had made. If I kept pushing them away, I'd soon lose them. My thumbs went to work on typing my reply. *"Hi, Peter. That sounds great, but can we meet up next week? I think I might be coming down with a cold. Isobelle."*

There . . . that should buy me some time.

He was quick to respond with, "*Oh no. I hope you feel better soon.*"

What a nice chap.

It was only a little white lie, but it felt like a dirty secret. I couldn't exactly tell him the truth, could I? The reason I couldn't meet up was because my schedule was packed to the brim with quadruplet cock. I don't think that conversation would go down well with male friends. Now female friends . . . that would be the highlight of our discussion.

Lucas

Time always dragged whenever I waited for something. Unable to keep a lid on my excitement, I

submerged myself balls-deep into an art project —
my mating gift to Isobelle.

The sun's rays cast a glittery streak of dust motes
through my shed window, the light kissing the canvas
with a rich golden hue. My keen eyes flicked back and
forth as I applied the finishing touches to my muse —
the blonde-haired angel who was sitting on the porch
under the shade of the wooden canopy. She buried
her nose deep into one of her science books, her
brow scrunched with extreme concentration, her eyes
descending each page with a tenacious thirst for
knowledge. It was the sexiest sight I had ever seen in
my life.

My brothers voiced their agreement through our
private bond. We all agreed, we struck gold when
Alex found Isobelle. Mason lounged upon the
wooden steps, guitar in hand, strumming out some
insane chord progression like he was Ed fucking
Sheeran. It was hard to compete with a guy like
Mason. He was a woman's walking fantasy. The
embodiment of perfection. Alex could easily be
mistaken for a hotshot CEO by the way he dressed,
the confidence he oozed, and how leadership came
naturally to him. People listened to him. They valued
his opinion. He was the kind of guy who kept a cool
head in the time of a crisis. Grayson had husband

material written all over him. The smut and filth he tended to spew from his mouth was just a smokescreen for what he truly wanted — and that was someone to cherish. I had always felt like the odd one out — like a fraction of me was missing. The same as a partially completed jigsaw with one puzzle piece short. My shed was my den — a place for me to unwind and just be myself. Oil paintings took up most of the space in my linseed oil-infused environment. An array of colored spatters coated the floorboards, staining the wood like imprinted memories. Artistry was almost the same as glimpsing into the future but with a definitive end in mind. Some might even say that a person's artistic style reflected the chaos within their soul. Maybe there was truth in that. I liked to think of it as an expression of how a person truly felt but couldn't always convey it with words or music. Maybe that was how I saw my art . . . to express all the music and poetry within my soul.

"Hey, Lucas!" Grayson called out.

Two seconds ago, he and Alex had been discussing plans for the extension, walking around with a notepad and measuring tape. I cluttered my solitary space with bike parts, artwork, and unwashed mixing palettes, so that Alex would sooner cut off his dick than step foot inside my domain. Here, in the confines of my shed, I could unleash the real me.

"What do you want?" I yelled back, agitated at being interrupted.

Grayson could talk the head off a horse, so the chance of me finishing my painting within the hour looked rather slim.

"What are you doing?" he asked, peering around the doorframe.

I threw a dust sheet over the easel.

"None of your business," I snapped back.

Grayson arched his brow with mock sympathy. "Did I ruin your happy time?"

I jerked my head back in outrage, tempted to punch the patronizing look off his face. "Happy time?! Don't talk to me like a fucking kindergarten teacher. Get the fuck out!"

Alex's husky laughter rumbled through the shiplap walls.

"I came here to let you know it's almost time for us to leave. Do you think you can heat-up some leftovers without burning down the cabin?" Grayson finished sarcastically.

I rolled my eyes, scrunching my nose to display my distaste.

"Fuck you and your leftover meatloaf. I'll be

grilling our girl some prime steaks out here under the starry night sky," I commented, crossing my paint-smeared arms across my bare chest. "Alex isn't the only one who can cook, you know."

Boisterous chortling filtered in through the open shed door. My brothers seemed to find the concept of me preparing a meal amusing. Maybe if Alex ever let me near the stove, I could show them a thing or two.

"Lucas's concept of preparing a meal consists of him hunting down a live kill," Alex remarked with dry humor. "What are you going to have her do? Fuck first, then hunt deer later?"

I wiped my clammy palms against my combat shorts, then stalked out to face the assholes head-on. Little did they know I purchased the meat from the butcher's shop today. I even bought a supermarket marinade to brush over it while it cooked. I just hoped that Izzy liked Texan food and didn't compare it to a *Fear Factor* trial.

"Go ahead and laugh. I won't be thinking of you guys as I'm sinking my teeth into all that sweet juicy tenderness." I flashed them a cocky smirk. "And just so you know, I'm not talking about the food," I retorted, watching their grins fall from their faces.

Alex held my gaze with one of his nuclear glares.

Grayson wrinkled his nose as he imagined the

scenario, then turned to Alex. "Well, at least you won't have to wash the bedding," he commented dryly.

Alex arched his brows as if he agreed with him. "True. That'll save me a chore." His eyes flashed back to me. "Don't forget to wipe your dick on the doormat on your way to bed."

I tried to mask my amusement by rolling my shoulders and stretching my arms over my head. "Did you get that thing I asked for?" I threw in the question, lowering my voice so that Isobelle couldn't hear.

Alex nodded his head subtly. "Yeah, it's laid out on the bed so that she can change into it later."

Blood rushed straight to my prized possession as I recalled my ultimate fantasy — Isobelle dressed all in red, telling me what a big cock I have as I plunged it deep inside her.

CHAPTER Twenty Four

Isobelle

I had been on the phone with my mum for an hour; the handset was hot against my ear. Each time I opened my mouth to speak, Mum would butt in with more questions.

"Do you go out much?" she quizzed.

I was about to answer, but she cut me off with another question. "Or do they keep you hard at it night and day?"

Holy shit, how do I respond to that?

"I get a break now and again," I answered, fighting the urge to laugh.

"Are you eating properly?" she inquired.

"Yes, Mum. I'm being thoroughly cared for," I assured.

Strong arms snaked around my waist, and Lucas playfully nipped at my earlobe.

"Ouch, Lucas!" I scolded.

"Izzy, who's Lucas?" My mum asked, her voice dragging with curiosity.

I swatted him away and pointed toward the open door, mouthing, "Get out."

"Oh, he's just the neighbor's dog, Mum," I lied quickly.

Lucas's face flooded with amused shock as he stood there, open-mouthed in the doorway. I shrugged, trying to excuse my comment as a fast improvisation.

"Aww, what breed?" Mum inquired fondly. "I've always had a soft spot for dogs. They make splendid companions."

"This one is a right pain in the ass, Mum," I continued to joke as Lucas shook his head at me, grinning with mischievous intent. I knew I would end up paying for that comment later tonight.

"Izzy, don't be so mean," Mum defended what she thought was an adorable, furry lapdog.

There was nothing cute and cuddly about Lucas. Dangerous and sexy — yes. But certainly not cute. Right now, my muscle-bound bad boy was eyeing me up like he wanted to fuck me raw. Whatever Mum wanted to waffle on about could wait until tomorrow.

"Mum, I'm sorry, but I've got to go. I'll catch up with you tomorrow. Love you, bye," I rushed my words and hung up the call.

I squealed as Lucas hoisted me over his shoulder caveman-style and delivered a rough slap to my backside.

"I'll give you a pain in the ass!" he threatened playfully.

Through a paroxysm of giggles, I tried to justify myself. "I'm sorry! She was almost suspicious. Put me down. I'm dizzy."

Lucas carried me around the cabin, twirling me around in circles.

"Oh, come on, I need to get ready for our date," I whined.

He placed me down and wrapped me in a tight embrace. After a pussy-pulsing kiss that lasted several minutes, we broke apart, panting for air.

"I'll be out on the front porch, cooling off," Lucas rasped, adjusting his nether regions in his jeans.

"Okay, I won't be long," I replied, then pressed one last lingering kiss to his lips.

Butterflies fluttered around my chest as I darted inside the bedroom to get ready. I had never felt so alive in my entire life.

My eyes homed in on the unmissable costume he had laid out on the bed for me to find.

Oh, my goodness.

I approached it cautiously, clamping a hand over my mouth to muffle my surprise. Lucas was quite a fan of fairy tales, and I could guess which one was his favorite.

The filthy dog.

I slid the sex-shop Little Red Riding Hood outfit over my naked body, dismissing the need for underwear. Lucas was rather rough during sex and would rip them to shreds anyway. My pussy purred with approval, moistening her lips, ready for the treat. The soft satin material warmed from the heat of my skin. My nipples puckered beneath the fake white bodice. Lucas's eyes rounded in a silent *wow* as he saw me emerge onto the porch. His breath caught in his throat, and his green eyes bounced all over my body as he drank in the view.

"Are you ready for me, baby?" he asked, his voice dropping to a sexy husk.

"You have no idea," I replied, lacing our fingers together.

The sky had already started its transition from light to dark, and that only enhanced the glowing flecks of gold around Lucas's irises. It was a deadly sign to anyone that he wasn't fully tame, but to me, it was an invitation to come out and play with his beastly side.

I was about to venture into the woods with the big bad wolf for company. He wrapped his arm around my shoulders, possessively staking his claim. His eyes darted down to me, sparing hungry side glances like he couldn't wait to skip to the good part of the story and eat me.

"You ought to stay close to me, Little Red," Lucas warned playfully. "The forest is a dangerous place at night. Especially for such a sweet little lady like you."

Another one who likes to role-play.

I huffed with amusement. "All right, I'll play along," I replied, humoring him.

My acting skills were dismal at best, but I faked a gasp and wriggled out of Lucas's clutches as if I was a terrified, helpless girl. I almost gagged thanks to the potent scent of vegetation. I could taste it on my tongue. Smells, tastes, sight, and sounds. My senses were heightened.

Lucas narrowed his brows at my momentary repulsion. "Are you feeling all right?" he asked, sounding genuinely concerned.

I swatted the air as if it was no big deal. "It's fine. Let's start again," I insisted, ignoring my churning stomach.

Lucas stripped off his T-shirt, displaying the muscles of a gladiator. My eyes darted to his nipple piercings, wanting to run my tongue around the soft tissue and titanium steel.

"I thought we could start with a little game," he mentioned, plucking open the top button of his combat shorts.

I almost choked on thin air, my eyes bulging wide as his cock sprang free.

"What sort of game?" I asked as he toed off his footwear.

Fuck me, he looked hot, standing there in all his buck-naked glory. The body of a Titan, sun-bronzed and inhumanly beautiful. The evening breeze billowed my slutty skirt a few inches higher, passing a cool draft around my shaved pussy. Lucas's eyes closed as he scented the air around us, and when he opened them again, he had a predatory glint in his eyes. My adrenaline raced around my body, creating a frisson of excitement. My nipples pebbled beneath the cheap material, and my sex clenched, desperate to be stuffed full of werewolf cock.

"Little Red, I want you to run, and run fast because I'm going to chase you down," he spoke with a dark raspy husk.

His cock gave a jerk in approval, his length thick, veined, and creaming at the tip.

"One, two, three," he counted.

Shrieking with delight, I darted deeper into the forest. We were nowhere near the red zone. The boys made Lucas promise not to take me there. Instead, he lured me to the familiarity of the nature trail. I knew of a decent hiding place. A tree that looked easy enough to climb.

Adrenaline pumped through my body, fueling me onward. The second Lucas stopped counting he would come for me. There was no way I could outrun him as much as I was going to try.

As if I want to get away when the fun is getting caught!

Lucas counted slowly, allowing me extra time to put some distance between us. I could imagine how fierce he looked right now, his wolf eyes glowing, saliva pooling into his mouth as his canines elongated, pre-cum dripping from the tip of his cock.

Remind me why I'm running again?

A piercing howl cut through the forest as he got to ten, exploding my ovaries to smithereens. Then the ground shook with a tremor of footsteps. He was coming for me. My lungs were on fire as I pelted toward the tree, leaping far enough to grab the lowest branch to hoist myself up onto my chest. With one leg left dangling, I dragged one knee up, then reached for a higher branch to climb to safety.

"Argh!" I screamed as his strong fingers seized my ankle, immobilizing me.

Lucas let out another triumphant howl that rattled my ears and sent a warm gush of juices rushing straight through my core. He tugged lightly, causing me to lose my balance and hang there, suspended from the tree. I kicked out with my other leg until he grabbed that too, then spread them apart and pressed his face against my bare pussy. His hot breath gusted my lower lips as he positioned his mouth against my slit.

"My, my, what a delicious cunt you have," Lucas murmured salaciously.

His dark chuckle felt as if it was vibrating straight through my pussy.

"This is the part where I beg you to eat me like the book says," I whimpered desperately. "Do it; give me that big, wet . . . oh my god!" I mewled as he dragged his drenched muscle through my folds.

"Oh, oh," I moaned breathlessly.

Lucas growled as his tongue swirled around my clit, tasting everything my pussy offered. My legs quaked, and my head reared back open-mouthed. Bits of bark crumbled beneath my fingertips as I clung on for dear life.

Rough, calloused hands held my thighs steady as he feasted, pushing his taut tongue into my pulsing cavity so that his nose pressed against my solid nub.

"Luca . . . Luca . . ." His name ghosted past my lips in broken sequences.

As he lapped up my cream, my walls constricted around his tongue. His nose rubbed against my pleasure button, making my stomach pull tighter. My legs clamped around his head like a vice, but Lucas continued his relentless assault until my come face replaced my expression.

"Uh, uh, uh," I grunted, letting go of the tree to ride his face.

Lights flashed behind my eyelids as if I had soared straight to the heavens above. Amidst Lucas's growls and my ragged groans, we filled the forest with the orgasmic sounds of sex.

Lucas hummed "mmm" as he pressed kisses to

the inside of my thighs, then set me down onto unsteady legs. His eyes were wild with desire, his chest heaving with shallow breaths. My god, Lucas looked magnificent when his pleasure consumed him. This mysterious, powerful beast of a man was mine. All mine. After tonight, I would get a lifelong VIP pass to the Lucas show. No refunds, until death do us part.

His hypnotic eyes danced back and forth between mine as if he couldn't quite believe it. It was the same way I was looking at him.

What does someone like you see in me?

I don't even know which one of us made the first move. Our lips seemed to draw together like magnets. My arms crossed at the back of his neck as his snaked around my waist. As we both lost ourselves in the rapture of our passion, I could taste myself on his tongue. The length of his cock pressed firmly against my stomach as we kissed; his hands trailed down to cup my bare ass, and my fingers tangling with his fawn-colored hair.

"I want you so badly," he groaned against my lips, freeing one of my breasts and squeezing the nipple between his finger and thumb.

"Then take me." My breathing was tremulous.

Lucas pulled me down to the forest floor with him, pressing my back into the loose chippings. The way he was looking down upon me like a victory prize was almost my undoing. His firm hands gripped the top of the cheap, slutty outfit and tore through it as if it was nothing but paper. My chest heaved haphazardly, drawing his eyes toward my bobbing breasts. Lucas crawled over me, moving his mouth against either side of my neck like a wicked game of eenie meenie miney mo. I already had one mating bite on both sides, so it seemed like he was savoring the choice.

Just when I thought he might bite me before fucking me first, he dragged his lips down to my left breast and sucked the nipple into his mouth. It was brutal and meant to make me squeal. His rough hands pinned me to the ground like a dog torturing his play toy.

Each time he inflicted pain, he caressed the area with his tongue. My nipples turned to stiffened peaks, pointing up at him as if begging for attention. Lucas stopped to scent the air — no doubt my pussy was kicking up a fuss at being left out.

"Let me touch you," I pleaded, reaching between us to find his cock.

"Nah-ah." Lucas jerked his hips away. "Tonight, it's all about you."

I had half the forest stuck to my hair, but at that

moment, I couldn't care less. I wanted my man, and I was going to allow him to take my body however he pleased.

"On your knees, Isobelle," Lucas commanded.

His voice sounded like a raspy growl, but that seemed to turn me on more. I got off on the fact that he was part man, part wolf. It was sexy as hell. Just like those fantasy erotica books I liked to read when I was feeling frisky, this was one of my wildest fantasies that had come to life.

How many women get lucky enough to experience this shit for real?

With the base of the forest biting into my soft skin, I positioned myself on all fours, offering myself willingly. My pulse sped up as Lucas knelt behind me and nipped my earlobe, reminding me he was in charge.

His furious breath fanned the side of my neck, billowing against my skin in short, warm blasts. My entire body thrummed with arousal. I lowered myself down until I could rest my chin on my hands, keeping my behind high in the air for him to mount me with ease.

Lucas readied himself into a comfortable position. He teased my entrance with the tip of his cock, pushing it inside my folds, then dragged it along my slit.

"Little Red Riding Hood wants the Big Bad Wolf to fuck her hard," I enticed him, grinding my pussy against the crown of his cock.

Air gusted against my center, cooling the wetness. Lucas placed his hands on my hips, angling me back even farther, and completely exposing me to him.

He growled, seeming as if I had just said the magic words that he so desperately wanted to hear. "Oh, baby, you do not know what this wolf wants to do to you. I'm going to fuck you till you can't walk, and then I'm going to fuck you some more."

He ran two fingers down my soaking wet swollen folds, reminding me he could see everything I offered, and he knew how badly I craved him.

"This is beautiful." He pushed two fingers into my hot channel, pulled them out, and then licked them clean, smacking his lips. "Tastes fine, too."

One second I was empty, then he was there, pressing the bulbous head of his cock against my folds, teasing me open before pushing it in an inch, then another. My pussy parted for him even more. He held one hand on the small of my back, gentling me as he slid another few inches in.

"Lucas," I gasped as my walls stretched wide.

He went slowly at first, letting me adjust to his size, then rotated his hips just to bring that perfect balance of pleasure and torture.

"Please," I urged him.

He was huge and thick, and I begged him to fuck me fast and hard, but Lucas made me wait first. He let me take him in at a slow pace, and once he had pushed in halfway, I felt so full.

"Yes," I moaned, thrusting my hips backward.

"Greedy." Lucas chuckled.

I want it, all of it.

"Fuck me, please, Lucas, I need you."

Lucas obeyed my command, ramming the last few inches into my hungry, aching channel so that his balls slapped against me. He held me like that for a moment, letting me adjust. Then — *slap* — another hard thrust. And again, *slap*, pause, *slap*, pause.

"Oh God, Lucas! Yes!" I moaned. "Just like that!"

"Are you ready for me, baby?" Lucas's voice was guttural, animalistic, and rough with need.

My pussy clung to his meat like a jungle cat guarding a prize kill. Now it was Lucas's turn to take his pleasure from me, and I was only too eager to brace myself and let him take it.

"Uh, Jesus, you feel so good," Lucas grunted.

"Fuck me rough," I blurted. "Don't hold back."

Lucas kept one hand on my back to steady me as he started his slow, pounding rhythm.

Once he built his momentum, he drove into me with pure masculine abandon. His balls slapped hard against my folds as his hips crashed into me, reminding me he could fill me to the brim.

I screamed out loud as he pummeled me from behind. He was so big. My walls stretched, clenched, and trembled as I struggled to keep still and take him as he delivered his delicious torture, spearing into me, dangerously close to smashing through my barrier. I balled my fists into the ground, gripping the earth as I braced myself each time that he drew his hips back.

Lucas held me in a perfect balance between pleasure and pain. With each new thrust, he forced more of me open, as if his cock somehow grew even bigger as he fucked me. Erotic noises and the salacious sounds of flesh slapping against flesh were swallowed by the forest.

Lucas settled into a punishing but steady rhythm, growling out his pleasure. My breath came in short, sharp pants. Crying out whenever he gave a forceful thrust.

The heat between my legs grew, and he had me so wet I felt a trickle of my juices sliding down my legs, coating both of us and easing his passage. He had primed me ready for a hard fucking. Up to now, he has let me ride to the rhythm of his movements. He delivered the perfect amount of friction as he thrust in and out. Then he pulled me back a little farther. My knees trembled as I struggled to take even more of him. He picked my rear up as high as it would go until my nose touched the ground. He growled in the back of his throat, then drove his cock into me with unbridled savagery.

Something wild seemed to come over Lucas. Guttural growls slipped through his lips as his fingers dug into me, his nails pinching my skin. I screamed once more, "Harder, faster!" It was enough to tip Lucas over the edge.

His other hand went to my shoulder, pinning me in place as he fucked me with abandon, not even pausing to let me adjust to his girth. I clenched and stretched around him, screaming in ecstasy, feeling the rising tide of an orgasm building from deep inside me.

His furious breath heated my nape, making my hair stand on end. My skin rippled with goosebumps, and my pussy answered with a rush of fresh juices.

He nipped my earlobe, and I gasped, "Lucas!"

"You're mine now and forever . . . say it," he spoke in a rough, raspy voice, and it was at that moment I realized he had partially shifted into something that could only be described as beast man.

His body was covered with fur, and his face had morphed into that of a wolfman.

"Yes!" I cried out. "Fuck. Yes! God! All yours! Do it!"

"Come for me, Isobelle, come with me," he commanded.

Lucas jerked his hips, and from my peripheral vision, I saw him rear his head back. He let out a loud howl that was part-human, part-wolf, and raw sex.

When Lucas came, he filled me so completely I doubted there was any room left inside me. His thick, hot semen coated my womb as my body quivered and clenched around his length. Lucas growled again. A low, menacing rumble vibrated through his chest and along my spine.

I screamed with him from the pleasure and pain of his hard thrusts, my body stretched as far as it could go, impaled on his gigantic cock.

I'm yours, and you are mine.

Then Lucas bent down again, his teeth grazing the back of my collar and his hot breath on my skin. Just as I reached the crest of my orgasm, he pierced into my flesh, drawing blood. With each rapid hip jerk, my body jolted along with him.

As he drew his teeth away and sucked me there, his tongue sealed the wound. He pumped out the last of his seed in me as he lapped at my neck and pulled me close to him.

"God, woman, you make me feel whole again," he whispered softly against my ear. "My heart is yours. I fuckin' love you so much."

Feeling weightless as my orgasm waned, I let him pull me against him, shuddering as he gathered me into his arms and held me close. He was still inside me. His long, thick cock pressed deep into my quivering channel.

"I love you too, Lucas," I replied.

His stubbly kisses grazed my delicate skin. I watched as the fur coating his arms receded. His touch was tender now, but the message was clear — my body was his, and he was mine, and I loved him.

"Let's go home," he spoke reverently.

His voice had become smoother, more like his own. He reached out for me, lacing our fingers as we walked back to the cabin as husband and wife.

CHAPTER Twenty Five

Isobelle

"**H**ow's the steak?" Lucas asked as the tasty, meaty morsel slid down my gullet.

"Delicious," I replied, licking the smoky marinade from my fingers. "My dad is going to love you." I realized what I said as soon as the words slipped out.

I hope he will.

Lucas grinned, then flipped another steak on the grill. The yellow flames licked up the sides, the juices falling onto the white-hot coals with a hiss. Orange embers danced amidst the curling smoke, drifting away like fireflies.

"Ten bucks says the boys will smell this from miles away and come running home for supper," he mentioned, listening for any movement in the trees.

I glanced around us just in case he was right.

"Is it another quiet night?" I inquired, hoping that it was as dull as dishwater out there.

Lucas's brows furrowed as he took a seat on the log beside me.

"Stop worrying. They'll be fine," he assured me.

That's not what I asked.

"Don't do that," I pointed out his error. "Please don't deflect my question. I specifically asked if it was quiet out there, and your response was *'don't worry.'* Of course, I'm going to worry."

Lucas sighed with resignation. "What do you want me to say? That they crossed paths with hunters?"

My food churned in my stomach.

"Did they?" I dreaded the answer to my query, but not knowing the outcome felt much worse.

Lucas nodded, making me swallow thickly.

"Yes, but no one was hurt. That's why I told you not to worry," he reiterated. "Hunters are known for laying traps, hoping they'll get lucky and catch something. They may be scumbags, but they're not suicidal. It's not like they can outrun us or outmaneuver us." He shrugged.

"I suppose not." My shoulders slumped as I pondered that. "How are they getting past all the rangers in the first place?"

Lucas wagged his finger as he spoke, "That is an excellent question. If we knew how they were doing it, we could put a stop to it immediately."

We became lost in our thoughts amidst the sound of cracking firelight.

Something occurred to me, and I couldn't hold my tongue for a moment longer.

"Let's just say for shits and arguments sake that hunters are not finding their way in by accident," I suggested, throwing that idea out there for Lucas to digest.

He mulled that over. "What? Like an inside job?" he replied doubtfully.

"I don't think you should rule it out," I added, supporting my claim. "Money is the root of all evil," I quoted one of my father's favorite sayings. "You never know what people will do if they're desperate or just plain greedy . . . just saying."

"Shifters would never sell each other out,

especially not to hunters," Lucas cited as if the thought was preposterous.

"I'm not suggesting that it has to be a shifter," I defended my theory, standing by what I said. "You guys told me that Lakewell is a mixed-species community. The traitor could very well be human."

"Hm," Lucas hummed, thinking that over. "It's a possibility, I suppose."

I tapped my full stomach, unable to handle another bite. Lucas picked the steak bone clean, then tossed it into the flames.

After licking the grease from his fingers, he announced, "I made you something."

My brows raised with surprise. "You did?"

I was feeling rather spoiled by my new partners. Mason's bracelet, Grayson's sex toy collection, now a gift from Lucas. I wondered what it could be.

Lucas hauled himself up, then held out his hand to help me up. "It's in my shed."

An invitation to Lucas's shed.

I felt honored. That was like winning a golden ticket to Willy Wonka's chocolate factory, minus the calories. My stomach fluttered with excitement. Lucas led me to his treasure trove, then dropped my hand so he could fish for his keys inside his pocket. I didn't quite know what to expect as he unbolted the latch.

Maybe a mass of tools, a graveyard of bike parts, gym equipment to maintain those delectable abs. But as he opened the door and flicked on the light, I realized I was only half right. It wasn't a tomb of dismantled bikes, but an exhibition of unfinished projects. Stacks and stacks of art canvases. My jaw slackened, awed by his impressive collection.

Not only was Lucas a motorcycle fanatic, but he was an artist too. He painted landscapes depicting mountain ranges, forests, and large bodies of water. It proved Lucas had an eye for detail, making each painting seem almost real. My eyes journeyed through all four seasons, spring, summer, autumn, winter, seeing Whitehaven through Lucas's eyes. These paintings belonged in an art gallery somewhere to be enjoyed by millions. Not to be gathering dust in a stuffy old shed. I glanced at Lucas and saw the self-doubt etched across his handsome face.

Madness.

"Babe, you're so talented," I stated a fact. "Why are these not hanging on the cabin walls?"

Lucas shrugged and scuffed the floor with the edge of his boot. "It's just a hobby. Something I do to blow off steam. It's no big deal."

"No big deal?" I spluttered, my eyes bulging with

amazement. "You don't realize how good you are . . . it's insane."

Then my eyes drifted to the pile of sketches on the workstation, and my throat thickened with emotion. Warmth filled my heart, and I was so damned proud of him I could have cried. He watched me silently as I checked them out, not saying a word, making no attempt to stop me or conceal them from me. My man was a talented soul, but why was he keeping this side of him a secret? He captured the expressions of random folk going about their daily business . . . men fishing at the lake, families playing on a picnic field, an old woman sitting on a park bench sharing a sandwich with her dog. Then there were some of his brothers, Mason strumming his guitar, Grayson snoozing on the porch, Alex standing at the stove with a dishtowel slung across his shoulder.

"Lucas," I breathed, completely mesmerized. "These are incredible."

Lucas said nothing. He just stood there motionless as I continued to explore. My fingers trailed across the scattered papers, stumbling upon a closed sketchpad. I spared a side glance, seeking permission to peek inside.

Lucas returned a shy smile. "Go ahead. I don't mind."

I lifted the cover page and gasped. He had sketched me. There was one of me at the guest house, frowning as I stared through the open window, jet-lagged and sleep-deprived.

"Oh, no," I muttered, cringing with embarrassment. "I looked like a right mess that night."

"You were beautiful," he corrected me.

I scrunched my nose, thinking otherwise. As I flicked through the pages, I realized that they were all drawings of me, and my cheeks flushed with heat.

"Oh my God," I gushed, feeling flattered and overwhelmed. "Lucas, these are all of me doing random things around the cabin."

His muscular arms snaked around my waist, and his chin came to rest upon my shoulder.

"Just appreciate how sexy you look folding laundry," he answered, his husky rumble lighting the wick of my heart and detonating it.

An image of myself lying on a fancy chair, completely nude popped into my head, and I couldn't resist saying, "Lucas, will you paint me like one of your French girls?"

"Huh?" Lucas grunted, having not understood

what I was talking about. "I don't know any French girls."

"Never mind," I muttered, grinning to myself.

He must not have seen the Titanic movie with Kate and Leo. I made a mental note to change that.

Oh, Lucas, you're in for a treat.

Releasing a contented sigh, I relaxed into his warm embrace and counted all four of my blessings. Alex, Grayson, Lucas, and Mason. I could never leave them now. Not when each of them owned a piece of my heart. Each day our bond grew a little stronger, and each time my heart became a little less homesick. If my parents could only see just how happy they made me, then they would eventually love them too.

"Are you ready for your gift?" Lucas asked.

"You mean, this wasn't it?" I replied.

Wasn't it enough that he had allowed me to peek inside his cave of wonders? I was more than thrilled with what I had learned about him. Behind Lucas's shroud of mystery, there was a pure-hearted sensitive soul who saw the world through unveiled eyes.

"Nope, turn around," he murmured, holding me by the shoulders.

There was a paint-splattered dust sheet concealing something beneath it.

"It's not exactly gift wrapped," he mentioned, and from his apologetic tone, I got the impression that he wished he had put more thought into it.

Excitement burst through my body, and I couldn't wait another second. I removed the covering, then slapped a hand over my mouth. My eyes marveled at the canvas.

"Oh, Lucas." My elated gasp tore through my throat as the portrait came into focus.

Words couldn't describe the way it made me feel, but my soft gasp and my teary eyes said it all. Lucas had painted us as a family. My men were playing with our children, and I was admiring them from the porch.

Lucas raised his finger and explained. "I saw you standing there the other day, and it inspired me. This is how I envision us years from now," he started, his eyes flicking down at me, then toward the painting. "A perfect loving family. I paint what I see in my heart." He blushed, ferociously. "Was that too much?" he asked, afraid that he had overstepped and scared me off.

"No," I threw in quickly, "I love everything about it. It makes me feel safe."

Lucas exhaled a subtle breath, looking relieved about that.

I placed my palm against his chest, meeting his gaze. "It's not staying out here in the shed," I stated firmly. "That's coming inside with me, and you can hang it on the wall first thing tomorrow."

I would have insisted that he put it up tonight, but I wanted to drag him off to bed and thank him properly.

CHAPTER Twenty Six

Isobelle

The bedroom was stifling when I woke. I knew it was close to lunchtime by the strong sunlight seeping in through the curtains. Sweat coated my skin, causing the sheets to cling to my body. I was sticky and gross in all the wrong places; my pussy and ass had been the source of Lucas's entertainment until the early hours. My god, I ached. I desperately needed a bath and then a deep tissue massage to recover.

Alex would destroy me tonight. My thoughts

drifted to his bag of tricks and wondered if they were going to be part of his plans. I lifted my head, cracking an eye open to see a bed full of naked muscles.

My boys came home.

"Good morning, Princess," Grayson croaked.

He sounded bone-tired, and because he didn't bother to open his eyes, he looked tired too. No wonder it was hot as Satan's asshole in here, with four humongous muscle men nestling alongside me.

I pressed a kiss to Grayson's forehead, and a dreamy smile curved his lips. As the mattress dipped, I disturbed the others.

"Morning, babe," Lucas rasped in a sleep-drunk husk.

I twisted to face him and gave him a good morning kiss. Mason brushed his fingertips against my thigh.

"Morning, love," Mason spoke in a groggy murmur.

It was a stretch to lean over Lucas, but I gave Mason a kiss, then turned to greet Alex with equal fervor.

"Morning, sexy," Alex rasped. "Did you have a fun night?"

"Yeah, thanks," I replied, smiling a lazy smile.

"How was your dinner?" he inquired, rising on one elbow. "What insipid monstrosity did my brother serve to you on your mating night?"

"Fuck you," Lucas growled.

"Actually, it was delicious," I answered honestly. "You missed out."

Alex grunted doubtfully.

Grayson's stomach rumbled. "Don't. I'm starving here. My stomach has started to digest itself. I'm too weak to move."

Alex rolled his eyes with a click of his tongue. "How about you, Fido?" He prodded Lucas in the side of his ribs. "Do you think you could handle some bacon and eggs?"

Lucas made an "Mm" sound. "Fuck yeah."

"Be a darling and put the kettle on," I asked, smiling sweetly at Alex.

His lips twisted into a wry smirk before he rolled off the bed and staggered into the kitchen. His loud, exaggerated yawn filtered through the cabin.

"All the more room for me," Lucas chuckled, sprawling out.

Mason scrunched his face as Lucas impersonated a starfish. "Hey, move over!" he complained.

Grayson spooned me from behind, sniffing my

hair, then released a contented sigh. "Do you want me to run you a bath, baby?"

"Are you trying to say that I smell?" I jested, although I knew I must have reeked of sex.

Each time the sheets wafted warm air my way, it wafted the fruits of our passion up my nostrils.

Yeah, more like overripe, fermented fruit.

The unpleasant sweaty sex smell was enough to turn my stomach.

"Yes, please," I replied. "The sheets need burning."

Grayson's deep belly laugh shook the bed. "It's a good job we have some more. The washing machine hasn't stopped spinning since we brought you here."

Lucas and Mason joined in with the boisterous chortling.

"And on that note . . ." Grayson rolled to the edge of the mattress, and as he stood, he almost spring-boarded me off the bed. "We could all use a scrub in the tub. That was one long-ass night."

His tone was a little clipped toward the end of his sentence. He sounded fed-up and agitated. It reminded me of when my dad came home stressed about work. Their ranger roles were like that of a police officer. My men patrolled the night shift, warding off danger so that people could sleep safely in their beds. My father joined the police force for the same reason. I decided that after my night with Alex, I would tell my parents about my four husbands, and to hell with the consequences.

Except for the werewolf part.

It was going to be a lot for my parents to digest — me admitting I was in a relationship with four brothers. Polyamory wasn't a subject that had ever been discussed around our dinner table. Mum and Dad were happy inside their monogamous bubble. They were old school, married at twenty-one, then moved in together, leaving it a year before they conceived me. My thoughts drifted back to when one of my mum's relatives had fallen pregnant out of wedlock. They considered it the scandal of the century. But putting my reservations aside, it was the first time I had experienced true happiness before. I had always been happy; I just didn't know what I was missing out on until I met the Bennett brothers. It was time to tell the truth. I loved my men. Mum and Dad would just have to come to terms with it.

The boys joined me in the bath, then left me to soak for a while. I needed this. My body tingled as I scrubbed myself clean. The bacon and sausage-infused air made its way into the steamy room, making my stomach rumble. It smelled so good; I could almost taste it on my tongue. That was my cue to pull the plug and grab a towel.

"I saved you some fried bread," Mason mentioned as I stepped out of the bathroom.

"Ah, you're a star," I praised, grateful for the sweet gesture.

I never used to eat it because of the fat content, but Alex had nailed making fried bread to a T. He let the bread soak up the bacon grease, and that complimented a poached egg like a charm. So much for watching my weight. I had been eating like a horse just lately. My appetite was on par with the boys.

"Get it down you, woman," Lucas muttered with a mouthful of toast. "Never mind the calories."

He didn't have to tell me twice. We ate, and we chatted, avoiding the subject of hunters. Their clever distraction obliterated that worry from my thoughts.

"I saw Lincoln Anderson last night," Alex announced. "He scored some VIP tickets to The Vortex club in Lakewell, and he asked if we wanted to tag along."

"Will Chloe be there?" I inquired.

As much as I loved spending time with my men, I didn't want to intrude on a boy's night out.

"Yes," he answered. "Her mom and Lincoln's dad are taking the cubs for the night."

I flinched my eyes. "Both parents are looking after the kids? That's nice of them."

Grayson nodded. "Yeah, well, they're mated, so . . ."

"Oh . . ." I bobbed my head awkwardly.

Lucas's eyes danced with humor as he studied my expression. "Chloe and Lincoln are stepsiblings, and mates. So, they'll be cool about hanging out with us in public."

His statement raised another question. It occurred to me that not everybody was going to be so accommodating. I remembered all the gossiping about the four men in the woods. All the scaremongering, the derogatory, spiteful comments calling their chosen mate a two-bit whore.

Me — now they could put a face to the name.

Chin-up, Izzy. Hold your head up high and show them what you're made of.

"Yeah, I'm up for that," I responded enthusiastically.

The thought of grinding on the dance floor between a quadruplet sandwich seemed like a perfect night out.

"Sweet," Mason muttered. "I'll see if Chloe will

take you into town to shop for a new outfit." He fished his wallet out of his jeans pocket and pulled out a credit card. "Here," he said as he slid it across the table.

"I'm not taking that," I refused, not wanting to accept his money.

"It's yours," Mason prompted me to accept it. "What's ours is yours now."

What?

I glanced down and saw that he was telling the truth. The name Mrs. Isobelle Bennett was spelled out in embossed letters.

"What's this all about?" I asked, picking up the card and wagging it between my fingertips. "I have my own money." Fair enough, it wasn't much to shout about. My days of living like a poor student, funded by the bank of Mum and Dad, were now behind me, but I still had my university budget to rely on. I wasn't exactly rolling in dosh, but I wasn't penniless either.

The boys blinked back at me, taken aback by my declaration of independence.

"But we're mates," Grayson asserted. "We will be a real family unit when Alex makes his mark."

I pursed my lips in protest, bouncing my gaze between them. Each injured look plucked at my heartstrings like a harp.

"Fine, I suppose I could use it for bills and food shopping," I relented. "But I'm having my wages paid into this account," I insisted, making my intentions clear. "If we're going to do this properly, we're in this 50/50."

"We're still paying for the dress though," Alex mentioned. "I'll write down the pin for you to memorize."

"And shoes," Grayson added. "She'll need new shoes to match her outfit."

Lucas nodded. "And sexy lingerie."

There were lewd chuckles all around. I flung my eyes up and down with a click of my tongue.

Typical men.

"You might as well go all out and get your hair done too," Mason suggested. "It is our first proper date together, and we want to celebrate it."

"Bloody hell," I chuckled. "Don't blame me when the bank statement hits the doormat."

They didn't seem fazed by that.

Lucas shrugged. "We come from a wealthy family. Our money won't run out in a hurry."

The nosey parker in me wanted to ask them what they were worth, but that just seemed rude. I would just find a cash machine and take a sly look at the balance later.

"I better dress to impress then," I replied, tucking the card into the breast pocket of my flannel shirt. "I suppose we're going to raise a few eyebrows by stepping out in public."

"Fuck 'em," Grayson commented, shrugging.

The others smirked in agreement as if Grayson had spoken on behalf of them all. I felt eyes on me and glanced across the table to find Alex staring. He responded with a coquettish wink that sent my heart bouncing around my chest like a pinball machine.

My phone beeped with an incoming text right at that precise moment, startling me out of my lust-driven haze. Huffing in annoyance, I snatched it up to see who it was from. Swiping my finger across the screen, it surprised me to find another message from Peter.

"Hi, Isobelle, I hope you're feeling better. Perhaps we can meet tomorrow at lunchtime to discuss an idea I have. It would be great to have your input. Regards. Peter."

Ugh! I suppose I could meet up for coffee.

"Hmm, it's Peter," I mentioned, witnessing their curious frowns. "He wants to talk to me about the conservation project."

Alex nodded, taking an interest. "He's passionate about his work, and he seems genuine, but he's still an outsider. If he wants to collaborate, just politely decline his offer. We don't let outsiders research our land. It's all kept '*in house*'." He flexed his fingers to air quote.

"That's fair enough," I agreed, understanding that. "I'll keep it civil and discreet."

"Speaking of discretion," Grayson muttered, stretching his arms with a yawn. "We'll be out of your hair before dinner. Alpha needs to see us about the minor mishap last night."

That comment prickled the underside of my skin. "What mishap?" I asked, sounding worried.

Mason rolled his eyes. "Oh, that." He huffed a sigh.

"It's nothing to worry about," Alex reassured me. "One of our rangers was clipped by a silver tip and had to be taken to the infirmary. We caught the perpetrator trying to skip town, but he won't be coming back, that's for sure." There was a gruffness to Alex's voice that chilled and thrilled me at the same time.

He had a heated look in his eyes that could melt the polar ice caps. My pussy clenched with the promise of a good, hard fuck, but not before Alex had his fun. I couldn't wait.

CHAPTER

Twenty Seven

Isobelle

An hour had passed since Mason, Lucas, and Grayson left for patrol duties. The humid air had made me sweat like a bitch in heat for most of the day, so I took a quick rinse beneath the make-shift shower at the back of the cabin. The sun resembled a squashed satsuma as it faded into the horizon, casting lilac ripples across the sky, and with the fading light came a swarm of pesky flies that seemed to love me. I got sick of swatting my hands in front of my face. The cool water stung my sun-kissed shoulders a little, but that was my fault for forgetting to reapply sunscreen. Freckles erupted all over my face — a feature of mine I hated, but my men seemed to find adorable.

"Ah-hem." A not-so-subtle cough made me whirl around, startled.

It was Alex. Who else could it be out here in the middle of nowhere? We were miles from the red zone, tucked away out of harm's reach. Alex smiled, flashing his pearly white teeth.

"Sorry, I didn't mean to scare you. Do you know how much longer you're going to be?" There was a lascivious glint in his eyes as if he couldn't wait for the fun to begin.

Using the pads of my fingers, I cleared my vision. "I'm finished now. Could you hand me that towel, please?" I replied, pointing to where it was hanging on the washing line.

The last of the water cascaded from my body, and I stood trembling in the evening breeze. I wrung out my hair, then ran my hands along my skin to check I rinsed off every last trace of soap. The point was to capture Alex's attention and give him an eye full, and it worked too. His eyes popped out on stalks as he saw my erect nipples. Every woman loves to feel desired, and there was no mistaking what Alex wanted to do to me right now.

"Here you go." His voice was a dark husk.

Spank you very much.

"Thank you." I accepted the towel, chuckling internally.

Bad girl, Izzy.

His lust-filled eyes watched the water droplets cascading down my body like a hawk that had just spotted a mouse — hungry, and hellbent on carrying me off to his nest to devour me. I was playing a game of dare without even realizing it. That was a dangerous game to play with Alex. If there was one thing I learned about him, it was that he loved to play games. It didn't matter if they were big or small. He had to be in charge, and if you did as you were told, my god, he would reward you for it.

Then again, the thought of defying him was thrilling, sending shivers down my spine. In all honesty, I had been having concupiscent dreams about being punished, tied up, and spanked, then forced to choke on his dick.

"Get dry, but don't bother putting on clothes because you won't be needing them," he ordered, his voice trailing away as he turned to leave.

I dried quickly, leaving my hair tousled and damp

after rubbing it through with my towel. Alex left the cabin door ajar, just enough for me to peek through. Wrapping the soggy towel around me, I tiptoed across the wooden floor. He pulled the curtains across the windows to darken the room, that way, we could appreciate the candlelight. Flames flickered in the fireplace, crackling softly as they feasted on the chopped wood and lint. It grew colder at night, but I didn't always notice because my men kept me warm in bed. He placed scented candles of assorted sizes around the room. I recognized the subtle hint of jasmine and chamomile, and there was one burning on the coffee table alongside some of Alex's Dom tools. It was red and stood out from all the magnolia ones. Something heavenly was simmering away on the stove, tantalizing my tastebuds.

My eyes scanned the room, drinking in the erotic scene that Alex had organized while I had been cooling off. My eyes drifted to the two chains dangling from a wooden beam on the ceiling, both with leather wrist cuffs attached at the ends. I hadn't taken much notice of the fixings on the beam before, wondering what else I might discover in this raunchy little sex den.

"Isobelle," Alex spoke as he came out of the bedroom, startling me.

Somehow, he always caused my heart to jump as if an electric current shot through it. My eyes raked over him, admiring how sexy he looked in his dark-gray suit and crisp white shirt. He looked every inch the Alpha male he portrayed himself to be.

"Turn around," he commanded, his smooth voice full of authority.

I obeyed. He held a long piece of red silk and placed it around my eyes, tying it in place at the back of my head.

"Now, I'm going to make sure you can't see anything," he spoke, in a chocolate-smooth voice.

He kept his word. I couldn't see anything. Then I felt him tug on my towel before it dropped to the floor, leaving me naked, vulnerable, blindfolded, and completely at his mercy.

"Alex, I . . .," I spoke.

"Silence, Isobelle. I will define the rules. Let me guide you to where I want you to stay, and I'll explain what I'm going to do, all in good time," he instructed.

His sensuous and alluring voice made me shudder with anticipation. This was the sexy side to Alex that I yearned to see, having only been shown a glimpse during that one occasion at breakfast. Whatever I thought I knew about Alex's kink, this just reminded me I had yet to explore the corners and shadows of

BDSM. He was seducing me into his world, one erotic step at a time, offering me a bite of the forbidden fruit with the promise of something sweet in return. My god, I wanted a taste of it. My mouth and pussy were salivating profusely.

"Lie down and hold your wrists together in front of you," he ordered.

I crouched down to my hands and knees, feeling the soft rug beneath me. The heat from the fire licked against my bare skin, caressing me with warmth. Positioning myself on my elbows, I rolled over onto my back, doing as he asked, then held out my wrists obediently.

"Good girl," Alex praised in a firm, controlled voice.

Alex bound my wrists together with the same silky material, once, twice, three times until I felt it pull taut as he tied a knot.

"Whenever we share private moments, you'll call me master. I will make love to you as Alex whenever you want, but your Master will bring you more pleasure than you've ever encountered before. Tell me you understand," he rasped.

His sexy voice acted as a match, lighting the wick of my ovaries — *boom* — blown to smithereens. He had me soaking wet already, shivering with desire and with a willingness to do anything he wanted, even if it was pushing me out of my comfort zone. My heart produced a slow drum roll as I waited for his next move.

"Yes, Master," I answered. My tone sounded thick with lust, almost desperate.

"Now for a safe word," he mentioned, not as a question but more of a request. "One that you will use whenever you wish to stop what we're doing."

It wasn't as easy as that, trying to come up with a word on the spot. After a few moments of thinking, he added, "It could be anything, but not something you'd shout out with pleasure or else that'll just get confusing," he chuckled softly.

"Um, all right." I racked my brain, struggling to think of a good one.

Everything I came up with just sounded cheesy or ridiculous. Then one word just popped straight into my head from out of nowhere.

"What about *abstinence*, Master?"

Alex's soft husky chuckle filled the room, having found that amusing. He probably thought I meant it as more of a threat.

"Then abstinence it is," he replied, satisfied.

"Not that that'll ever happen," I muttered under my breath.

That would be considered a swear word among the boys.

"Silence," Alex rasped.

"Sorry, Master," I apologized for talking without permission.

His fingers brushed the sides of my arms, causing me to shiver and covering me in goosebumps.

"Good girl. Now sit up. I'm going to feed you first," he ordered.

Alex's footsteps were soft as he moved around the room. There was the distinct sound of cutlery clashing together, and whatever the food was, it smelled appetizing. It was so good my mouth watered with anticipation, knowing how well he could cook.

"Open up," Alex requested.

I parted my lips, allowing him to feed me the fragrant meal. It tasted delicious, exotic, but I still couldn't tell what it was. Just like when you held your nose and couldn't appreciate anything, I couldn't see it, and therefore, it could have been several things.

Alex waited for me to swallow, then pressed a chilled glass to my lips. From the subtle vanilla bouquet with oak undertones, I could smell that it was wine. The deep-bodied taste clung to my tongue; it tasted expensive and complimented the food. Alex was classy and sophisticated. He had an element of mystery about him that lured me in, granting me a glimpse of what he offered; it left me with a feeling that the best was yet to come, keeping me on my toes and panting for more.

He continued to feed me the food and wine, and I allowed him to do so, just as he wanted, offering him my submission, just like I wanted. It was a two-way thing, building the confidence between us before we moved on to bigger and more adventurous things. That was what BDSM was all about. Trust. Not the sort of abusive crap I had read about or had the displeasure of witnessing in films.

"Good girl, now lie back and take your reward," he commanded, brushing his mouth against my breasts, causing my heart to palpitate.

The coarse feel of his short, groomed beard and soft lips against my skin set off a maelstrom of sensations that affected every inch of my body, especially between my legs. I laid back as instructed, my body thrumming with anticipation of what was about to happen next. I would love what he was about to do, or I wouldn't.

Here it comes.

Something soft brushed down the full length of me, and I let out a soft surprised gasp. It was silky and cool like the petals of a rosebud trailing from the top of my forehead, tracing my nose, lips, and chin, caressing the dip in my neck before continuing its journey to the valley between my breasts. My breath stuttered as a plethora of sensations trailed along my body, past my navel until its delicate petals brushed along my folds. It was there one moment, and then it was gone, replaced with a warm gust of breath as Alex pressed his lips against my labia, taking me by surprise. I gasped, arching my back off the floor.

"Ale — uh, Master," I almost mewled his name, feeling his tongue delve inside my pussy, then drag itself along the length of my slit. The taut muscle then began writhing around my solid clit in a lover's dance.

"You taste exquisite, baby." There was a soft purr in his whisper that almost flung me over the edge.

"Each time you obey me, you'll get a reward. If not, you'll be punished. I don't want to have to punish you by spanking. I would rather you associate that with pleasure," Alex explained, his voice quivering as if driven insane with need.

Shaking with desire, unable to guess his next move, I lay there submissively. It was thrilling and erotic, waiting for him to touch me, yet powerless to see anything.

"I'm going to start with a little wax play. I won't hurt you. It'll feel pleasant," he promised.

The minute he mentioned *wax* I froze. Bracing myself for the hot sting against my skin, my body tensed. Within moments, a hot drip landed on my chest, and my back arched, jolting my hips as each droplet hit my stomach.

"Master, ahh," I hissed, gritting my teeth at first, then relaxing the moment I realized it didn't hurt like I thought it would.

My skin warmed everywhere, anticipating the next sweet, burning sting. The wax landed, hitting the sensitive slope of my breast and licked a fiery trail toward my nipple.

Alex massaged the softened wax onto my skin using his large warm hands, working it in with his thumbs. The feeling sent heat flooding through my channel, and a gush of moisture pooled between my legs.

He settled himself before me, pressing my thighs wider as he knelt between me, and I knew what was coming. Anticipation licked through me as I waited to feel his touch. I expected him to drip candle wax there, but he didn't. He didn't use the candle. Instead, he stroked a wax-painted finger over my clit, and I lost myself in the inferno of ecstasy, writhing among the flames that spread throughout my body.

"Master, that feels so . . . so good."

Alex circled his finger around my solid bud, earning helpless, yet grateful whimpers from me. His wax-covered pad sent a tremulous sensation through my clit, and my body juddered with pleasure, threatening to come undone with the first few strokes of his finger.

"God, you're so responsive. Good girls get the best rewards," he promised.

I could sense his salacious grin, convinced that he was reveling in this right now. I wriggled my hips to grind my clit against his fingers, only for him to pin me back down with one strong hand.

"Greedy girl, Isobelle. Master gives pleasure to you for your obedience but will punish you for being impatient by not allowing you to come. I'm going to torture you now, my submissive mate," he warned.

His shoulders bumped against my thighs, spreading me wide open. Then his hot, pointed tongue speared between my folds, licking me from bottom to top before fluttering over my clit.

How is this a punishment when it feels so good?

My breaths came out in desperate, sharp pants. Alex made sure my thighs were pinned wide apart as he delivered sweet torture on my pulsing bud, leaving me helpless and vulnerable. I was reaching the point of no return. The pressure built in my stomach and the first orgasmic wave rippled. Just as a rough moan tore through my throat, he paused.

"Please, Master," I begged.

"You don't give the orders, Isobelle. If you want it, beg me for it," he commanded.

This was so unfair. I needed it. He couldn't deny me this.

What must I look like? Lying here, spread legged and begging to be licked like a shameless harlot.

"Please, Master, let me come," I bleated.

Alex gripped my thighs and held me there, opened to him, split wide and completely at his mercy. Then he moved over me, his muscular body pinning me to the floor. I couldn't move at all like this, barely able to breathe, and what little oxygen I had in my lungs was driven from me as he pinned my bound hands above my head.

He nipped at the skin along my neck, trailing down my shoulder and across to my chest, encapsulating my nipples with warmth each time he suckled them. My body responded to his touch, thrumming with pleasure as he toyed with them, letting them go with a pop, and repeating the action until they were no doubt dark with pressure and begging for mercy.

His hands gripped my thighs, rubbing the skin under his thumbs in small circles. "Beg me," he demanded with a growl.

"Please, Master," I begged breathlessly. "I beg you to let me come."

"Good girl," he seemed satisfied. "As a reward, tell me where you want to be touched," he asked, knowing full fucking well where I needed him to touch me.

My body ached and trembled with need. Almost painfully. My heaving chest rose and fell with short, shallow pants. My swollen clit pulsed between my legs, desperate for release.

"Please, I want to come on your tongue," I pleaded, my voice sounding needy.

"Please, what?" His firm tone, admonishing me for my mistake. I knew what he wanted to hear, what I had forgotten to say during my desperate plea for release.

"Please let me come on your tongue, Master," I corrected my error.

I sensed Alex move away from where he crouched over me. He lifted me off the rug and helped me to stand. I braced myself for the sound of rattling chains, still unable to see what was happening around me. Alex tugged at the binds, freeing my wrists. Not that I would be granted freedom for long. Within moments, both of my wrists were buckled into the leather cuffs, my arms raised above me like a prisoner, chained up in a dungeon. My heels were unable to fully touch the ground.

Alex spread my legs apart using his foot, so that I was completely outstretched like a star. My ears attuned to the jingle of his belt buckle, the rustling of clothes as they hit the sofa. My senses were wild and alert, dragging in a lungful of his woodsy cologne and the scent of raw masculinity.

He's naked, I just know it.

"You want your Master's tongue on your pussy, submissive?" he asked in a sharp, raspy voice. My pussy twitched and pulsed as he spoke.

"Yes, Master," I replied obediently.

His warm breath billowed around my ear, sensing that he was only a hair's breadth away from me.

"That's right, I'm sure you do. You love the feel of your Master licking your sweet little pussy, don't you? I bet you're dripping wet, desperate for my tongue."

"Yes, Master," I responded, quivering with need.

His warm lips nudged against my folds and my legs shook, knowing what was to come next. Alex's groan vibrated through my center as he tasted me. His tongue slithering around my clit like a starving creature.

I threw my head back open-mouthed as he curled a finger inside my soaked channel, pushing in a second, then moving and stroking against my constricting walls until he found my G-spot. Lightning flashed behind my eyelids as he hit my detonator, combusting me into flames.

"Uh, uh, uh," I mewled, undulating my hips to ride out my release.

Alex ate my pussy like a rabid animal who was feasting on a prize kill.

My legs gave way as the feeling became too much. A tight constriction bound my stomach muscles into a coiled spasm, my legs shook, my fists clenched, and my eyes squeezed shut behind the blindfold.

"That's right, babe, squirt for me," Alex murmured, lapping up my cream.

All I could do was hang limply, suspended in chains. Lewd squelching sounds played out as he pumped two fingers in and out of my pussy, coaxing me into another earth-shattering climax. His lips were there again, drinking the nectar of my release.

"Yes, oh god, Master feels so good," I panted between exhausted breaths.

The leather restraints bit into my wrists, delivering me a slow-burning pain to accompany the thrill he was giving me. I don't know why, but I breathed out a "thank you" as my body relaxed, slumped midair. Alex let out a genuine laugh in response.

"Female ejaculation twice in a row. Told you your Master knows how to deliver pleasure," he spoke in a smooth, sensual husk.

I let out a breathy chuckle, unable to string together a coherent sentence.

Fuck . . . I squirted into his mouth . . . twice.

If I wasn't so high on oxytocin, thanks to the dynamite orgasms, I would have died of embarrassment.

"Stand up straight," Alex ordered.

I sensed him walking around me, then felt a sudden slap against my ass cheek. I yelped, jolting forward.

"Up!" he commanded, then landed another sharp slap to the other ass cheek.

I shrieked at the sting. Whatever he was using had a flat surface that lit my skin on fire. He delivered firm alternative slaps on each side, causing my hips to buck with each blast. The skin burned where he struck, blazing red-hot.

The soft clattering sound of rummaging came from the left side of me. Then I heard the squelch of something being squeezed from a tube.

"Relax for me," Alex cooed.

Using one lubricated finger, he massaged the tight knot of my asshole, working his way through the ring of muscle. My stubborn hole put up a fair fight, resisting his intrusion and making him work for it. I gasped at the burning sensation, my lips parting into a silent O as he wriggled all the way in before working in another finger. The heat from his warm breath caressed my shoulder over the place where he would mark. Soft lips versus coarse stubble brushed along my nape, teasing every nerve ending with a maelstrom of sensations.

"Your body is so responsive," Alex praised. "You were made for this."

"Yes, Master," I agreed.

"I've got a gift especially for you. I had it crafted before your arrival. Diamond encrusted with the only word that matters."

"What word is that, Master?" I was curious to know.

"Mine," he replied, removing his fingers and replacing them with a smooth, blunt object.

Fuck, is that a butt plug?

It soon warmed to my body temperature after he secured it snugly into place.

"I'm going to take your ass after I have your pussy," he said, twisting the plug before tapping his finger against my soaking wet entrance.

Alex held my body close, pressing my back against his chest. Fuck, he was Herculean. He nudged the head of his enormous cock at my cunt, rimming it, teasing it just an inch. Delivering pure torture, he kept it there, barely inside. My pussy lips clung to the bulbous head, ready to suck him down.

"Tell your Master what you need," he breathed. His palm splayed out against my soft stomach, pressing me closer into him.

His pelvis knocked against the flat handle of the butt plug, reminding me I was full there too.

"Deeper, Master," I begged him.

Alex drew back, almost pulling out before slamming in hard. Stars burst in my vision, and I gasped, having not expected him to enter me with such ferocity. He dragged his cock through my loins, then waited at the point of slipping free before spearing into me with another firm slap.

"Tell me what you want, Isobelle," Alex growled, losing restraint.

"Uh, I . . . I . . . uh," I grunted, unable to think straight.

Drag — pause — slap. Drag — pause — slap.

"Use your words," he insisted, pausing his cock at my opening.

"Just like that. Exactly like that, Master," I replied breathlessly.

"Tell me what else," Alex groaned, pressing his mouth against my soft skin.

"Harder. Deeper," I moaned, wriggling my hips to create friction.

"My girl wants it harder?" he growled with approval.

Alex clutched my hips, then slammed inside me.

"Fuck," his voice strained.

"Yes, Master!"

The erotic sound of flesh slapping into wetness, harsh grunts, and ragged moans filled the room. Alex thrust like a maniac, fucking me into oblivion.

"Do you think you can take me harder?" His raspy voice tickled my ear.

"Yes, Master, harder and faster," I moaned, wanting it all.

He smiled against my neck, then yanked the blindfold from my eyes, tossing the red silk to the floor. Using both hands, he picked me up by my hips as if I weighed nothing and lifted me off the floor. He granted me a moment's grace before pounding into me with pure masculine abandon, pulverizing my pussy with his huge monster cock.

"Take all of me, Isobelle. Feel me fucking you hard. You like it fast like this?" He grunted with each slam of his hips, his heavy balls slapping against my soaked cunt. I could hardly breathe, loving it way too much. My eyes rolled in the back of my head, watering at the corners. Alex tore the chains clean out of the ceiling and forced me onto my hands and knees. The flames crackled in the fireplace, the heat causing me to sweat from its proximity. Alex lined his cock against my pussy, mounting me like an animal. He reached around to rub my clit, causing my walls to flutter around his length. The pounding commenced, but this time Alex wanted to finish.

"Fuck, Alex, Master, oh god, I'm cumming, don't stop," I panted, the words skittering through my lips.

"Not until I say so. Wait for me. Cum with me," he asserted.

"I don't think I can . . .," I groaned.

Alex increased his momentum just as I reached the pinnacle of ecstasy. Fireworks burst behind my eyelids as Alex sunk his teeth into the groove of my neck, staking his claim on me. Although I expected it, the sharp pain hurt just as much as it did the first time. His powerful hips jerked with each ejaculation. Sweat dripped from his hair onto the back of my neck, then trickled down my spine.

"Love you, babe," he whispered against the place where he marked me, lapping the area with his rough tongue to clean the wound.

"I love you too," I replied breathlessly.

"Are you ready to explore some more?" he encouraged.

I trembled in his arms.

"Mm," I managed as he withdrew the butt plug from my asshole.

We spooned until he was fit to go again, then he lubed me ready to take him. He parted my cheeks to push into me from this angle, and my ass opened to accommodate him. Alex propped himself up, leaning on his right forearm, then held me with his left hand, rocking himself into me until I opened more. His fingers wandered down to my clit, and I whimpered, unable to cum anymore.

"I can't yet, it's too sensitive," I whined.

"Yes, you can. I'm going to wring one more out of you," he promised.

He then rotated his hips and circled his fingers around my swollen clit until he felt me tremble against him. I whimpered, feeling too sensitive to take any more but too weak to do anything about it. I was his to please. His to adore. I let out a rough moan as my pussy convulsed, squeezing my ass around his cock. He gripped my hips and gave three more sharp thrusts before spilling more of his seed into my tight hole. His body shook against mine, wrapping his big powerful arms around me to hold me close.

I couldn't feel my legs. I knew I wouldn't be able to walk after this. Alex must have sensed what I was thinking because after he cleaned me with a soft, wet cloth, he swept me into his arms and carried me off to the bedroom. He exhausted me, and I couldn't keep my eyes from closing. Alex put me to bed and crawled beside me. Unlike the others, he was just content to hold me throughout the night. I appreciated this, having been left drained after such an intense week.

"Alex?" I asked, choosing to refer to him by his name now we were done playing.

"Uh-huh?" he answered me.

"Why didn't you approach me at the conference?" I raised a question, having wondered this from the beginning. "You could have said hi and invited me here yourself."

He let out a wistful sigh, "I don't know. I wanted to. But I didn't want to scare you off."

"So, you thought by luring me here I wouldn't have a choice?" I replied teasingly.

It was an excellent query. One that he couldn't argue his way out of. Alex groaned, no doubt thinking of a great excuse. "Yes and no. You're not being held against your will. I just wanted you to give us a fair chance. I hoped that if you got to know us, you'd fall for us, and that nothing else would matter."

He was right about that.

"I'm glad you brought me here. Falling in love with you has been the best thing that has ever happened to me." And I really meant that.

Alex responded with a passionate kiss. We lay together in a lover's embrace, then drifted into a deep sleep. When I woke the following morning, I found myself squished in between all four of my men.

My husbands.

CHAPTER Twenty Eight

Isobelle

I hummed along to the song that was playing on the radio as Mason drove me into town. We were almost late, thanks to the boys playing rock-paper-scissors to decide who would drive me there. Mason won, much to the boys' dismay. It meant he got to spend some quality alone time with me down at the harbor. He parked and spent fifteen minutes kissing and cuddling me before it was time for me to meet up with Chloe and Peter at the coffee shop.

"I better get going," I said, pressing my lips to his one last time.

"One more for luck," he pleaded.

"Have fun," Mason urged, stealing another cheeky kiss.

"I will," I acknowledged, feeling extra lucky.

"Text us when you need us to pick you up," he instructed. "We have plenty of errands to run, so one of us will be around to swing by and meet you."

"Okay, will do," I responded, exiting the car.

I smoothed out my maxi dress, closed the door, and waved goodbye through the passenger side window. My heart fluttered in my chest as he drove away.

Oh my gosh, I have four gorgeous husbands.

It felt like I had lost a penny and found a pound. I glanced around me. Lakewell was bustling with life, busier than the first time I visited. Families were picnicking on the luscious grass, watching all the small yachts sail by. Kids were forming a disorderly queue beside an ice cream van. Elderly residents were taking a moment's rest upon the lakeside benches. Today was a glorious day. The sun was shining, and my heart was full.

"Isobelle!" A cheery voice called out.

As I turned to look, I saw Chloe waving at me

from across the street. I returned the gesture with a friendly smile. As soon as I spotted a gap in the traffic, I hurried across to the opposite side of the road.

"Hi," Chloe greeted me sheepishly. "I hope there are no hard feelings. It was much easier to play *'let's pretend'* with a stranger. Then we got along so well." Her contrite tone told me she was being genuine. "I felt terrible when I went into your room and found you were missing. But by the glow of your skin, and all those teeth marks on your neck, I'd say you're living your best life." Her lips stretched into a suggestive grin.

I jerked my head from side to side, swishing my ponytail around my shoulders as if wearing the mating marks like badges of honor. By some strange magic, they had healed overnight. Now they just looked like four crescent-shaped scars that had repaired a shade lighter than my natural skin color. I had stretch marks across the tops of my thighs that didn't look as pretty.

"I was a little apprehensive at first, but they soon persuaded me," I replied, keeping the conversation clean for this time of day. The smutty details were best shared over a bottle of wine or whatever tickled her fancy.

My mind was now dirtier than a pub carpet, and my knickers were just as sticky.

"I bet they did," Chloe's voice snowballed with excitement. "You have landed yourself a harem. I have enough on my plate with Lincoln."

We continued to talk as we walked.

"Thank you for inviting us out tonight. I'm looking forward to it." It was true. I looked forward to going out and having fun. I had been single for such a long time, and even before then, my previous boyfriends weren't big on the club scene. My party posse usually consisted of me, Joanna, and a couple of friends from uni.

"It's our way of saying sorry," Chloe mentioned apologetically. "And besides, I hope we can be buddies. Lincoln knows the quads rather well with them being rangers and all. It'll be good to have another girlfriend around. This reminds me . . . I've invited my friend, Danna, to meet up with us to go dress shopping. I hope you don't mind?"

"Of course not," I answered.

"You'll like her. She's human too. And she's mated to Josh, who's also a ranger, and Lincoln's best friend. They'll be joining us tonight, too."

It thrilled me at the prospect of making more friends here. It felt as if I was settling in.

"The more, the merrier," I replied, upbeat.

"Slut!" The word was disguised as a cough, but it was still distinguishable. As soon as I heard it, I knew it was deliberate and intended as a nasty insult.

Chloe and I both turned to look but failed to spot the culprit. We shared a baffled look before we continued to walk. Neither of us paid any attention to it. Instead, we just picked up our conversation where we left off. We smelled the coffee shop before we reached it. The aromatic scent of ground coffee beans, toasted bagels, and bacon floated past my nose and grew stronger the second that we stepped inside. A plethora of mouth-watering scents hit me all at once, and suddenly, I felt dizzy and lightheaded.

"Whoa!" Chloe grabbed my arm to stop me from falling. "Easy there, Tiger."

I rubbed my forehead, feeling a little silly. "Blimey, I got dizzy suddenly. I don't know what happened." The white mist that had formed in front of my eyes began to dissipate.

"Is she okay?" a male voice inquired about my wellbeing.

I knew that voice. It belonged to Peter Munroe.

"Ugh, Peter," I muttered, embarrassed by what just happened. "I'm not drunk, I swear." I tried to make a joke out of it to mask my humiliation.

Peter held his palms out in front of him. "Hey, no judgment here. I'm guilty of throwing back a couple of scotches before lunchtime, especially coming up to the end-of-year exams."

Chloe and I chuckled. "Honestly though, I rushed out without eating much for breakfast. It's my fault," I gave a reasonable excuse.

Alex would flip a lid if he found out about this. Mason would give me a lecture about breakfast being the most vital meal of the day. Lucas would stand over me until I agreed to eat something substantial, and Grayson would spoon-feed me. Nope, I'm not going to mention this.

"Why don't you ladies go find us a table, and I'll order us some coffee?" Peter offered. "And something wholesome to snack on."

Chloe led the way to a vacant table that could accommodate four people. We each dragged out one of the white plastic chairs and placed our purses by our feet as we sat down. My eyes danced across the open-plan space that was packed with identical tables and chairs, tall potted plants that provided a little privacy between the customers, and the rustic artwork that lined the walls. The serving counter comprised a long glass display unit laden with sandwiches, cakes, and pastries. The backdrop was an enormous blackboard that had the menu written in white chalk.

Chrome espresso machines were situated between the assortment of cups that ranged from small, medium, and large on tiered shelves, and the multitude of flavored syrups.

"So, how long have you and Peter known each other?" I asked Chloe.

The sound of idle chattering and the grinding noise from the coffee machine filled my ears. The metallic clatter of a spoon being dropped snatched my attention momentarily.

"Oh, not that long. I only met him several times before you came here. He stays the night when he needs to meet with Alec White about the Forestry Commission. Alec is suspicious of everyone, but for some reason, he lets Peter visit. Lincoln thinks Alec has another agenda, and that you are part of it."

I raised my brows as I nodded, surprised by that. "Oh, I just assumed he was a friend of yours. And yeah, I'm starting to think you're right about Alec juggling several balls at once. I think he is using me to get the humans off his back."

Chloe gave an ambivalent shrug. "Peter seems nice enough. I'm sure he's genuine. Lincoln just gets a little cautious when it comes to outsiders. And to be honest, I can see his point. Nothing good can come from humans knowing about shifters. Peter doesn't know about them, so be careful what you say in front of him. I take it that you've been given the low down on the hunter situation?"

I nodded, feeling a chill trace my spine with its icy tongue.

"Yeah, I was shown some of their handiwork," I revealed, shuddering with disgust. "

Chloe grimaced. "God, I wish we could figure out a way to stop them from getting into the state. It scares me to think that my children could hurt themselves in one of their traps, or that my husband will get killed in a hunter attack. When will it end?"

I wished I could pluck the answer out of the air, but that would be like trying to catch smoke with my bare hands. Nobody had any clues, and that made it even more terrifying.

"Well, maybe when I begin my assignment working with the Alpha, I might dig a little deeper into the mystery. I haven't met him yet. The guys are scheduling an appointment for us to meet. I must accept him as my Alpha."

It seemed odd talking about meeting Mr. White like this was a regular job interview, when in fact, I wasn't sure what I was supposed to expect. The boys told me I needed to recognize him as my Alpha, which felt strange because I wasn't a wolf. It was a rite of passage that I couldn't get out of, no matter how hard I tried. By accepting the guys, I had to accept their way of life, and by doing that, I had to swear an oath to their leader.

Chloe cast me a serious frown. "I don't envy you. He's a scary-looking bastard. He doesn't have a lot of patience either. Put me in front of the Clan Elder any day of the week. I would rather face a grouchy old bear than a scary-ass Lycanthrope."

"Well, that doesn't inspire much confidence," I breathed out apprehensively.

Chloe nudged my elbow. "You'll be all right as part of his wolf pack though. It's super cliquey."

We changed the subject before Peter got within earshot, switching the discussion to current affairs.

"So, you girls like reality TV shows, huh?" Peter muttered as he placed the tray of coffee and sandwiches down onto the center of the table.

It must have cost him a small fortune.

Chloe responded with an enthusiastic, "Yes," whereas I made a *Meh* face and shrugged. "I tolerate *Love Island* at a push," I added.

I used the term *tolerate* loosely. What I meant was, I ogled at all the tan-tastic muscled men and ignored all the stick-thin Barbie dolls. Now I had no reason to sit through another season because I had died and gone to muscle-man heaven.

"I can't let you pay for all of this," I mentioned, motioning at all the food. "Let me give you something toward it."

"Me too," Chloe added, insisting on paying a fair share.

Peter waved his hand in dismissal. "Nonsense. I insist. I rarely get the chance to sit and relax."

"Well, your evening meal is on the house," Chloe told him, not taking no for an answer. "I'll tell Joe to let you pick whatever you want from the menu."

"That's kind of you," he muttered awkwardly.

No matter how hard I tried to shake the replay of my mating nights from my mind, they refused to budge. They were making me feel hot and frisky, and that had to stop when I was out in public. It was a good job the boys were not sitting here with me, or else I wouldn't be able to keep my hands to myself. During my post daydream haze, I noticed a group of women who were standing at the counter. While the barista was busy completing their order, one of them muttered something snarky, then they all started snickering. Curiosity had me wondering what they were making fun of. It wasn't until they cast their sly eyes my way that I became paranoid they were talking about me. They did the same thing to Chloe. A wretched uneasiness crept over me and stagnated in my stomach. Chloe followed my gaze and made a *tsk* sound. The first time, I might have been mistaken, but the second time, there could be no mistaking what I saw.

Choosing to rise above it and maintain the English stiff upper lip, I sipped on my coffee and ignored them. They were obnoxious pricks, and I refused to give people like that the time of day.

"Is it me, or does it smell of cat piss in here?" Chloe muttered, sniffing the air as if she detected something pungent.

I frowned, confused, then saw the grin spread across her face as the group of women huffed with outrage.

Ahh, so they must be cat shifters then.

Peter sniffed the air but was baffled by what Chloe said. "So, Isobelle," Peter began making conversation. "How are you settling in? You weren't feeling too well the last time I checked in with you. I don't want to press you, but I'm looking forward to seeing what you find out here."

I wiped away my froth mustache and smiled. "Yes, I'm settling in rather nicely. I always get a little iffy whenever I travel." That wasn't a complete lie. I always needed a few days to recover from flying. It was like my body needed to acclimatize, because the last time I flew to Spain, I swear, my shit turned snot green. I kid you not, it was like Kermit the frog had been squatting up my asshole and did a kamikaze landing into the toilet. Mum said it had something to do with the altitude messing around with my bodily functions. Dad claimed I was an alien. I missed his sense of humor. "Now that I'm feeling much better, I can't wait to explore the forest and see what I can find."

Peter nodded sympathetically. "How come you checked out of the guesthouse?" he asked, his brow creased with concern.

Chloe looked at me with flared eyes, signaling for me to lie on the spot. I came up with an excuse that I knew he would swallow. "Ah, well . . . you see, it's easier for me to stay in the cabin next to the ranger station. That way, I'm right at the heart of the forest. I have a greater chance of finding a wolf pack out there, and the rangers let me tag along with them on the nature trails so there's zero chance of me getting lost."

I was never any good at coming up with random bollocks on the spot. To be a great liar, you had to have an excellent memory, and I had a brain like a sieve.

My news seemed to spark Peter's interest. "Oh, okay. That makes sense. They know the forest like the back of their hands and can show you around better than anyone, I suppose. Have you seen or heard anything yet?"

"No, nothing yet," I replied, not giving anything away.

If Peter didn't know about shifters, then there had to be a reason for that. It meant that my husbands didn't trust him enough to share that information with him. Maybe even Alec had told them not to, and they were in on this plan of his. Even though Peter seemed like the nicest guy in the world, a secret like that wasn't just theirs to share. It would compromise the safety of the entire state. It seemed to me that Alpha Alec only agreed to let Alex bring me here to throw Peter Munroe off the scent. *The sly dog.* He knew I would succumb to the mate bond and help to protect their secret. That's what Mason meant by keeping the research *in house.* I just need to wait a few weeks, then send Peter a bogus report, telling him that there are no rare wolves here in Whitehaven, just regular ones. I'm guessing that's what the Alpha wanted when he agreed to let me come here.

Peter made a face which suggested that he wasn't so sure about that. "Really? Nothing?" he sounded disappointed.

"I know, it's weird. I thought I was here to study a rare species of wolf, and all I've found so far are white-tailed deer, beavers, and hares," I lied some more.

"Oh . . ." Peter sounded a little crestfallen. "Well, I'm sure you'll have better luck now that you're feeling better."

We finished cheese and ham sandwiches and a plateful of miniature cakes between us. The gaggle of geese, who had been making fun of me, had thankfully fucked off when they picked up their food order. I felt the atmosphere in the room shift for the better as soon as they stalked through the door.

Peter wagged a finger at me as he hurried to chew his food and swallow. "I just had a thought. When was the last time that you had your blood sugar levels checked?" he asked, bringing up the subject of my health again. "That could be the reason you were all light-headed a moment ago."

"I had a routine medical check before I flew out here. My doctor said I have a clean bill of health," I informed him.

Peter scrunched his face as if he had just been

stumped out. "But would you consider a second opinion?" he pressed the matter further. "It might be nothing, but at least it'll put your mind at rest."

Needles petrified me, so I shook my head in dismissal. The urine test I did before I flew out here had come back fine, and that was good enough for me.

"It's unnecessary. My doctor was rather thorough," I stated, unwilling to budge on the matter.

Peter didn't push the subject any further. Instead, he suggested it was something for me to think about if any more symptoms persisted.

It's only one dizzy spell, for goodness' sake. What a worrywart.

"As much as this was a pleasure, ladies" — Peter rose from his chair and dusted the cake crumbs from his slacks — "I have got to dash." He bounced his cheery gaze between Chloe and me as he thrust his arms inside the sleeves of his blazer. "We should meet up again sometime."

"Sure," Chloe agreed pleasantly.

I nodded. "Yeah, well, you have my number."

Peter made his excuses and left us to chat. I saw him taking a call outside the coffee shop and watched as he hurried down the street.

"We ought to get going too," Chloe mentioned,

reaching down to grab her bag, "or else we won't have much time to search for a dress before our salon appointment this afternoon."

My stomach fluttered with excitement. "I need to find a cash machine first." Sue me, I wanted to take a sly glance at the balance before I risked purchasing an outfit. I needed to know what kind of budget I had to work with. It wasn't like I was going on a mad shopping spree, but I still had to know my limitations. Nobody ever gave away magical debit cards with an unlimited credit limit. This was the real world, not some fantasy billionaire CEO romance novel. I followed Chloe out into the busy parade of shops to find the nearest cash point. I shoved the debit card into the card slot and typed the pin into the keypad, hoping that I memorized the numbers correctly. Lucky for me, I had. Then as I saw the account balance, I had to blink my eyes several times and peer closer to the screen.

Wow! That is a lot of zeros.

My forefinger pressed the button to eject the card. I didn't need to take out more cash. I already had some in my wallet. Not only that, but I was also shocked at how much money they had accumulated as forest rangers. My hands were shaking as I shoved the card back inside my purse, unable to believe what

I had just seen. I considered myself to be a privileged middle-class woman. My parents owned our family home outright with no outstanding mortgage. We also had a beachside holiday home in Ilfracombe, in Devon. I was set to inherit my grandparents' equestrian center when they died, and my parents had several policies in place to set me up for life. Even with our combined net worth, taking everything into account, it was nothing compared to what was on that screen.

How come they have so much money?

"Is everything all right?" Chloe asked. "You're not having another dizzy spell, are you?"

I shook my head as I turned, then moved to let someone else use the machine.

"No, I just had a bit of a shock, that's all." I thought Chloe would be the best person to ask about this. "Are all rangers paid a decent salary, or does it depend on what town you're from?"

Chloe laughed. "Ahh, I get it. I saw the look on your face when you looked at the screen. The answer to your question is yes, it is an excellent salary, but it doesn't equate to a six-figure bank balance. Not by a long shot. The only poor wolf shifter you'll ever meet is a rogue. Your wolf pack derives from old money. The foxes are the wealthiest; the bear's wealth is in real estate and the construction industry. The cats get by with the resources they have. The cats are all a bunch of religious fanatics if you ask me. Take those bitches in the coffee shop for instance; they consider our way of life a sin. I'm still the girl who fucked her stepbrother, and you're the woman who fucks four brothers." She shrugged.

Saints and sinners, Lakewell was full of them. The mixed community was like a variety of cultures thrown into one town. People would either get along or they would quarrel.

We met up with Chloe's friend, Danna. The three of us were on the same wavelength of *live and let live.* The shopping trip and the pamper afternoon were just what I needed to unwind and decompress from everything. We enjoyed massages, then were able to shower and change into the clothes we bought. I got my hair, nails, and makeup done as part of a pamper package deal. Alex sent me a text to say that he would be the one to meet me and asked if I minded whether he waited in the lounge area. I noticed him sitting there, dressed like a dream in a black dinner suit that hugged his broad physique. He was perusing the magazine stack like he was bored out of his wits. Feeling sorry for him, I trotted over to him in my glamorous new heels, giving him a twirl as his eyes bounced up to greet me.

"Be honest; what do you think?" I asked, turning from side to side in my red figure-hugging plunge dress. The vibrant material matched my varnished nails and glossy lips; my voluptuous boobs looked fabulous, and even Alex's eyes popped out on stalks as he saw them. The dress was by some designer I had never even heard of, probably because they weren't known to the human world. I wore matching red peep-toe stilettos that complimented the outfit; the six-inch heels were made from twisted gold and were embellished with hundreds of tiny Swarovski crystals.

Alex's jaw flopped open and closed like a fish out of water. "Holy shit, you look incredible," he muttered, sounding awestruck. "Do we have to go out tonight?" he murmured, something between a whine and a plea. "We could cancel the dinner reservation and eat at home."

The heat that I saw burning in his eyes told me I would be the only dish on the menu.

"Yes . . . yes, we do have to go out actually," I answered adamantly. "This took a lot of work, and I'm not about to let it all go to waste."

Alex swept me into his arms and brushed his lips

against my ear. "Did you choose some sexy lingerie for me to take off with my teeth?"

I arched my left eyebrow as I pulled back. "Who says I'm wearing any?"

That statement blew Alex away. It was only a slight fib. The scrap of lace that I was wearing resembled more like a cheese wire, and not worth its material value. I left him wondering about that as I picked up my purse and sashayed out of the salon.

"See you tonight, girls!" I chirped with a cheery wave to Chloe and Danna.

It was all about letting loose and having fun tonight. I needed this. We all did.

CHAPTER

Alex

J ust as I thought, my brothers were all stunned into silence the moment they laid eyes on our mate. She looked breathtaking in her glamorous red dress, and I couldn't wait until the night ended so that we could all take turns in worshipping her sexy body.

Lucas let out a low whistle that brought a blush to Isobelle's cheeks.

"You are beautiful," Mason exclaimed, taking her by the hand so he could bring it to his lips to kiss.

"The most stunning woman on the planet," Grayson added.

A middle-aged couple walked into the restaurant before us and grimaced in our direction. Luckily for them, Izzy was too wrapped up in us to notice them. My family had been putting up with these bigoted assholes for decades. People either respected our lifestyle or they didn't. Our mother had been reduced to tears, alienated, treated like a whore, and heckled in the street. When we were young, kids used to run inside their houses whenever they saw us playing outside. Their parents shunned our parents at the school gates. We never got invited to birthday parties or playdates. The only place where we felt we belonged was with each other. That was the beauty of being a quadruplet and growing up in a reverse harem family unit. We were never alone and became our own little community. We didn't want Isobelle to suffer as our mom did, but I'd be damned if the prudes would stop us from leading a full and happy life with her. Our days of solitude were long behind us. We refused to be the taboo subject that everybody whispered about. Isobelle deserved better than to be treated like that.

"You all look so handsome," Isobelle expressed as she greeted my brothers with kisses.

"You just had to wear red, huh?" Lucas grinned wolfishly.

Izzy shook her hips, making her tits sway from side to side. "All the better to tease you with, my dear," she joked.

Lucas sucked in a bead of drool from the corner of his mouth. We all ended up with tents in the front of our slacks, thanks to our wife's womanly wiles. I had to think of something nasty so I could turn around without poking someone's eye out.

As we stepped inside the Mediterranean-themed restaurant, I heard scattered gasps coming from across the room.

"Look who just walked in," someone whispered.

"Oh my God, she's their shared mate," another guy murmured.

"Lucky bitch," someone else commented.

"Each to their own . . . leave them be," another person muttered in our defense.

We were getting mixed reactions. Some people just didn't know how to keep their opinions to themselves, and it was becoming increasingly difficult not to retaliate. If it wasn't for Mason thinking on his feet, taking Izzy over to the floor-to-ceiling fish tank that divided the front counter from the dining room, she might have overheard what people were saying.

Thankfully, she was more engrossed by all the colorful fish swimming around the reconstructed coral reef. I stood guard alongside Lucas and Grayson, shooting pointed glares until each gawking prick looked away and focused on their food. They received our message loud and clear. We were not to be jeered at like a freaky circus attraction. The next person to snicker at us would join the lobsters in the boiling pot.

Lucas

The atmosphere was so intense I could have snapped it in half. The last time I saw a room fall this silent was when Grayson stripped naked in the school canteen, stood on the center table, and did the dick helicopter as a dare.

"Are we being seated today or what?" I voiced my frustration out loud. "I'm starving over here."

I can't believe I skipped lunch for this.

The servers had seen us standing here taking up the front entrance. There was no way that they could miss us, so there was no excuse for the shitty service. We had a reservation. Alex called ahead and booked a table for five. Even though a few of the server dudes were wolf shifters like us, they seemed uncomfortable with us being here. Their boss didn't seem to mind much. Bear shifters generally didn't. The flustered wolves could have informed us that someone would be with us shortly, but they had been whispering with the manager for several minutes. I didn't like how they were throwing anxious side glances at us every few seconds, as if all the diners were going to walk out in protest. It was the same fucking scenario everywhere we went. Everybody passed judgment on us as if our lifestyle was contagious.

"Babe?" I called out to my wife. Izzy flicked her gaze to me. "Pick an empty table, sweetheart. I guess it's a matter of *'sit wherever you want'* tonight."

That made the fuckers move. Their eyes almost bulged from their skulls as they heard what I just said. One server hurried over to us as if the manager had shoved a lit firework up his butt hole.

"Good evening, gentlemen." He flicked his beady eyes to Isobelle and swallowed hard. "And to the lovely lady."

A male diner choked on his mouthful of food at that statement. I was about to stalk over to him and lift him by his throat, but Grayson was first to retaliate.

"That's a nasty cough you got there, buddy," he

growled, his brow set into an infuriated scowl. "Maybe you need a rough pat on the back, or maybe you should try sipping some water."

Grayson's hint was obvious that he would be the one to deliver a harsh pat on the back. Knowing my brother, he'd hit him hard enough to make him cough up a lung.

Mason gripped the bridge of his nose and huffed with annoyance. Alex balled his hands into tight fists. Izzy was bouncing her gaze between us in a state of bewilderment, wondering what the hell was wrong.

"Did I miss something?" she asked. The jubilant sparkle that was present in her eyes had already diminished, and with it went the last of my resolve.

I gave the server dude a look that demanded he better fix this fast.

The gulp that bobbed in his throat told me he had registered that loud and clear. "My manager and I wondered whether you would prefer to dine on the balcony terrace?" he asked, trying to keep everyone happy.

Alex looked at me and winked. I took that as confirmation that this was a suitable compromise. Alex, being the fancy snob that he was, had been here plenty of times, whereas I was more than content to eat at the truck stop by the forest road.

Alex turned to the server with his poker face intact. "That would be splendid, thank you."

As they led us to the VIP table, exclusive to town leaders, the disgruntled diners vented their outrage.

"That hardly seems fair," an unhappy diner voiced. "Just because she's new around here and bagged herself four of our eligible bachelors, she's being treated like royalty."

"Well, if you weren't such a nasty bitch, they would dine in here with the rest of us," another wolf shifter stood up for us. "And they're mated. Look at her neck and think before you disrespect the will of the Goddess."

To be honest, it was less stressful being seated away from all the hustle and bustle. At least people wouldn't have to watch me chew my steak like a bloodthirsty carnivore.

"Wow," Isobelle murmured as soon as she stepped out onto the lakeside terrace. The balcony backdrop was lit with a curtain of sparkling lights. Soft music filtered through the wall-mounted speakers and merged with the sound of the lazy lake. The sky was already turning a majestic shade of blue, deep purple, and pale violet with blended white contrails scoring through it. The view was incredible. Despite the minor hiccup in our evening plans, the delicious food, the champagne, and the relaxed atmosphere quickly made up for it. This date hadn't turned out to be a colossal disaster after all.

I reached my hand across the table and laced my fingers with Isobelle's. "Have you thought about what you're going to tell your parents?" I asked, noticing that she kept glancing at her phone.

"I'm building myself up to it," she replied, eyeing each of us with a silent apology. "I know I'm a chicken, but I don't want to hurt them."

We all agreed through our unique bond that Isobelle should not feel guilty for keeping us a secret, and she should tell her parents when she felt ready.

"There's no rush, love," Mason reassured her.

"We understand," Alex reinforced. "There's no pressure."

Grayson nodded to show that he felt the same way. Isobelle let out a long sigh of relief.

"Let's just enjoy tonight," she suggested, raising her champagne flute in a toast. "It's our first night out as an officially mated harem. Our problems will still be there waiting for us when we've all sobered up."

We each raised our glasses and brought all five flutes clinking together above the tabletop.

"To us!" We chorused. "And whatever the future may hold."

Isobelle

"Brr, it's cold outside." I shuddered, rubbing my arms for warmth.

The buzz from the two glasses of champagne I had at dinner had started to wear off. I put on a brave face in front of the boys, pretending not to have heard all the insensitive whispering, when in fact, I picked up every word that was spoken. Not all of it was bad. Some of it was reassuring.

Grayson was the first to remove his suit jacket and wrapped it around my shoulders. I snuggled into it, loving how his woodsy scent infused the material. Chloe, Lincoln, Danna, and her ranger husband, Josh, met us outside the Vortex club. Josh was a blond version of Lincoln, big and bulky, but with less facial hair. They dressed more for comfort, donning stonewashed jeans, boots, and plaid shirts. The girls stood out from their husbands. Danna opted for a glitzy blue two-piece skirt and strappy top and silver heels. Chloe looked stunning in a pink halter-neck mini dress and white patent open-toe pumps.

The queue to get in the club curved around to the side of the building, but lucky for us, we didn't have to wait behind the stanchions like everyone else. Lincoln had VIP tickets that allowed us to bypass the queue. A bouncer came over to unhook the rope, and after checking off our names on his clipboard, he let us go inside. My skin looked tanned beneath the neon blue lighting, and anything white glowed even brighter. Our teeth looked super white. The fast-paced music absorbed into my body, the beat thumping straight through my chest. This was the best part of going out, the adrenaline rush.

"I need to pee," Danna announced. "My bladder isn't used to holding on to this much liquid after having kids."

"Again?" Josh side-eyed her with disbelief. "You went before we came out."

"It's all your fault that my pelvic floor is completely fucking floored after giving birth to your offspring," she whined, her palms pressed flat against her stomach.

Chloe chuckled. "Okay, let's make a pit stop to the bathroom while the guys fetch us some drinks."

We took a detour to the ladies' restroom, and I checked my makeup in the mirrored wall above the black glitzy vanity counter. The soft lighting made me look flawless.

"What is this wizardry?" I chuckled, admiring the

airbrushed reflection of myself. "I want this mirror. I think the one in my bathroom hates me."

The restroom had everything a girl needed to spruce up her appearance, straightening irons, curling tongs, complimentary dry shampoo, hairspray, makeup, and perfume. If this was London, or anywhere in the UK, I could guarantee that girls would fill their purses with freebies. It was bad enough we were renowned for robbing the shot glasses from the Revolution bar, but this was like walking into a Selfridges beauty counter and it being a free-for-all.

"This club is owned by the Reaper Cartel. Trust me, there's no expense spared," Chloe explained as I sifted through the products.

Well, on that note, I better not pinch anything in case they frisk me on the way out.

I followed Chloe and Danna into the exclusive lounge and saw that our husbands were waiting for us in a huge private booth. The cut-out section in the middle of the table was filled with ice. Champagne and spirit bottles were poking out from it. We shuffled around the circular seating and put our clutch bags onto the bench beside us. It amazed me when Grayson showed me that each cube of ice had either a crystal or tiny golden nugget inside them.

"It's rather posh in here, isn't it?" I mentioned, raising my voice over the music. "I've been to some fancy places in London, but this blows them all out of the water."

Grayson nodded as if he had heard me perfectly and tossed some ice into the empty tumbler glasses. "It's an ostentatious display of the Reaper's wealth. If you melt those cubes down, you get to keep as much as you can fill your pockets with, but most people who come here don't."

Josh poured large measures of Johnnie Walker whisky, and between him, Lincoln, Alex, Grayson, and Lucas, they finished the bottle in one go. Mason was happy to stick with beer and declined anything stronger.

Alex rummaged through the selection of liquor bottles. "Pick your poison, ladies."

"Vodka and coke, please," Chloe chirped without hesitation.

Danna glanced at what was on offer. "Uh, I'll go for a Bacardi and lemonade."

There were too many choices. Not that I was complaining.

"I'll have a gin and tonic, please," I answered.

Even though gin tends to shoot to my head faster than some of my best ideas, it always got me pissed quickly. Yes, it was the devil's juice, but needs must. There was no way I was brave enough to walk onto the dance floor without a little liquid courage.

"Make it a double," I encouraged.

As the alcohol started to take effect, I could feel myself loosening up and I started to enjoy myself. The atmosphere inside the Vortex club was buzzing and carefree, and nobody seemed to care that I was here with four lovers who were taking it in turns to flirt with me, nuzzle against my neck, whisper lewd sexual remarks in my ear, and snatch hot kisses occasionally.

"We should do this more often," Lincoln suggested as he topped up his tumbler with a generous measure of whisky.

I would be flat on my back in an alcoholic coma if I drank half of what they were knocking back. Jesus Christ, shifters could drink.

The fourth gin and tonic had gone straight to my head, making me slur my words. I was such a fucking lightweight.

"I'm up for that," I snapped up the opportunity for another night out.

Even though I barely knew these people, I felt at home with them. The conversation just seemed to flow without a struggle. We got along fine, and they took no offense when someone said something in jest.

"Who wants to dance?" Danna asked, aiming the hint at her husband.

I saw the flinch in Josh's, Alex's, and Lucas's eyes when she suggested we all get up to dance. Dancing wasn't for everyone. It wasn't hard to distinguish between the Kevin Bacon wannabes and those who preferred to stand at the bar and tap their feet.

"I do," Chloe volunteered. "Come on, Linc. Get your cute butt onto that dance floor."

Josh grimaced as he scooted out of the booth to let Lincoln out. Now that he was up, Danna seized his wrist and dragged him to the dance floor.

I threw my husbands a pleading glance. "Are any of you coming?" I asked, hoping that one of them would.

Grayson and Mason seemed keen, but Alex and Lucas needed a little more convincing.

"Ah, come on," I pleaded with them. "Let's make a club sandwich."

Mason took my hand and guided me to the illuminated floor tiles. They lit up purple, matching the neon theme around the room. Dry ice curled around the gyrating bodies like clouds of white smoke. I saw Chloe dancing with her wrists crossed behind Lincoln's neck, and Danna slowly grinding against Josh. I swayed my hips to the music, feeling the beat pulsing through my chest. Alex and Lucas drained their glasses and ambled across the dance floor, not wanting Mason and Grayson to have all the fun. They closed in around me, stalking me like prey. The mixture of cologne and body heat served as an aphrodisiac, turning me on. Their hands were on me, sliding across my midriff, and caressing me as we danced. Soft versus rough kisses grazed against my lips, neck, and cleavage. It was so good to get out and have fun, I lost track of the time. People looked . . . and I knew they would, but I didn't care. They weren't me. I was happy . . . so happy that no one could spoil it. It felt so right. In ten years from now, I'd still remember this night, the way it felt to feel loved and to be in love, the freedom of being myself, and how much my confidence had grown.

"I'll be back, I just need to nip to the loo," I mentioned after four more drinks.

The boys sauntered back to the booth as I retreated to the restroom. I didn't ask Chloe and Danna to accompany me. Being the big girl that I was, I didn't require somebody to hold my hand as I peed.

After relieving my aching bladder, washing my

hands, and checking that my makeup had stayed intact, I ventured out into the hazy corridor. A firm hand snatched at my wrist, and I found myself flat up against the wall, staring into a pair of strange reptilian eyes. I couldn't tell what color they were beneath the neon lighting, but this guy was huge. His brow set into a deadly scowl with a bar piercing on the right side, a scar sliced through his socket, but left his eye undamaged. Tattooed arms pinned me into place, his muscles bulging beneath the white cotton shirt, the ink disappearing beneath his rolled sleeves. My eyes bulged. His shirt collar gaped open at the neck, revealing the tattoo R.I.P across his chest. A dangerous vibe oozed from his pores like a noxious fume, making my hair stand on end.

"You ought to watch what company you keep," he spoke in a grave Cajun drawl.

This guy looked like an inked version of the Hulk and sounded as though he had swallowed a bag of rusty old nails. I wasn't stupid enough to suggest that he should mind his own business. He looked as if he could murder me with his bare hands.

"We're not doing anything wrong. We just wanted to enjoy a night out with our friends," I returned, not wanting to start any trouble.

I assumed he was one of those people who disapproved of our lifestyle.

His vertical pupils flickered with a silent analysis. "You don't know what the fuck I'm talking about, do you?" he rasped, pushing back from the wall.

I swallowed thickly. "Know what?" I asked, feeling myself sobering up.

"A word of advice… choose your friends more wisely. You'll be surprised what lurks behind a friendly smile. Just lately, these parts are full of them . . . smiling assassins, waiting for you to turn your back so that they can take their pound of flesh." He grimaced at the words as if they left an unpleasant taste in his mouth.

Uh, trust me to stumble into the midst of an aggrieved drunkard with a grudge.

"My friends, and the company I keep, are none of your concern," I spoke in their defense.

"What does a hunter look like?" he asked, cocking his head to one side. "Go on, enlighten me."

Yep, an angry drunk.

He didn't seem to take my shrug as a reasonable answer, so I muttered, "Like anybody, I suppose."

To be honest, I didn't know what to think. He had a point. *What does a hunter look like?* In my mind, I envisioned the cast of *Predator* lurking through the woods and setting traps. To be fair, I didn't have a clue.

"When a guy asks you for a sample of blood around here, that ought to ring alarm bells," he finished, taking a step back. "Think about it."

His comment baffled me.

"But I'm human! I'm not like any of you," I countered.

The only person who sprung to mind was Peter, and he was a geeky university professor who lived with his grandma and his pet Chihuahua. I'm sorry, but he hardly gave off hunter vibes.

"This is too fucking precious, even for me," he snickered as he turned to leave.

I could still hear him cackling as he disappeared down the hall.

"What a weirdo," I muttered, scrunching my nose.

"There you are!" Lucas exclaimed. "We were about to start tracking your scent."

He glanced around the hall as if he was looking for something, but he soon gave up when I kissed him. After the weird ordeal with the inked stranger, I needed this.

Lucas rested his forehead against mine. "We have to hurry; Grayson is doing shots."

"Why is that bad?" I pulled away, wincing.

Lucas flared his eyes. "Oh, it's bad all right. No one wants to see him do the helicopter." He narrowed his eyes. "Babe, are you all right? You're trembling."

A weak smile flickered across my lips. "Yeah, I'm fine," I lied.

The green-eyed creep had freaked me out, and I couldn't shake the bad feeling that started to grow deep inside me.

CHAPTER Thirty

Isobelle

The mid-morning sun stung my eyes as I cracked them open.

Ouch, my head.

The light dazzled me. My feet throbbed from dancing in heels all night, and it felt like someone had taken a jackhammer to my skull. I smacked my parched lips together to revitalize my withered tongue, but it was no use. I needed water. My stomach gurgled like an active volcano, and my breath smelled as if I had brushed my teeth with dog shit.

I'm never drinking ever again.

I had no recollection of getting home last night. One glance beneath the sheets confirmed we were all naked. The warm, musky odor of bodily fluids wafted up and offended my nostrils, confirming my suspicions. We'd had sex. Although, I couldn't remember the details. My memory was hazy, the room was spinning, and I just wanted to hang my head out of the window and breathe in some fresh air. It had been such a long time since I vomited and suffered from a hangover. The last time was during freshers' week. A mass of tangled limbs stood between me and the bathroom, forcing me to decide whether to wriggle free or risk waking the guys. The problem was . . . they always woke up horny, and my poor pummeled pussy couldn't take another beating without relieving my aching bladder first. It seemed like a strenuous endeavor, so I gave up and sagged back onto the bed with a whine, my bladder throbbing with the urge to purge.

I'll just die here instead.

Half an hour later, I couldn't take it anymore. "Who wants to get me a drink?" I croaked, hoping that one of them would take pity on me. "I would get it for myself, but I'm desperate to go to the loo."

Silence . . .

"If no one volunteers, I'm just going to choose one of you," I cautioned.

"Oh, yeah?" Lucas tickled me in the ribs.

A tender tummy and a full bladder were not a great combination. Something was bound to erupt whether it be up or down or from both ends at once.

"Don't," I groaned. "I don't feel very well."

Lucas rolled on top of me and pinned both my arms above my head. "Well, that'll teach you to do shots with Grayson," he reminded me, his words evoking an embarrassing flashback that made me cringe.

"No . . . I'm way too fragile for this," I whined, recalling how I danced on the bar and flashed my ass to the entire club.

Not only that, but I also didn't like Lucas being so close to me because my breath smelled like a silage tanker.

"Just let me die of shame," I groaned.

"Not until you give me a kiss," Lucas demanded, gazing down at me with a boyish grin.

I sucked my lips between my teeth in protest. There was no way I could kiss him without scrubbing my tongue with bleach, caustic soda . . . Cillit Bang, the best British cleaning agent in history.

Okay, maybe that's too dramatic.

But my breath smelled bad, and he always seemed to smell minty fresh, even after a night out on the booze. He pressed his lips against my tightly sealed mouth and rolled off the bed like a stuntman.

"Are you brewing up?" I asked, shocked he had volunteered himself.

"Someone has to," he muttered sarcastically as he left the room. "Considering those lazy bastards won't move."

That impressed me. Weren't bad boys supposed to run around breaking hearts, not causing them to flutter?

"Aww, thank you, babe. I'll make it worth your while." That was a subtle hint to the others that if they pleased me, they would also be in for a treat.

My plan seemed to work.

Alex cracked an eye open and angled his face to peer at me. His gray eyes were bloodshot, his hair was a mess, and he had remnants of red lipstick smudged over his lips. He looked like a vampire who had just risen from his coffin.

Grayson poked me in the small of my back. "Hey, that's not fair. You can't play favorites, you know?"

Mason was fast asleep. His brothers had pulled the covers from him, revealing his naked body. My eyes took a slow journey south, landing on the lipstick smudged cock between his legs.

I must have had an eventful night. It was a shame I couldn't remember.

"I'll tell you what; why don't you give me a hand to make breakfast?" I suggested, considering that Alex was feeling as rough as a badger's ass this morning. "Nothing too heavy. Just something to settle our stomachs."

"Speak for yourself, I feel fine," Grayson responded proudly.

I wish I could say the same.

After throwing on my bathrobe, I abandoned the search for my slippers. The cool wooden floor was such a relief underfoot. I ambled into the bathroom to relieve my bladder and rested my tender head against the wall. The past few nights were beginning to catch up with me. After finishing my business, washing my hands, and splashing some cold water onto my face, I scrubbed my teeth until my gums tingled. I stared at myself in the mirror, shocked that I resembled a zombie who had crawled out of an earthy grave. Only a strong cup of coffee would resurrect me from the dead. Not tea. Not yet.

I slumped at the kitchen table and buried my head in my hands. Just the thought of putting bread into the toaster seemed like a strenuous effort. Even the jingling sound of a spoon hitting the inside of a mug was a decibel too loud. I raised my weary head, and Lucas presented me with a hot cup of coffee.

"Thanks, love," I mumbled appreciatively.

"Be careful. I think I've overfilled it," Lucas warned.

"I'll leave it to cool for a bit." I pulled him down for a kiss now that my breath smelled fresh.

"Easy," Lucas reinforced, widening his eyes with a wicked glint. "Or I might just have to eat you for breakfast."

"Have you seen my bag? I need some aspirin," I asked, remembering that I had packed extra.

Lucas walked over to the storage cupboard and retrieved my purse from off the coat hook.

"Thanks." I went to take it from him, and he pulled it away, making a big deal of how heavy it was.

"What are you carrying around in this thing? It weighs a ton," he teased, holding the strap with two fingers.

I flashed a sarcastic grin. "Women's secret things," I replied as I grabbed it from him.

Setting it down on the table, I rummaged through

the graveyard of receipts, leaflets, half a packet of chewing gum from years gone by, spare tampons — in case of emergencies — and lots of other junk I hoarded in there.

"Why do women like to accumulate crap? Our mom is the same. Her purse could sink a battleship too. Oh look, you've rescued some hidden treasures," Lucas muttered with typical male sarcasm as I picked up a lip gloss that I thought I'd lost, and an old ten-pound note I didn't remember having.

Knowing me, I had stuffed it in there during a drunken night out. It made a change from finding notes screwed up after washing them in my jeans' pockets.

"Lucas, I've got something in here for you." I pulled my hand out of my bag and stuck two fingers up at him.

A very English way of telling him to *fuck off.*

He stared open-mouthed in amazement. "That's it, you've asked for it," he threatened, stalking around the table to ambush me with tickles. "Argh, Lucas! It hurts when you tickle me like that. You're so heavy-handed," I complained, attempting to shield my sore ribs.

"What's going on here?" Grayson inquired, walking through to the kitchen in a pair of shorts he used for lounging in. His eyes sparkled with mischievous intent after catching sight of Lucas who had me bent over the table in such a compromising position.

"He's assaulting me. Help!" I joked, earning myself another round of painful tickles.

"Can I join in?" Grayson asked, grinning.

"Oh, for fuck's sake. Mason! Alex!" I screeched through fits of laughter, hoping that one of them would rescue me.

Grayson's hand dove straight to the crease of my inner thighs, causing a high-pitched scream to erupt from my throat.

"Bastards! The pair of you. Let me drink my coffee," I spluttered.

Lucas flipped me over so that he pressed my back against the table and positioned my ass at the edge. He spread my legs apart as Grayson pulled my robe open, leaving me bare and vulnerable. Grayson moved the mug onto the kitchen counter out of the way. He turned his attention to me and devoured my breasts. His mouth was all over them, nipping and sucking my nipples into stiff peaks. Lucas pressed kisses along my inner thighs, my legs quaking with anticipation of all the pleasures that were yet to come. As his journey reached its destination, his hot breath gusting warmth against my mound. Lucas's relaxed tongue delved between my lower lips, lapping slowly, and humming his approval as if this was the best thing he had ever tasted.

"She tastes amazing, doesn't she?" Grayson spoke in a sexy husk.

Lucas was too busy feasting to muster words, replying with, "Mm."

"I still can't believe you're real," Grayson mumbled, trailing kisses across my jaw, then claiming my mouth.

The kiss was rough and urgent, and as my fingers found the waistband of his shorts, I felt the reason why. Straining beneath the thin material, his solid cock was battling to break free.

Grayson pinned me down onto the table while Lucas speared inside my tunnel, slurping my juice with his long, wet tongue. My legs shook, my clit throbbing with pain and pleasure, so intense, both sensations felt the same.

Lucas used his tensed muscle to stroke my inner walls, lapping at my essence as the juices gushed into his waiting mouth. The wonderful intrusion made me buck with pleasure, his skilled muscle reaching high into my cavern and making me moan at the pressure. My back arched off the table, only to be pinned back down by Grayson. Lucas was more primal, more animalistic than the others. Sex with Lucas was one wild ride. You were getting just as much of his wolf as you were getting of him as a man, and he didn't disappoint.

Lucas pulled away, leaving me a panting mess on the table. His pupils dilated with lust and his full, swollen lips glistened with the essence of my arousal. "Do you want a taste before I finish off inside her?" he offered, stepping aside for Grayson.

Grayson took his place, going straight for my sensitive clit and sucked it into his mouth. Several strokes of his tongue had me flying apart for a second time. My entire body quaked as I climaxed again. Tears rolled down the sides of my head, disappearing into my hairline as the intensity left me sobbing. I had forgotten how many times I had come during the past few days. There had been too many times to count.

Grayson mumbled something to Lucas about going easy on me, then helped him to flip me over onto my stomach. I wasn't sure if Lucas knew how to go easy with anything. Then right there at the entrance of my pussy, the thick, hard bulb of Lucas's cock pressed against me.

My backside and thighs tensed as his manhood drove my walls apart. I sucked in a gasp, hard and sharp as he forced his way through my opening and filled me up to my bursting point.

"Do you like that, baby?" Lucas asked, delivering a rough slap against the side of my thigh. The skin stung where he struck, leaving behind a fiery print.

"Yes," I mewled as he dragged his fat shaft back out again, then yelped as he rammed it back in with a slam of his hips, smashing his pelvis against my rump.

I was already pivoting on my tiptoes, bent over the table, impaled upon his cock, but the force of his thrusts was enough to lift me off the floor. With each hard slam, the table skipped and creaked until it rocked back and forth.

"Uh. Uh. Uh," I moaned with pleasure, loving the way he fucked me to smithereens. He reached around and fingered my clit and I exploded. My eyes rolled into the back of my skull and lightning bolts erupted behind my eyelids.

"God, Lucas, I'm gonna . . . cum," a loud guttural moan, sounding nothing like a noise I would make, left my throat as I roared out my release with Lucas following behind me, growling out his climax as he emptied his balls.

My limbs were left limp and boneless as he pulled out of me. Grayson scooped me up and carried me back into the bedroom. "Move over," he called out to Alex and Mason who were now fully awake.

Grayson placed me gently down on the bed, climbing over me with his huge cock rearing and ready to go. I winced as he sheathed himself to the hilt.

"It's sore," I whimpered.

"I'll go slow," he promised.

Grayson kept to his word, rocking into me with gentle, slow thrusts, his kisses matching the pace. He threaded his fingers through mine, bringing my hands above my head. "My favorite place is inside you." His low husky voice was barely a whisper, but it held so much meaning.

He coaxed another powerful orgasm out of me as he circled his hips, his own body coated with glistening sweat.

"Grayson!" I dragged out his name with an orgasmic moan.

My walls constricted against his girth, milking his climax.

"Fuck, I'm there!" he grunted, his body tensing as he ejaculated inside me.

He slumped against me, and we stayed like that, cuddling until we felt able to move.

"So much for me making breakfast," I uttered.

"Did we fuck with your plans?" Grayson chuckled, pointing out the obvious.

He draped his arm around me.

"You know you did," I answered, shoving it off me.

We were too hot and sticky, and I needed to breathe.

His salacious chuckle implied he didn't care. It didn't matter how gross we were, he still craved the closeness.

The clattering noise of pans hitting the stove meant Alex was cooking. I looked around the bedroom and noticed that Mason had gone too. Moments later, the sizzling sound of bacon accompanied the heavenly smell. My stomach rumbled, telling me to get up and feed it. I stumbled around, snatching my dressing gown and finding my slippers. My hair resembled a bird's nest. I tried my best to rake my fingers through the snags as I chose a seat at the table.

"Here, I made you some fresh coffee," Alex announced, holding out the mug with the handle pointing toward me.

"Thanks." I took it gratefully, bringing the mug to my lips and taking a small mouthful. It was too hot to sip, but I was too thirsty to care.

My dad could drink a scorching cup of tea within minutes. We used to joke that he had a cast-iron gullet.

"Do you want one of these?" Alex held a plate out with a delicious-looking bacon sandwich on it.

"Daft question; give it here," I answered, practically snatching his hand off for it.

He pulled the plate away as I tried to take it. "What's it worth, hmm? What do you say, Mason? Lucas got sex just for brewing some coffee, and Grayson had some for doing nothing at all." He shrugged, pressing his lips together.

I rolled my eyes.

"Hand over the sandwich." I beckoned with my palm outstretched, curling my fingers back and forth. "Or else I won't be held responsible for my actions."

Mason, who was finding the entire exchange hilarious, stood beside Alex, folding his arms across his bare tattooed chest. "They got some. It's only fair," he added.

My eyes narrowed into slits as I huffed, "Fine. Now feed me or else nobody is getting anything," I warned, ready to fight to the death for that sandwich.

Alex chuckled, flashing his perfect white teeth, his eyes crinkling at the edges. "Here, eat it before it gets cold."

"Don't worry, I will. It will not be a pretty sight, so don't watch me," I forewarned before cramming half of the cut-up sandwich into my mouth.

I let out a satisfied moan as the smoky flavor hit my taste buds with a bang.

Alex and Mason paced the kitchen, waiting for me to finish my breakfast. I took my time, nibbling at the crust and enjoying how much it frustrated Alex.

Do they mean they want their turn now? My poor abused pussy.

All this sex worked faster than any other hangover cure. The second I swallowed my last bite and washed it down with a last gulp of coffee, Alex grabbed the mug from me. He passed it to Mason, whose eyes were darkening with lust, then he picked me up and carried me into the bedroom. I bounced flat on my back on the bed.

"Spread her legs, Mason. Just like that," Alex rasped, exerting his usual masculine dominance.

"Do you want to go first?" Mason offered, giving Alex the green light.

"Down here? Absolutely. You can enjoy her mouth if she'll let you in there," Alex replied, removing his shorts.

Mason did the same, then turned my head as he

kneeled beside me. I realized what he wanted and twisted at the waist. Alex pinned my thighs apart as he slipped between them. I looked up at Mason's flushed face, meeting his glimmering gaze as I brought my lips to the tip of his erection, flicking my tongue out to taste the pre-cum that had beaded there.

At the same moment, Alex lined himself up at my entrance. I moaned as I sucked Mason's length, fluctuating between bobbing and licking him. Alex speared inside me and began to fuck me in slow, controlled thrusts. I groaned, undulating my hips to match his rhythm.

"God, Izzy," Mason growled, one hand wandering over to caress my breasts as the other tangled in my hair, the three of us continuing to move together as one entity.

Breathing through my nose, I swallowed Mason's cock down my throat, not even stopping as I gagged on it. It felt like a victory to take him so deeply, swiping my tongue against the base. Alex screwed himself deep into my pussy stirring up another tsunami of pleasure. My clit was as solid as a pebble, relishing the scruff of his pubic hair grazing against it. It was a delicious synchronization of gentle thrusts and forceful slams, low grunts, and moans. Each movement pushed me that bit further toward the finishing line.

Mason withdrew from my lips, his glans an angry shade of purple. "I'm saving the ending for when I'm inside you.

He stood back, stroking his huge veiny length. Alex's pelvis slammed against mine, sending a hot gush of sticky seed deep inside my womb. He dug his fingers into my thighs and squeezed, throwing his head back with a roar. I felt the warmth flowing within me. The sound of sloshing water meant that someone was running a bath. I couldn't wait to scrub myself clean again.

Alex pulled away and stepped aside for Mason, who wasted no time in filling me again. We kissed as we fucked, and Mason lifted my ass to bury his cock as deep as he could go. I let him use me however he needed to, watching his face scrunch with pleasure as he came. Sperm gushed from my gaping hole as he rolled off me, trickling down the cleft of my ass and absorbed into the bedding. My pussy burned from the stretch, and my loins ached as my muscles retracted back to normal. I waited until I caught my breath, my tits heaving upon my chest, my nipples as hard as bullets. The room reeked of sin and our sheets needed to be boil-washed in holy water. But most of all, I needed a break from all the sex.

"There's no way I can walk after that," I panted.

"We wouldn't expect you to," Mason chuckled.

He carried me into the bathroom where he and Alex bathed me. Lucas and Grayson floated lazily in the water. My men took turns to kiss me, their hands massaging my shoulders, caressing away every ache, every pain until all I could feel was bliss.

CHAPTER Thirty One

Isobelle

nother day passed, and I still had mentioned nothing to my parents. I avoided social media altogether, partly so I didn't have to reply to any messages. At one point, I considered updating my relationship status to *"It's complicated"* just to wriggle out of divulging all the details. My daily phone calls were brief, making awkward small talk about the weather. When my mother asked me if I had made any progress with the research project, I froze, unsure of what to say on the spot. This was more than a little white lie; it felt deceitful, withholding a huge part of my life from my family. The guilt consumed me like an ugly parasite, feeding off every insecurity that resurfaced. People would judge me. Nobody would understand. I wasn't ashamed of the Bennett brothers, so why was I keeping them stashed away like they were a dirty little secret? It wasn't fair to them. Throwing caution to the wind, I grabbed my phone from off the arm of the sofa and began typing out a text message.

"Hi, Mum. Are you working tonight? Let me know when it's best to call. There's something I need to tell you about."

The delivery report flashed at the top of the screen, letting me see she had received it. For all I knew, Mum could be in surgery, so I didn't expect an immediate reply. It was always easier to talk to my mother about men. It felt awkward discussing my private life with Dad. I swear that he still viewed me as his little girl, despite me being a grown woman. It was going to be difficult for him to hand me over to one man, let alone four.

Just as I was about to lay my phone back down, it rang. At first, I thought it might be Mum replying to my message, but instead of my mother's name and picture on the home screen, an unknown number flashed in its place.

I answered with a wary, "Hello?"

"Mrs. Bennett?" It was a male voice on the line. He sounded confident, charming, and Italian.

I was just about to ask who it was when he introduced himself.

"It's Alpha White. I hope you don't mind me calling you out of the blue, but Alex passed on your number. Can you spare a few moments of your time?"

Knowing it was him forced me to sit up straight. There was no disguising my nervous tone as I stammered, "Oh, hi, yes, hello."

"Mrs. Bennett, how are you settling in?" he inquired, sounding every inch the patriarch as I believed him to be.

"Please, call me Isobelle," I insisted. "I'm settling in rather well, thank you for asking. It's beautiful here. I've even made a few friends," I told him.

Alec's courteous manner put me right at ease, and as the telephone conversation continued, I learned he and I shared many common interests. Alpha Alec explained someone had called him away from the state on an urgent business matter, and he planned for us to meet as soon as he returned. He didn't go into detail about his circumstances, but he told me he would only have two hours to welcome me into the pack and show me around his laboratory before he attended to other matters. I appreciated he was an extremely busy man who was pressed for time.

"Perhaps you could solve a mystery that was brought to my attention last night," he mentioned, handing me the first task as his assistant. "The bear community has raised concerns about the possible contamination of White Lake. They have reported an influx of dead fish and animal carcasses in and around the falls. Then residents claim to have suffered from skin rashes after swimming in the lake. Fortunately, shifters have rapid healing abilities, but the family pets who had been swimming with the children have since become sick . . . some even died. It's got the clan riled up as to what could've caused it. I'll leave it in your capable hands to collect a sample from the lake and conduct a toxicology report to source the root of this issue. No major shifter casualties have been recorded, but until we can rule out the cause, who says that won't change in the upcoming days ahead?"

"Are you saying that this could be down to hunters poisoning the water supply?" I asked, feeling that this was a possibility.

There was a momentary pause as Alpha Alec sighed. "Yes, that is the consensus among the community. I'm hoping it isn't the case. We had a few issues with pesticides being dumped into the water a couple of years back, so I'm hoping this is down to some careless farmer and nothing more sinister. But until we expose the culprit, we must explore all avenues of inquiry. I'll get everything you need sent over to you by this afternoon."

"Thank you," I replied. "I'll ask the guys to take me there. I'll need to collect some blood samples from the dead animals so I can run them through the screening process," I explained, needing to compare my findings.

It sounded as if he sucked in a breath through his teeth. "I called ahead, warning the clan to hold off with the disposal of carcasses, but they were keen to begin the clean-up process. The residents of Forest Hills are sentimental about the way they handle their dead . . . I can only hope that the rangers haven't incinerated everything yet. As for the domestic pets, the bears consider them as a part of their family, the same as humans cherish theirs. They've probably buried them already."

I was about to comment that it was understandable for people to value the life of their pet, the same as a member of their family, but I had to stop myself from blurting it out. He sounded amused that the bears kept animals as pets. Maybe Alpha Alec disapproved and believed that we should leave all beasts to roam the land freely as nature intended. This wasn't a human state, so therefore they didn't all adopt the same customs as one another. I had to keep reminding myself that I was just a guest here. Who was I to pass judgment on what they did or didn't do? Alpha Alec rescheduled our appointment, telling me he would see me two days from now. That was fine by me. It gave me plenty of time to inspect the lake water.

I better hurry.

Mason, who had been loitering around waiting for me to finish, plopped down on the sofa beside me. "That wasn't so bad, was it?" he commented, referring to the positive phone call.

"He seems nice enough," I replied, turning to face him. "Everyone speaks about him as if he's a great, big, scary monster, but when he talks, he sounds like one of my university professors. I can't believe we have so much in common."

Mason chortled. "It depends on what time of day you catch him, but you'll find that out soon enough. He is a clever man, Izzy. You'll be working with a scientific legend."

That could very well be true. The boys dropped it

into one of our conversations that Alec White had led a lengthy and eventful life, and that he was a little over five hundred years old. That was a long time to spend studying the world. My new boss was a fountain of knowledge for me to learn from. I couldn't imagine having such a large aggregate of information stored in my memory bank. It would be such a privilege and an honor to work alongside him.

"Wow," I breathed, awed by that statement. "I still can't believe how lucky I am."

"Of landing your dream job or being mated to four smoking hot guys?" Grayson butted into the conversation as he perched on the arm of the settee.

He grinned in a way that suggested he wanted my answer to be both or for me to choose the second option.

"You just want me to say it, don't you?" I muttered dryly.

From out of nowhere, all four of them had me cornered on the sofa, threatening to tickle it out of me.

"Both," I answered, "but mainly because I'm mated to four smoking hot guys," I finished, earning myself approving grins all around.

In the time that it had taken for Alex to nip to Whitevale and return with all my equipment, we had completed our chores and changed into suitable walking attire. Alex, who for once was dressed for a hike in the mountains, started putting together a picnic while Lucas loaded some essentials into the trunk of Alex's car. When everybody was ready, I rode in the back seat between Mason and Lucas, leaving Grayson to ride shotgun beside Alex. All they did was argue over what music we should listen to, and every time Grayson went to touch the radio, Alex slapped his hand away from the dials and growled at him not to touch anything.

"Hey, there's no need to get all aggressive," Grayson complained. "I was only trying to put on some decent music."

"Do you call that music? It's just noise and excessive screaming," Alex protested, half a mile into the journey. "For the love of the Goddess, spare my ears until we get to Forest Hills."

"How dare you insult my favorite rock band, you orchestral-loving freak. Let's see what else you've got on the USB," Grayson muttered as he began flicking through the albums on the digital display screen. "Crap, crap, and more classical crap. Oh, what is this? Enya's greatest hits." He chortled, surprised by his findings.

Lucas chuckled quietly. Mason looked visibly

uncomfortable as if he expected them to fight. Alex stared ahead, stony-faced, choosing to rise above the teasing.

"Put on the radio," Mason spoke up as the voice of reason. "Lakewell Central plays back-to-back chart music at this time of day. Isobelle might appreciate it."

Grayson did as he suggested, which made for a peaceful journey. We all fell into a comfortable silence as we listened to the radio, all of us enjoying the ride as we gazed out at the scenic country view.

Grayson

It was good to see Izzy so enthusiastic to work for our pack. She would be the first human besides Victoria Grayson allowed to travel in and out of Whitevale. It was only because Victoria mated with the late Beta, Arron Grayson, that Alec granted her permission to stay in town. Mixed-species couples moved to Lakewell. I don't even think Isobelle realizes what an honor this was for us.

The second we arrived at the ranger trail, Izzy

hopped straight out of the car and retrieved her things from the trunk.

"Get your paws off," Isobelle insisted. "I'll carry my things. You can get the picnic basket." She swatted Lucas's hand away as he reached for her backpack. It was a good job she traveled light because it was a four-mile hike down to the lakeside.

It wasn't as hot today as it had been all week. At least we would have a comfortable stroll through the woodland while the weather was good. The aroma of clean forest pine filled my lungs as I walked alongside Alex. He was still wearing his dark-tinted aviator shades and was casting critical glances from left to right, muttering under his breath about the substandard maintenance of the nature trail.

"It's beautiful here," Izzy commented, glancing around at all the picturesque scenery.

"It would be even better if they cut the ferns back a bit," Alex grumbled, "Just look how far they are encroaching onto the trail. If I was their chief, I would get somebody to deal with this immediately."

Aside from the overgrown foliage that liked to trip you as you walked, Forest Hills was the place to visit if you wanted to be at one with nature. The residents were mostly humble country folk, some of whom spent most of their time working their ranches or up at the timber yard. This town was renowned for its craftsmanship and supplied the entire state with handmade furniture. It also boasted an unrivaled construction industry that no other community could compete with. Our kind owed a lot to the bears. They were a vital ally to every species of shifter within Whitehaven.

"We used to come camping out here when we were cubs," Lucas revealed to Isobelle.

Our parents brought us here every year. I remembered this one year, we came here during mating season. An innocent trip to the falls turned out to be a pornographic biology lesson that we didn't forget. The bears liked to get down and dirty in the great outdoors, and they didn't just come to the falls to admire the stunning view. There was also a remote beauty spot high in the mountains that played host to mass orgies. We had never been to one, but some of our friends had. I refused to share my wife with anyone other than my brothers, but the thought of fucking out in the open with other people watching us turned me on. I knew the guys would back me up on that subject. It was an all-time fantasy that we shared between us.

"I'll show you the exact spot where Grayson

pushed Alex into the Lake," Lucas promised, earning a disgruntled snort from Alex.

"That was so funny," I cackled in remembrance. "He was splashing around and screaming like a cat who had fallen into a watering hole. It was only after our mom yelled at him to stand up that he realized the water level reached up to his waist."

"It's no laughing matter. I almost drowned," Alex preached. "You can drown in a few inches of water, irrespective of whether I could stand. It was foolish of you to push me in, and the fact that you continue to mock me shows you're just as immature now as you were back when we were seven years old."

"I can't imagine you all being little," Isobelle mused.

I cast a side-glance so I could read her expression. The humor sparkling in her gorgeous blue eyes suggested she was craving all the details. Our mother could fill her in on some of our wildest antics, as could the retired principal of Whitevale High. We were the reason he retired early. We were rebellious. Me especially. Mom said I should have been born with devil horns. Lucas was always the quiet one, spending most of his time with his sketch pad or taking things apart. That didn't mean he was an angel. Not by any means.

He was just as impish as I was. Mason was the clever one because he never got caught. He only had to flutter his eyelashes at our mother, and she would defend him to the hilt. And Alex . . . well, he hasn't changed much. You could say he has grown into his attitude.

"There was never a dull moment in our childhood," I assured her. "It helped to shape the men we are today."

Izzy hummed, "Uh-huh," as if she didn't doubt that for a second.

"Out of curiosity, did you ever have any pets?" she asked off the bat.

I could answer that question in a heartbeat. "No, our mom had enough on her hands with the four of us."

"That's not entirely true, is it?" Alex spat, glaring at me.

"Uh-oh," Mason muttered as if dreading what was coming next.

I knew exactly what my brother was getting at, and I was ready for it.

"Dude, I'm over it," Lucas was quick to add, trying his best to keep a straight face.

But Alex was like a dog with a bone. He couldn't resist the opportunity to make me look like an asshole in front of our girl.

"Guinea-pig killer," he accused, his voice full of contempt.

"What?" Isobelle gasped, her face contorting with horror.

What could I say? I was guilty as charged. But in my defense though, I was five years old, and the homemade parachute worked perfectly fine for the cartoon mouse I saw on TV. Poor Lucas. He adored that little fur-ball. From the very first moment he stole it from the petting zoo, he had been feeding it night and day. That was why he named him Goliath. He grew to the size of a bowling ball and was almost as round as one. It gave our mom quite a fright when it landed in the yard with a splat.

"He who is without sin shall cast the first stone," I shot back at Alex. "Cheater, cheater, goldfish eater!"

Fair enough, this was idiotic immaturity at its finest, but he started it, so I was going to finish it.

Isobelle flicked her admonishing scowl over at Alex. "Is he joking?"

Alex dropped his gaze to the ground as we strolled. I noticed the flare in his eyes as it pushed him to justify himself to our wife.

"Our principal caught Lucas and I sneaking some test papers from his office, and I accidentally knocked over the goldfish bowl. It fell off the desk and shattered onto the carpet, and in a blind moment of panic, I scooped up the fish, intending to find a glass of water to put it in. But then the door flew open, and the principal walked in. He started yelling and screaming and looked like he wanted to tear us limb from limb. To hide what happened, I stuffed the fish into my mouth. He demanded an explanation, and Lucas elbowed me in the ribs, causing me to swallow the fish. It traumatized me." Alex shuddered with a grimace. "That put me off eating sushi for life."

The look of pure revulsion etched itself across our wife's face as she glanced between us in disbelief.

"My conscience is clear," Mason boasted, holding his hands up as if butter wouldn't melt in his mouth.

Lucas made the noise of a cow mooing distantly, calling him out on all his bullshit. Alex breathed out a breathy chuckle, his broad grin stretching wide across his face.

"I fully own up to all of my misdemeanors," Lucas stated. "There are just way too many to count."

"Why do I feel that you were all a bunch of downright little bastards?" Isobelle mentioned.

"We were awful," Alex answered, confirming her assumption. "It didn't get any better when we reached adolescence. I'm pretty sure they still have a certain someone's photos plastered around every bar in Whitevale, don't they, Mason?" he lifted his shades, eye-signaling our brother a subtle hint to come clean.

Mason scrubbed his hand across his face with an embarrassed groan.

Mason

I wished it would start raining so we could change the subject and run back to the car. It seemed unlikely . . . now that we were a couple of miles in, and the gray clouds had dispersed.

Isobelle's questioning expression meant I couldn't wriggle out of this even if I wanted to. It was only fair that I came clean considering my brothers had all decided to *share*.

"When I was twenty-one and old enough to drink, I earned a lifetime ban from every bar in Whitevale for disorderly conduct," I admitted, much to my wife's surprise. "Alcohol brings out the inner Loki in me."

Lucas pointed at me. "It makes you fucking awesome," he complimented me.

I shook away the mental imagery. "The most

humiliating part wasn't how I behaved," I explained. "In all fairness, I could never remember it. But it was the fact they placed my photos where everybody could see them, and in bold red letters they stamped the words 'Banned' and 'Do not serve this wolf'." I cringed. "Then to make matters worse, they used my image in the Alcoholics Anonymous campaign, slapping my face onto every billboard and bus shelter in the entire fucking state. I was lucky they let me into The Vortex club the other night."

Isobelle laughed. "So that's why you stick to beer."

Stone-cold sober, I was the paragon of virtue, but after a few tequila slammers, I got a little uncouth. Hence, the reason I limit my alcohol intake nowadays. We were all spoiled, overprivileged pricks in our hometown. If Isobelle had known us back then, she would have rejected us right there on the spot.

"I'm such a boring bitch," she commented, "I'm a goody two-shoes compared to you."

"And now you fuck four brothers at once," Lucas pointed out. "Guys, we've corrupted an angel."

Izzy giggled. "It wasn't like I took much convincing."

Alex entwined his hand with hers and brought it

to his lips to kiss. "Now your halo has well and truly slid around your ankles."

"Along with her panties," Grayson quipped, making us all chuckle.

"Hey, cheeky!" Izzy playfully slapped Grayson's arm.

She didn't seem to mind listening to our stories. We hoped it would make us sound like regular men and allow her to relate to us a little more. It didn't matter that she was a human, and we didn't want her to think of us differently. Sharing secrets was the key to a healthy, sustainable marriage. But there was one secret we had yet to reveal. We were sitting on something huge — something we were all anxious to share with her but didn't know how. The truth was bound to come out one way or another. We knew that. But when the time came for that bomb to detonate, it was going to cause an almighty explosion.

MORE BOOKS BY KELLY LORD

The story continues in Ravished by the Beasts

More books in the Whitehaven Shifter series:

Taken by a Beast

Rescued by the Beast

Loved by the Beast

Read more books by Kelly Lord:

One Night with Pops

Living with Pops & Daddy

One Man Show

The Contingency plan (only available in paperback and hardback for now)

Check out my website and sign up to my newsletter:

www.kellylord.co.uk

Printed in Great Britain
by Amazon

45192733R00225